Scandalous Housewives
Mumbai

Madhuri Banerjee is a bestselling author, a blogger with CNN-IBN, a screenplay writer for Bollywood films, an Ad film director, a columnist with *Asian Age* and a mother. She has her own production house, Gray Matter Solution, that makes ad films and TV shows. She has also won a National Award for her documentary on women's issues called Between Dualities. Currently, she is the face of Revlon as their Relationship Expert.

She tweets with the handle @Madhuribanerjee and has over 12,000 followers who love her relationship advice. Her personal blog www.madhuribanerjee.blogspot.in has over three lakh views already. She is a traveller, an avid reader, a coffee addict, an amateur photographer and a chocoholic.

ALSO BY THE SAME AUTHOR

Advantage Love

Scandalous Housewives
Mumbai

Madhuri Banerjee

RUPA

Published by
Rupa Publications India Pvt. Ltd 2014
7/16, Ansari Road, Daryaganj
New Delhi 110002

Sales centres:
Allahabad Bengaluru Chennai
Hyderabad Jaipur Kathmandu
Kolkata Mumbai

ISBN: 978-81-291-3114-0

First impression 2014
10 9 8 7 6 5 4 3 2 1

The moral right of the author has been asserted.

Typeset by Saanavi Graphics, Noida

Printed at Thomson Press India Ltd, Faridabad

Bala—For your incredible ideas, amazing sense of humour, and continuous support. I'm so lucky to have you in my life. This book would not have been possible without you.

Milu—For being a terrific housewife, a great friend, and an incredible photographer.

Ariaana—For working quietly on endless activity sheets while I wrote a few chapters every day. I'm super proud to be your Mama.

A Facebook page called **Indian Married Unsatisfied Housewives** has 150,000 'likes'. And this is just the people who have access to the Internet.

As per a 2011 consensus, 23 per cent of Indian women are employed. In a country of 58,646,9174 women, there would be about 392 million women who could be housewives.

This is a story of four of them that you might recognize.

Author's Note

Sapphire Towers is a housing complex in Mumbai that is fictional. It is based on the observations I made about several housing complexes across Mumbai. The new complexes in Mumbai all have a similar design. There are two or more buildings in a complex called a society. The society has a swimming pool, a gymnasium, a walking track or park with swings and slides for children, and a clubhouse where parties or society meetings are held. A few might even have a lake behind them with a swampland or a tennis court along the premises. Some towers are connected through a refuge floor if the buildings are very close to each other. This is a fire safety norm for the buildings. Each society has an office that looks into the maintenance of the society, and is run by members chosen by the owners of the flat at a General Body Meeting.

In Mumbai, apartments are known by BHKs, which means Bedroom, Hall and Kitchen. A 3 BHK would be an apartment with three bedrooms, a large drawing- and dining-room, and a kitchen.

The members can avail the complex facilities whenever they're free. Most times, the members of the society really have no time to partake in any of these, but sit in the playground near the swings where the children play.

1

As usual, Gita's husband was late. She looked at her birthday cake and sighed. She had thought that, for once, Shailesh would make an effort. That maybe today, just today, he would keep his promise and come home early. But now she knew; he really didn't care. It wasn't about work as he *always* had work.

'Mummy,' Gita's four-year-old daughter, Anu, came running out of their bedroom, one of the two in her in-laws' flat. She gave her mother a tight hug. 'When are we going to cut the cake? It's almost time to go to sleep.'

Gita pondered. Either she could wait for Shailesh to come, or she could cut the cake now with her two girls and then pack them off to bed. She looked at the clock. It was 9:30 p.m., way past their bedtime. She decided she might as well have a little fun with her girls instead of waiting for a man who might not even be back before midnight.

'Come, let's cut the cake. Should we light some candles? Where are the matches?' Gita smiled as she asked Anu.

'Let's call Dadi and Dada too.' Anu ran into the other bedroom to call her grandparents, and Gita wondered why she even bothered. After all, it was because of Anu that her relationship with her husband and in-laws had turned sour. They had wished for Gita to have a boy for a second child; Renu, their firstborn, was then six. But she had another girl, and when the doctor had told her, she was overjoyed: A sister bonding was exactly what she wanted for Renu. But her in-laws had refused to even hold Anu, much less distribute sweets to the neighbourhood, as they had done when Renu was born.

Now Gita refused to try for another child. She had secretly gone on the pill to avoid another pregnancy. The idea had come from her close friends in the Sapphire Towers society, who had brought her the packet and told her to start taking it forty days from Anu's birth. Thank God for those women, she thought. Otherwise, she would have gone completely mad in this building complex that sometimes felt like a prison.

Anu dragged her grandparents out of their bedroom for the cake-cutting. Gita shouted for her elder child Renuka to come as well. She came, playing a game on her mother's mobile phone.

'Mama, how old are you?' asked Anu.

'Silly,' said Renuka. 'You never ask a woman her age!' She had the smirk of a Didi (elder sister) that said she knew better. Renu was tall for her age, her athletic body outgrew clothes faster than Gita could afford to buy new ones. She had long wavy hair and was a stunner for her age. All the boys in the building loved to play with Renu since she could beat anyone at football or cricket and still be the prettiest one around.

Gita smiled for the first time on her birthday. 'Where did you learn that, Renu?'

Renu put down the phone for a brief second to look up at her mother. 'Sahil chacha,' she said.

'Sahil chacha' was Gita's unmarried brother-in-law; he lived a few floors below. She suddenly remembered she had promised to call him for the cake-cutting. She went to the landline and dialed the intercom to Sahil's flat. He picked up and said he would come.

Sahil had moved out of his parents' apartment as soon as Gita and Shailesh had their second child. He said it was too crowded for the entire family. For a while Gita's parents-in-law had insisted that he stay; they said he could sleep with his brother in one room, and the two girls and Gita in the drawing-room. But

Sahil felt that it was wrong: How could one separate a husband and wife? Besides, Gita needed some rest as well, and his parents woke up early to have tea. They would wake Gita up to make it for them. After a full night of looking after her newborn, she was in no position to cook for so many people. So he chose to not be a burden on anyone and look after himself by moving out.

His parents had thrown a fit but he insisted. He told them they could stay with him, too. Shailesh and he had a fight about how, as an elder brother, it was his prerogative to look after the parents. Gita had stood in the corner, secretly hoping Shailesh would see the logic in Sahil moving out and taking his parents with him. It would give her time with her husband, a say in how to bring up her children and more room for storage! But Shailesh asserted that Sahil could shift within the same building, and the parents could visit him whenever they wanted. The parents hated Gita even more for kicking their younger son out, even though she had nothing to do with it.

'Where's the birthday girl?' Sahil said, as he bounded up the floors and into Gita's house without ringing the doorbell.

'Here she is,' he said, and picked up Anu and twirled her around as she squealed. Then he looked at Anu and said, 'Hey, you're not the birthday girl!' He put her down and ran after Renuka who shrieked and went into her parents' room. 'It's not me either!' Sahil had a pleasant demeanour. He was tall, raw-boned with broad shoulders, and a hint of stubble that made him ingenuously appealing. His movements were swift, full of grace and virility. His brows and eyes were startling against his fair skin and light wavy hair. It wasn't that he was so good-looking that made Gita smile; it was his imminently captivating presence that made people happy when he was in the room.

Gita watched from a distance and smiled. How she wished Shailesh would be this happy with her kids. But most evenings he came home, took his dinner, and sat with his parents to chat before switching on the TV and zoning out. Then the next morning he would leave early for work. He barely saw Renu's homework or spoke to Anu about her day in Nursery. He either came home too late or else was too tired to do anything else. In this family, at least for Gita, Shailesh brought in the money and Sahil the laughter.

'Alright alright, all the wax is melting on the cake. Come now,' Gita said, as she asked her in-laws to sit. Gita's mother-in-law was in her late 60s. A plump woman with silver hair and weathered lines on her face, she never smiled, and berated Gita for most things she did.

Her mother-in-law remarked, 'Why such a fuss? It's not as if it's your first birthday.' She adjusted her sari and sat down as if her casual remark should not matter to anyone. But Gita bit her lip with the statement and held back her voice.

'Looks like an expensive cake. Where did you get it from?' spoke her father-in-law. He was in his early 70s and still fit as a fiddle. Unfortunately.

Gita chose to ignore their acerbic remarks. She knew by now that holding her tongue was better than falling into a full-blown fight in front of her children. It only left them traumatized and Gita in tears. And by the end of it, they wouldn't have changed their opinion at all.

'Mama, I want to blow out the candles,' said Anu. Gita put her in front of herself, near the cake. She held Renu to one side and they all blew out the six candles on the cake.

'Why are there six candles?' Sahil asked, though he already knew the answer.

Gita gave him a warning look from the corner of her eyes.

'Because Mama has turned six!' Anu said proudly. Gita laughed as she adjusted the red dupatta on her new Biba salwar kameez.

Renu cut the cake and fed a small bite to her mother, and then to her sister and Sahil chacha. She did not give any to her grandparents, and went back to the game on her phone. She said to Anu, 'Because Mama has turned thirty-three today. See, three candles on one side and three on the other? Thirty Three.' She left the party and went to her room.

Gita called after her, 'Aren't you going to have a piece?'

Renu replied, 'No, I'll get fat!'

Sahil burst out laughing. His parents were shocked. 'Have you been teaching her such nonsense?' Gita's mother-in-law berated her. 'Seeing how thin you are, she must also be wanting to go on a diet!'

Sahil came to her defence. 'Gita is naturally thin, Ma. She doesn't have our Gujarati genes. Renu must have learnt this from her friends in school. Kids nowadays are smarter than when we were at their age.' Gita flushed and looked gratefully at Sahil. Her large expressive eyes widened when he surreptitiously winked at her when his parents weren't looking.

Gita served them a piece of cake each. Her mother-in-law said, 'Give me a bigger piece. Why are you doing so much kanjoosi?'

Gita replied, 'You have diabetes. I don't want you to fall ill.'

Mrs Patel didn't say anything and helped herself to a bigger piece. Gita wiped her hands on the napkin that was kept on the table and looked at Anu, 'Come on, brush and bedtime.'

'Nooooo,' Anu complained. 'Sahil chacha has come! Can't we play a little longer?' She picked up the chocolate pieces from the sides of the cake and stuffed them into her mouth.

Renu also whined from inside the bedroom. 'I'm still waiting for Papa to come. He promised to see my score.'

'No,' Gita worked up a firm tone. 'Tomorrow is a school day. We can show Papa your score in the morning, Renu. And Anu, Sahil chacha will come back tomorrow evening again.'

The girls grumbled loudly, but in the end listened to their mother. They brushed their teeth and went to sleep in their respective places in the bedroom. Anu cuddled up to her mother on the master bed and Renu covered herself with a sheet on the mattress on the floor. Gita turned off the lights, and within minutes the two girls were fast asleep. She went into the bathroom and readjusted her clothes. A little chocolate had fallen on her white and red embroidered kurta and she took a little water and rubbed it off. Then she covered her bright red dupatta over the stain and smoothed down her hair around her ears. She stopped for a second to look at herself in the mirror. She wasn't bad-looking. Her quiet oval face was fair and delicate, her slim waist which flared into agile rounded hips could have made her a model. Instead, she chose to devote her life to her family. She applied some strawberry Vaseline that give her lips a hint of red colour and walked out of the bathroom. She turned on the night light and crept out of the bedroom.

She saw Sahil still sitting in the drawing-room and noticed that her parents-in-law were no longer around. She guessed they had retired to their own room. She gestured a question to Sahil: How did you manage to put them inside their room so quickly?

Sahil whispered to her, 'Simple. I told them they were missing an awards show on TV.' Gita smiled with gratitude. Getting a TV for her in-laws' room had made such a difference in her life. Sahil had gifted in to them for their fortieth anniversary earlier this year. Now they could just go into their room and watch TV instead of sitting in the drawing-room and looking over Gita's shoulder every minute of the day. And they were glued to every award show that came over the weekends. What a relief the idiot box could actually be.

Gita took the seat opposite Sahil. Good housewives maintained a distance from all male members in the family, no matter how close they were to them. Even though Sahil had a great camaraderie with Gita, she was always guarded around him. 'Have you had dinner?'

He smiled. 'I ordered some chicken from Sagar Shrot downstairs. I saved some for you, by the way. Just go down at lunchtime and gobble it up. You have the keys.'

Gita shook her head. 'I could have easily made something for you.'

'Thanks, but I'm tired of ghaas-phus,' said Sahil, referring to the pure vegetarian food that was made at home. Gita wasn't allowed to cook or bring in any non-vegetarian items into the Gujarati house. But she and Sahil both loved eating non-vegetarian. Since he didn't have a cook, he would order from the nearby restaurant and she would occasionally join him for a meal. It was their 'food' secret. She thoroughly looked forward to the impromptu luncheons with Sahil, when she could gorge on all the meat she wanted. He continued, 'Besides, it's your birthday. Why should you be cooking today?'

'How is today different from any other day, Sahil? The kids still need their tiffin. Ma, Papa still need their meals. Who's going to do all this? A birthday doesn't mean I get a day off. It just means I'm a year older,' Gita said, looking melancholy.

Sahil reached his hand across to gently pat her knee. 'Hey. No getting upset on your birthday. Where's that lousy brother of mine? Didn't he give you a present at least?' Gita shook her head and stifled a little laugh; Sahil could be funny.

'Well, how about I take tomorrow off?' Sahil said. 'You come over and we'll order some mutton biryani for lunch. The kids will be away at school and the maid can serve the parents lunch.'

Gita had a maid who came to clean the house and assist her in the kitchen. Sometimes, she stayed back to serve the food as well and clean up after that. It was a great help, as she didn't have to do the laborious, menial household chores.

'But don't you have work?' Gita asked.

Sahil dismissed her query with a quick wave of his hand. 'I'll work from home in the morning and leave post-lunch. I just need to work on a presentation and send it through email. One of the perks of being the boss at a production house.' Gita smiled. Just then, the key turned in the lock of the main door and Gita almost jumped up from the sofa. As if on cue, she ran to the kitchen to get a glass of water. Sahil picked up the TV remote and tuned into a news channel.

Even though they were comfortable with each other, it was an unsaid rule in Indian society that any other man besides a woman's husband could not be sitting alone with a wife while the husband was away. Gita knew she needed to adhere to that.

Shailesh entered and saw Sahil sitting there. 'What are you doing here?' he almost snapped.

Sahil shrugged. 'It's Gita's birthday. I came to wish her.'

Shailesh looked towards the kitchen and felt guilty. He had completely forgotten! Gita emerged with a glass of water for Shailesh. He took it silently and sat down. 'I've had dinner,' he said. He meant she need not make fresh rotis for him or warm up any food. It was his way of giving her some time to herself. Gita understood that he had forgotten her birthday altogether, and this was a way of saying she need not stay up any longer.

She asked, 'Cake?' He nodded. She cut him a slice. He took it with a smile. Gita wrapped up the cake from the table, put it in the fridge, and went to her room without giving either of the brothers another look. Sahil got up to leave. As he opened the door he turned to his brother and said, 'At least you could have got her flowers.' He shut the door and left.

Gita heard her brother-in-law's remark and wondered if this was what marriage was all about: a husband who worked constantly, a wife who only looked after his children and parents, and a lifetime of daily domesticity. If only she had a son. Maybe her husband and parents-in-law would love her. But she knew that she was too tired to have another baby as well as manage a house. She crept silently into bed and held Anu a little tighter. Her children were her whole world. She was so proud of having two girls. She wished that Shailesh would be proud of them, too. She made a wish for her birthday. 'Dear God,' she whispered aloud, 'Please give me back some romance in my life. I need something more than being a housewife and mother every day.' She closed her eyes and went to sleep, not knowing that the universe would grant her the wish.

2

'I can't believe your mother-in-law said that!' Natasha said, in shock as Gita narrated what had occurred on her birthday the previous day. Gita nodded as her friends sat and ate the cake she had brought them. She felt a close connection with the housewives of Sapphire Towers and met them every day in the lawns, where the children played and they sat and gossiped. The three towers were connected through a common lobby and the walking track that went around it. They were also connected through refuge floors that were to be used in case of a fire. It was a large hall that connected each tower. There were twenty-four floors on each tower, with penthouses on the top two floors of all three towers. The residents of those flats were rarely seen in the lawns. Their drivers opened the doors of their Audis and BMWs when the people entered and exited the building from the lobby area. The rest had parking on the three floors below the building, where the drivers sat and gossiped. There were common area bathrooms for workers in all the parking floors, and a canteen on one side where one could get hot samosas and milky chai. There were shops outside Sapphire Towers that the residents used. A dry-cleaners, a tiny tots school, an ice cream parlour, two grocery stores, several vegetable vendors and a hardware store.

Although Gita and her friends hardly walked on the track, they met around six every evening for two hours to chat about their lives. This evening, Gita, Natasha and Sarita were together. Aarti had said she would be a bit late. No four women could be as different as them. Gita was petite with slim hips, mid-length dark brown hair and tiny breasts that she hated. Natasha was tall and slender with a toned, bronzed body and a full pout. Sarita was of average height with wide hips and heavy breasts that she was quite proud of. Despite their physical differences, their mental connection was very strong.

Gita saw the cake vanish in seconds when she brought it down in a plastic box for her friends. It was the first time that she hadn't made the cake at home herself. She didn't want to do any work on her own birthday and splurged a little on a one kilo dark chocolate cake for herself.

'She didn't even finish the piece of cake I gave her before she took another one,' Gita continued. 'Of course, Shailesh didn't see because he came home much later. She told him she had been so good and not had anything. She's unbelievable!' Gita was selective in revealing the juicy details of her private life. She conveniently decided not to tell them about Sahil's visit or the fact that she had lunch with him in the afternoon.

'My husband would have told his mother not to lie. He's always taken my side,' said Natasha. Gita looked at her incredulously. Natasha was a forthright woman. It seemed as if her marriage was perfect. She always boasted about how her husband took her to overseas trips, and how she managed to balance her home and life perfectly. It probably also had to do with having only one daughter who was all grown-up and didn't need her mother.

'You won't understand family politics, Natasha,' said Sarita. 'It's very complicated to speak in front of your in-laws. One must keep the harmony at home as well.' Sarita lived with her in-laws as well, in a three-bedroom flat in another wing. Her grown-up children stayed in one room and her in-laws in another, while she enjoyed marital bliss with her husband in a separate room. She had often felt lucky that they had booked the three-bedroom place when the Towers were being built, even though her in-laws had complained about spending so much money. But space created peace, and they all seemed like a happy content family today.

'Hi guys, what have I missed?' said Aarti, as she joined them.

'Aarti, it's so good to see you after four days!' said Gita, giving her a warm hug. Aarti was the quintessential beauty amongst them. With a porcelain face and chestnut brown hair, she could easily have given any of the Bollywood heroines a run for their money. Even though she was slightly on the plump side, Aarti never shyed away from her sexuality and wore dresses and skirts, something that no other housewife did in Sapphire Towers.

'This new Sales role is so tough,' she said. Aarti had always been with Sales in a corporate job, and with the passing of time, her travels had increased. She was very tempted to resign and stay at home after the birth of her child Aryan, but her in-laws had insisted she keep her job while they looked after him. She was very grateful to them. They found purpose to their lives by looking after Aryan, and she found meaning to hers by working. Her friends envied her dedication to her career. Secretly, they wondered if the ambition would eventually wear off and she would decide to settle down to look after her husband and child, but she surprised them by climbing up the corporate ladder and earning pots of money for the family.

Natasha filled her in on their in-law bashing conversation. As they expected, Aarti didn't join in the fray; rather she said, 'I'm sorry to hear that, Gita. But not all in-laws are like that. Look at mine, they let me do what I want. In fact they're the best thing that happened to me after Aryan!'

'Let's drop all this bashing,' she continued. 'I have some big news!' They all kept their eyes on her. Aarti was known to be dramatic; she liked having an audience.

'The clubhouse is hosting zumba classes for women and it's only five hundred bucks a month. We can all join!' She clasped her hands and was extremely pleased with her news.

The women looked at her skeptically.

'I don't know Aarti,' said Gita, biting her lip. 'I'll have to ask Shailesh. I mean, he might not like it if I'm jumping around in front of other people.' The mere thought of discussing it with Shailesh tired her. She knew it would be pointless: she'd get his endless why's and how's before finally winning, and she would be left exhausted in trying to make her point.

Sarita agreed with Gita. 'I'll have to ask for money from the house and it just puts me in an awkward state. So I don't know, Aarti.' She knew her in-laws were supremely rich. They had crores to invest in properties all over Mumbai, but for small things within the house, they were tight-fisted. She didn't want to lose the peace in the house by asking for money and time away from her duties.

Aarti couldn't believe her friends. Weren't they modern women? Goodness! They were educated and literate, weren't they? And yet they behaved as if they were being held on puppet-strings by the men in their life. Aarti looked towards Natasha who hadn't said a word. But Natasha just said, 'Why do we need to exercise so much? We're married. It hardly matters if we put on some weight.'

Aarti was incredulous, 'It's not about weight. It's about being fit. And healthy. For ourselves.'

'You can afford to do all this, Aarti,' said Sarita. 'You have a job and you're earning. And you're in the glam industry where you need to be thin. It's too difficult for us to take out time to do all this.'

'What "glam", Sarita? Sales is hardly glam!' Aarti said with a snort that Gita thought only she noticed. Maybe Aarti was getting tired of her job and needed to do something more?

Gita said, 'At least you get to travel to different places and meet new people.' Look at me, Gita wanted to add; she had gone from her parents' home to that of her in-laws', and she had never seen any part of India as Shailesh hated travelling, especially with the children.

Aarti replied, 'Yes, there's travel but it's tiring as well. No job is easy, even if you love it passionately.'

'Tell them about the time you travelled with Kareena Kapoor?' Sarita suddenly remembered that story. 'The glam factor was there, for sure!'

They then found themselves talking about show business, and from there, they moved on to the latest movies. Soon the zumba class was forgotten and everyone was discussing if their husbands had taken them to the theatre recently. Sarita and her husband were movie buffs who watched the latest film every Friday evening. It was their 'date night', she said, and they always had fun. It was also the one thing that he would splurge on because he enjoyed films; otherwise, he opened his wallet very rarely, too.

Natasha said that she watched all her movies on pirated DVDs since she hated going to a movie hall alone, with Vikram, her husband, constantly travelling. Gita secretly wished to watch films but rarely got the chance, unless it was coming on cable TV late night and could watch once everyone had gone to sleep. Sometimes, she thought she needed to see them just to prove to everyone she did watch films, otherwise, they would consider her 'boring'. Aarti, meanwhile, was not fond of Hindi movies, which was fine, given how she rarely had time off work to go to a movie hall. Her family had an active social life, and whenever she was in town, she had to accompany them to parties.

'You're lucky, yaar,' Gita told Aarti. 'At least you get to attend parties.'

'It's not that fun anymore,' Aarti said. 'All I want to do is sleep when I get back, but as a wife, I need to be there for my husband and in-laws as well.'

'And your child,' reminded Natasha.

Aarti nodded. 'Yes. Aryan is seven years old and needs me.'

That's all the cue they needed, as the girlfriends then talked about their children and how they needed their mothers, whatever age they were. Natasha kept quiet. She had always felt that her daughter Diya was an independent child and did not need her as much as other children her age needed their parents. Now a teenager, Diya wanted to do everything her peers at the international school were doing, and Natasha had a hard time disciplining her. It was something that troubled her deeply. It would also lead to a great rift between them in the near future.

Before the group knew it, it was eight o'clock and they had to rush back home.

'What have you cooked today, Gita?' asked Aarti.

'Something simple. Veg pulao, sabudana vada, papad and boondi raita. I wasn't in the mood to cook so much.' Gita smiled. She was aware that among all of them, she had the best culinary skills; she was quite proud of that fact.

'Wow, Gita,' said Sarita. 'That's 'simple'? That's awesome. I've made aloo parathas.' Sarita had been forced to learn how to cook when she got married. It was a chore that she grudgingly did every day just to please her in-laws.

'It's easy,' Gita said. 'I have a maid who chops up the vegetables. I just throw things in then.'

'I wish my in-laws would keep a maid,' Sarita said. With great difficulty I forced them to keep a top servant to clean the entire house and come twice a day to do dishes.' Sarita suddenly recalled the early days of her marriage, when she did all the housework on her own, and then at night was also expected to pleasure her husband Jai. It was a tough six months. Her in-laws didn't like the fact that she found housework to be a burden, and her husband resented it when she denied him sex on nights when she was simply too tired.

Natasha chimed in, 'I've made a salad, and Vikram and Diya had better eat that tonight with leftovers from yesterday. I was in no mood to cook.' Natasha glanced at her phone to check if Vikram had called to even say when he would be back home, but there was no message from him. She was glad he hadn't reached home yet. If he had and she wasn't there, he would be extremely upset; she shuddered at the thought of what he would have done next. She looked up and smiled at them, not betraying any emotion. There were some secrets that could never come out of the closet.

'Rahul would love your salad, I bet,' Sarita said. 'That boy is obsessed with the gym and eating healthy! And he's only eighteen, for God's sake. Seems like yesterday I was giving him Smileys for tiffin.'

'This is why I pay a maid to cook, guys,' Aarti said. 'I make sure I contribute to the family income so I don't have to do any domestic shit.'

Sarita and Gita threw each other a knowing glance. This was the nth time that Aarti had thrown the fact that she was a working woman—the only one amongst them. It was tiring. They felt like she was looking down on them for being housewives, though she never meant it in that manner. Gita said gently, 'There's no shame in cooking for your family, Aarti. You know what they say—the way to a man's heart is through his stomach. It gives me great pride to know they rely on me for something. And the fact that they love my food makes me quite happy.'

Aarti seemed to have realized the crudeness of her words. 'Oh, I didn't mean it like that, Gita. I only meant that I'm so bad at it that, thankfully, I can hire a cook. Otherwise, I would burn everything in the kitchen!'

They all laughed. Gita said to Aarti, 'We're all good at some things and horrible at others. How does it matter if you can't cook? You're excellent at pampering your 'pati' and Aryan.' She gave Aarti a warm hug.

Somehow, no matter how close the women were, they rarely took each other's husbands' names, choosing to call them 'your husband' or 'your pati' and keep a safe distance, thereby acknowledging respect for each other.

Aarti, trying to make up for her faux pas, replied, 'But I would seriously like to learn.'

'I don't even know what to throw in if the maid chops up things! Maybe we can take a cooking class together?' asked Natasha. 'My maid takes so many days off that I feel I'm helping her instead of the other way around.' They all burst out laughing. The four pillars of conversation you could have with any housewife that would make you bond immediately were maids, diets, exercise, and children. The women in Sapphire Towers were experts on each!

'You can afford it, your hours are so flexible,' said Sarita, who had always been the plump one in the group. She looked at Natasha who protested, saying it was just because of genes and yoga.

Soon it was time for them to say their goodbyes and go home. As she walked to her flat, Aarti couldn't help but think that maybe the only thing she was good at was lying to her friends. Her entire life was a lie! Yes, she pampered her husband, but that was because of the guilt that ate her up. She worked hard, sure, but that was so she could get away from her house. And she laughed merrily because if she didn't, the shame would depress her. If the group ever got to know the truth about her marriage, she knew they would refuse to be her friend anymore.

It was a thought that sent shivers down Aarti's spine.

3

Aarti had always been pretty and she knew it. She had even been on a TV ad once, for Pampers diapers. Over the years, she would discover how that had made her parents extremely proud. They would tell her she would become an actress when she grew up. But she had always been plump, and acting meant a strict discipline with diet and workout. She had joined several gyms since turning fifteen-years old. But after the first three days of sweating it out, she became erratic and soon gave up altogether. She even tried dance and water aerobics once, but as was her habit, she quit when the excitement wore off.

Eventually, Aarti realized what she wanted to do: travel. At first, she didn't know how. She thought of joining an air hostess academy, but she realized that it would be short-lived. Not many private airlines continued to hire women after a certain age. She needed to fly for the rest of her life. An opportunity came in college when she got recruited by a multinational firm as a Sales trainee. She took a liking to her job, like fish to water. She had the clients wrapped around her finger, with her gorgeous looks and sharp intellect. Best of all, she got to travel across India. It was also a way to expand her boyfriend circle. Aarti had men following her since she hit her teenage years and started developing. With her pretty porcelain face and long brown hair she had men swooning for her from school through college. They followed her about and she basked in their attention. She never kept a man longer than a month, allowing everyone to have a chance to woo her.

But there was one man who captured her attention. He was unavailable, though, as he was already in a relationship and ignored her. He was a challenge; she loved it and played all her games with him. And this simple act of their flirting changed the course of her life forever.

'Aarti!' Amitabh said, as he snapped his fingers in front of her face. 'Come back to earth, darling.'

She smiled at her husband. 'Oh, just thinking about what the girls were saying today.'

'Oh? What were they saying?'

'Nothing special. Something about cooks. What were you saying to me?' Aarti felt special that her husband actually took an interest in her life. He asked her about her day and was a wonderful father to their son.

'I was saying that Mom has bought you a sari. She wanted to show it to you before she showed it to me. She was hesitant to ask you if you wanted to go for Chhaya's wedding this weekend.'

Amitabh went back to reading his comic book. They were sitting in their large master bedroom, while their son played in the hall outside with his grandparents.

'Amit, can't you read anything else besides comic books? You're a grown man!' She was honestly exasperated.

He playfully shoved the cover of the comic to her face. 'This just happens to be the first edition of when Batman met Joker. It's a classic. Grown men *should* be reading this.'

She shook her head with a smile and got up from the bed. 'And obviously, I will like what Mom has bought. And of course, I will go. For all that they've done for me it's such a small thing to do.' She went outside to find her mother-in-law, who was playing Monopoly with her son.

'Mom, you didn't have to buy me a sari! You've already given me so many.' She wrapped her mother-in-law in a hug.

'No, no. You need to wear something new. That is if you want to come?'

'Sure!'

Aarti sat next to her son and admired his features. For so long Aryan had looked like her and she did not have to worry about her terrible secret. Now he was beginning to take on his father's features and it troubled Aarti. Aryan didn't look like Amitabh at all.

She smoothed down Aryan's hair and said, 'Let Dadi go to sleep now, Aroo. It's been a long day. Mama will play with you.'

Aarti helped her mother-in-law up and walked with her to the adjacent house where her father-in-law was already fast asleep. He was a military man and his bedtime had always been 9:00 p.m., like clockwork. He woke up at five every morning, made his own cup of tea, and went for a two-hour walk before the entire household woke up. Then post-dinner, at eight o'clock sharp, he would sit and read a book and then, at nine, go to sleep. Thankfully, they lived in a separate house, even though the servants were common and they shared a kitchen. With Aarti rarely around, her in-laws looked after Aryan in either of the houses. And they gave enough space to their son and their daughter-in-law to call friends over or have some private time to themselves. It was quite an irony though, Aarti thought, because all her friends thought it was a perfect set-up, but she and Amitabh didn't even want privacy. Sleeping next to a man who didn't want to touch her was the loneliest thing in the world.

She went back to the drawing-room where Aryan sat waiting for her. 'Mama, tell me a story.'

'Not tonight, Aroo. I'm so tired. And you can read yourself now. You're a big boy.'

'I know, Mama, but you make up such good stories. Tell me one from your day yesterday.'

'Chalo, let me tuck you in and I will tell you a story.'

Aarti decided she shouldn't say no. She had been working for so long that the only way to assuage her guilt was to tell stories to Aryan every night when she came home, or in the morning before he went to school. So he looked forward to her leaving instead of clinging to her. And he soon enjoyed the fact that his mother worked and could still tell him interesting stories. He would relate these stories to his peers and everyone enjoyed listening to him, making him feel quite the 'dude'.

It was late when Aarti finished telling him about her travel to Delhi that week. Aryan had dozed off. She tucked him in, turned off the lights and went to her room.

She found Amitabh in bed, turned to his side; she decided he was asleep. Aarti wondered if she should wake him up to have a conversation but decided against it. It could wait until tomorrow. They had gone seven years with a lie; what difference would one more night make?

Aarti turned off the lights and stared at the ceiling. She wondered, how could her life that seemed so perfect have gone so wrong?

4

Sarita resented the fact that her in-laws had so much money but refused to even hire a cook. She was young at the time of her marriage, an arranged one, and had Rahul after their first anniversary. The in-laws were overjoyed. But she soon realized they didn't give her anything in return. They didn't even do any catering for the 'godh bharai' when the entire family came over to give her presents. She had to order pizzas and her father paid for it.

Her parents-in-law had taken everything she received at her wedding and kept it with them in the family locker. She was not allowed to wear any of the jewellery, even those gifted to her by her side of the family. And not wanting to spend on a nanny to look after the child, they had allowed her to go to her mother's house in Bhilai as soon as the gold was kept away. She had her delivery there and came back after three months.

For her second child's birth her mother trained a maid and paid her in advance to stay with Sarita and help with the baby. Even then, Sarita's in-laws grumbled that they were feeding a new member, while staying awake the whole night because of a newborn's crying. Sarita complained to her husband Jai but he refused to take sides, saying it was her own battle to fight. He occasionally took his children to the mall, giving Sarita some time to herself. But even for this, her in-laws begrudged her, saying their son was spending money eating outside when the maid could cook something for the children at home.

Sarita couldn't figure it out. The family had properties in several parts of Mumbai, and yet they behaved as if they didn't have money. They were extremely stingy. Their immovable assets were valued at crores of rupees. But they insisted she cook all the meals at home. Even if they went for a film occassionally, they would either come back after the film and have their meal, or eat before they left. They would not spend on popcorn and Coca-Cola.

So in the early years of her marriage she was a glorified maid, even sweeping the floors and doing the dishes. They told her that since she wasn't doing anything at home, she might as well do some work. But over the years her health deteriorated and Jai eventually agreed to keep a maid to clean up. A cook was more expensive, however, and so one was never hired.

How she wished she could work like Aarti and spend some of her income on paying for a cook. The maid her mother had given in the early years was a huge boon to Sarita. But as soon as Rhea had turned three, they had sent her packing, saying Sarita could manage things on her own. And now ten years later, Sarita still hated the fact that she couldn't keep her own maid. And she hated it even more that she didn't have the courage to speak out about it.

'Where did Rhea get a mango from?' asked her mother-in-law, as soon as Sarita walked in.

'I bought a dozen today.' Sarita walked to the sink to wash her hands to prepare for dinner.

Her mother-in-law suddenly raised her voice. 'There's no need to bring such expensive fruit at home. Kids will grow in any case. Bring bananas!'

Sarita sighed and quickly changed her statement so she wouldn't have to hear more about it. 'I meant I brought it from my mamaji's house. He gave me the mangoes for free.'

'Then it's okay,' said the father-in-law, who was sitting in front of the TV. 'Cut some for us also, Sarita.' She looked at both of them and wondered how such literate people could be so mean. She glanced at her husband Jai, who didn't say a word and was engrossed in watching *Kaun Banega Crorepati*. He had come home early today, a fact that her mother-in-law made sure to remark on in order to make her feel bad. 'Husband has come home, and wife is still out for a walk!'

Sarita didn't say anything but shot Jai a look that said he would hear about it later. She was quite the firebrand when it came to letting him know exactly how she felt, even though she kept her silence in front of his parents. He in turn would pacify her by pressing her feet or giving her a back massage. And since he had such lovely, soft hands, he gave the most amazing massages that soothed Sarita's body from head to toe. He was happy because he didn't have to spend any money on her, and she was happy because he pampered her.

'Let her be. She needs to exercise,' said Jai teasingly, aloud. And even though he meant it as a compliment, Sarita felt slighted. She decided not to have any sweets from that day forward. (A vow she would break the very next day.)

'Where's Rahul?' asked Sarita.

Jai got up from his chair in the drawing-room and headed towards the bathroom, without answering Sarita. She looked around at everyone and no one seemed to have a clue. Or weren't bothered to find out while glued to the television. She took out her phone and walked to the kitchen where she began preparing the parathas. Rahul hung up on her and sent her a Whatsapp message instead. Since he had bought himself a phone two years ago, Rahul had been perpetually sending his mother messages instead of talking. But Sarita hadn't figured out how to message back; she only knew how to receive messages and make phone calls. She realized she was technologically challenged but she hardly cared. His message said he was with his girlfriend and would be home after dinner. She frowned. Her boy, about to turn nineteen, was already dating! But she knew that if she tried to stop it, he would rebel and do things behind her back. So she let him go out with girls and drink, as long as he told her about it. She was aware that adolescents liked to do everything with alcohol; otherwise, it wasn't fun.

She recalled mentioning to her friends that she was an open-minded mother. They had berated her for it.

'How can you do that, Sarita?' Gita was completely shocked.

'I would never let my children drink till they're twenty-one,' Natasha had said, even though she had caught Diya sneaking a bottle from the bar to her room.

'And girlfriends should not be allowed,' Aarti said. 'You need to put your foot down. What he needs to be doing is focusing on school. Our children can't be distracted at such a young age. Don't be a friend to them. Be a parent!'

Sarita wondered if all her friends were really such strict disciplinarians with their own children.

As for her, she had given Rahul and Rhea complete freedom, and so far, they had not disappointed her. They did fairly well in school and were well-behaved children, unlike Aarti's child Aryan, for example, who was turning out to be quite a brat. He spoke rudely to his grandparents and Sarita wondered, as she made her parathas, if she should mention it to Aarti, who was rarely around to see how her child was growing up. It just went to show how a working mother indulged her child all the time, and a stay-at-home mom found time for her kids. But Sarita would never tell Aarti. Everyone had their own parenting style and it was an extremely sensitive topic between women. She didn't want to wedge a gap in their friendship by telling Aarti she had to find a different way to bring up her naughty boy.

Sarita served dinner to her in-laws first, then her husband and Rhea, and finally sat down with her own plate once everyone was done. The entire family had eyes on the TV while they ate. Their daily dinner ritual. Sarita tried to make conversation between the same ads that came every time for the two hours they remained glued to the TV. 'Jai, why don't you ask Rhea about what the teacher said today?' Jai looked up from the TV and raised an eyebrow at Rhea, who made a face at her mother.

'Maaaaa. Not now.' Rhea was not pleased at all with her mother.

Sarita spoke, in between mouthfuls of aloo parathas, 'Her teacher said she was a very bright student but she was always distracted.'

'Well, obviously if she watches TV while doing her homework, she will be distracted,' said Jai, chiding his daughter who wasn't in the mood to chat with her parents at all. She couldn't believe that they gave so much liberty to her brother and were so strict with her. She wasn't a baby anymore and needed some independence. She had been begging them for a mobile phone and her grandparents had refused to buy her one. Even her father, who took them all out for a movie once a month and had dinner at the food court in the mall, said it was too expensive to give her a mobile and pay for the monthly bills. And she had wanted a Samsung, the latest model, because all her friends had one. She felt completely out of place among her peers and she blamed her parents for it. But she dare not say anything or she would get the thrashing of her life from her father, who had once slapped Rahul in front of the entire family for saying the 'f' word in the house.

'Apparently, she is a computer genius,' Sarita said.

'Will you get me a laptop then?' Rhea asked, and Jai laughed out loud.

He gave his daughter a gentle pat on the back. 'I suggest you study Maths and get an MBA. Your father doesn't make enough money to buy laptops for you to study computers!'

Rhea sulked and went to the kitchen to make an intercom call to her friend, who lived in another wing of Sapphire Towers. 'Diya? Come down, na. I'm bored. Okay.' She hung up and announced to her family, 'I'm going downstairs to the lobby.'

She got up and left the room, shutting the door behind her, while Sarita called after her, 'Only half an hour, Madam!' Rhea heard but didn't reply.

Sarita cleared up and excused herself to go to sleep. It was ten o'clock and she had had a long day.

Jai joined her in the bedroom and locked the door behind them. Their nightly ritual thus began. Something that they had been doing, five days a week, every week since they got married. It had been twenty years, and they only missed their activity if she had her periods or they had a party to attend. The latter was so rare because he was quite antisocial. He would rather have sex with her than go to a party.

She smiled at him as he came closer and started kissing her. She loved the way he was so into her even after so many years. He dropped her on the bed and lay on top of her. His demanding lips caressed hers roughly. She closed her eyes, waiting for the regular pattern. He would quickly take off her clothes, strip himself, kiss her a bit more, enter, exit, and clean up. Then they would roll over and fall into a soporific slumber.

But then he said, 'Want to try something new?' It startled her because it had never been asked in all of their married life. She looked at him with wondrous curiosity. New? She nodded. What was wrong with the old? What did he mean?

She felt the heady sensation of his lips against her neck, the spot where she got aroused the most. He whispered, 'First, let's have a safe word.'

'A what? A 'safe word'?' she asked between her moans. 'What do you mean?'

'In case you get uncomfortable.'

She stayed quiet as he slipped his hand under her shirt and squeezed her breasts. 'It'll be 'surrender'. Say surrender when you want me to stop.'

'Okay.' She had no idea where he was coming up with all this. Was it something he had heard about? Or worse! Was it something he had already done with someone? Her mind went into a tizzy trying to figure out. But when he grabbed hold of her ass and smacked it hard, her eyes popped out in amazement. Should she enjoy that? She smiled feebly and said, 'Yup, that was new.'

'Did you like it?' he asked, as his lips bent down to cover her mouth hungrily. And surprisingly, she did. She had no idea that the wave of emotions that were going to follow would leave her in a mixture of pleasure and pain over the next few days. This was so unlike Jai. What had gotten into him? Jai suddenly stopped kissing her neck and sat up. He took out a pair of handcuffs from his back pocket and looked at Sarita keenly. Her jaw dropped. 'Where did you get those?'

He smiled secretly, leaving her more befuddled. He slid off her green kurta and white bra and gently sucked her nipples. She loved every moment of it. This was the foreplay that she had only read about in magazines. It was now actually happening and she relished the entire idea. He picked her up and threw her gently on the bed as she let out a little giggle of excitement. He held her hands to the back of the bed as he took out a pair of handcuffs from the side table drawer.

Her heartbeat throbbed against his chest as he clasped the handcuffs behind her on the bed. Then he took out a handkerchief and blindfolded her. She whispered, 'The parents are in the next room!' They might be able to save her from this man who didn't seem like her husband!

He murmured back, 'That's what makes this more fun!'

Lying there, tied in the darkness, Sarita felt a small wave of fear race through her body. She murmured, 'Jai…' She didn't know if this was the right thing to do. Had he really tried this with someone else and was experimenting with her to see how she would react to it?

She felt reassured by his slow kisses, from her neck and down her body, caressing her nipples, her stomach and her thighs. Suddenly, she felt a shock go through her body that was both intensely cold and deeply hot. Jai had put an ice cube in his mouth and was running his lips around the same spots he had gone a moment earlier.

'Ayeee Ma!' she squealed, wanting to please his attempt at this new form of lovemaking but feeling very cold in all the wrong parts. He removed the ice cube and used his fingers to feel the length of her neck and breasts, going down to her navel and circling it, and slowly slipping his fingers into her as she arched her back and felt the wave of pleasure sweep through her body.

With his other hand he held on to her nipples as he clasped them tight while sliding into her. He kept the blindfold on to increase her pleasure and Sarita realized, by not looking into her husband's eyes, she could imagine this man on top of her to be anyone! She had the first of what would be multiple orgasms. This was nothing like she had ever had. He soared higher and higher, and gave her ass another spank. Yes, this was very different from the missionary position they had been used to. She let out a little yelp, and he covered her mouth with his hand as he continued to make love to her. She was elated. It was all new, and bold, and terribly exciting. Her body tingled as it split into a thousand splintering pieces in pleasure. He moved off her and she was left panting. How would she ever enjoy the old missionary routine again?

'Was it good for you?' he asked, with a knowing smirk.

She could only nod her head. He jumped off the bed, looking extremely pleased and smug, and walked to the bathroom, while Sarita examined her body after this newfound circus act. She didn't know where he had found out about this new way to make love. And suddenly, her mind went spinning. Who was giving him advice? Was he seeing someone else??

Just before dozing off to sleep he murmured, 'I could do many more things if you were a little thinner.' He gathered a few pillows around him and went off to bed, leaving Sarita with flaming cheeks and a deep sense of guilt for every item of food she had put into her mouth in her forty years. How amazing and yet cruel could a husband be? With one statement he could chop a woman's confidence down to smithereens, and with one kiss he could build it up for a high that lasted a week.

That night Sarita decided on two things: she would start going to the gym, and she would start spying on her husband.

5

'The General Body Meeting will now come to order!' the Secretary of the Society said to a handful of people in the room. The husbands of the Sapphire Towers' wives had gathered in the common hall used for parties to attend the bi-annual meeting of the society.

The wives were sitting in the lawns outside the hall, chatting, leaving it to their husbands to attend the meeting.

'What do you think they're discussing?' asked Aarti.

'The pool,' Natasha replied.

'The pool? What's wrong with the pool?' asked Gita. She had never gone to the pool, in any case, but felt she needed to express outrage for some reason. She had only sent her children down to learn swimming every Wednesday and Friday evening, and she was afraid that if it was shut down, her children would not be able to go anymore.

'Apparently, the residents of the other building have a view of the pool, and the husbands don't like that.'

Aarti hadn't heard the entire sentence, so asked again, 'What?'

'People from different buildings staring at us. The husbands are protesting,' Natasha said with authority.

'But it's okay for our society to look down and see their women at the pool?' asked Gita, confused and partly relieved that the pool was not being closed down.

'I've been to the pool so many times now. Whatever the neighbours had to see has already been imprinted in their minds!' said Aarti. All the girls started laughing.

'I think they're planning to build a wall or something to cage us in when we're in our swimsuits,' said Natasha, who was a regular at the pool. She was an excellent swimmer, and hated the fact that several people who didn't know how to swim would go back and forth in the deep end, rather than take laps or stick to the shallow end. She vowed to go swimming one day at night when no one was there. A vow that she would keep, except she would be naked and with a man at the time.

Aarti waved her hand in the air, 'Ooff! It's not like we're wearing bikinis anyway. All the women wear full swimsuits that come with shorts. We're practically in our burkhas!'

The women agreed. They had seen how the women dressed and went swimming only after the husbands and children had left the building for work or school. They would come out fully clothed and quickly change into a swimsuit that covered their arms and half their legs before going for a swim. They might as well have worn jeans since none of them were good swimmers anyway.

'I would love to learn swimming though. It's great exercise and I've never had the chance to learn,' Gita thought out loud.

'You should,' Natasha said encouragingly. 'There's a ladies instructor who comes at eleven twice a week. Call the clubhouse and find out details. It's a lot of fun to learn in a class.'

Gita thought it was a good idea. 'Thank God they're not shutting it. Renu and Anu have swimming classes and I would have to find something else for them to do at that time then.'

Natasha ribbed her friend. 'You put your girls in too many activities, Gita. Let them be!'

Gita shook her head. 'They need structure in their lives, Natasha. The more you push them to do different things at an early age, the better they'll learn discipline.' Gita had seen Natasha's way of controlling Diya and how futile it was. She didn't want her daughters to end up spoilt like her.

Aarti suddenly remembered Sarita. 'Where is Sarita? Didn't we Whatsapp her that we were coming down?' They all checked their phone for the group they had made for themselves on a social site. They called themselves 'Lovely Ladies'.

'Ya, see, I told everyone we're meeting. Only she hasn't confirmed. What is she up to?' Gita said.

'Is she okay?' Natasha asked.

They wondered about Sarita. Their friend had not shown up for the last few days, and now that she skipped this meet-up too, they began to worry about her. If one of them called her house, she would say that she's doing something and would call back. But she never called back and they wondered if something was wrong.

Suddenly, they saw Sarita emerge from the gym opposite the lawns and wipe her head with a towel. Their jaws dropped, and Natasha was the only one who shouted out before Sarita headed towards the lift, 'Sarita!' Natasha waved to her as she looked in their direction.

Sarita walked towards her friends. She knew she was caught. She would now have to tell them everything and the words just weren't forming in her mouth. She reached them and they started talking without giving her a chance to figure out what to say.

'You? Gym? When? Why? How?' asked Aarti, who couldn't form the sentences but wanted to know all the details.

'Ya Sarita! How come?' asked Natasha.

Sarita sat on the bench next to them and drank a large gulp of water from her bottle. 'Look at your gym gear!' remarked Gita, who was quite astounded that Sarita, who hadn't exercised a single day in her life, actually had a Nike water bottle and wristbands. Thankfully, Sarita could cover the handcuff marks with sports products.

'The gym is free. Did you know that? Apparently, we pay a monthly maintenance that includes the gym. So I just thought I should use it,' said Sarita. She didn't want to give away too many details.

'Yes, I did know it was free. But *why* are you using it? You hate exercising!' asked Natasha, who never lost any weight despite the amount of yoga and swimming she did.

'You've never exercised in your life,' Gita added.

'And you're the one who always tells us that we shouldn't join any classes because we're married anyway!' Aarti said, feeling slighted that no one had joined the zumba class when she had suggested it, but everyone wanted to now head to the gym because Sarita had taken the lead.

Sarita stretched her legs and said, 'I know! My God, look at you people pouncing on me! I want to lose weight, that's all. I've been having so many back problems. Why are all of you jumping at me for trying to be thin? You can also join, you know, fatsos!' she teased, and they all laughed with her.

The others decided that they would leave the gym to her. Natasha said she wasn't a closed-door person. She liked exercising outdoors and would prefer playing a sport or go running than lifting weights at the gym. Gita said she never had the time. And Aarti said she would prefer a class like pilates or dance rather than go to the gym.

The conversation led from working out to yoga. And from there to instructors who came home.

'Baap re!' exclaimed Sarita. 'Once I got a yoga instructor to come home and my in-laws went on and on about how expensive it was to keep him. It was just one day and a free trial session, for God's sake, but they made me feel like I was selling their gold to improve my back.'

'Same here,' said Natasha, even though she didn't live with her in-laws or have money problems. 'My husband walked in on me doing yoga with an instructor and asked him to his face, 'So you like touching other women?' I was mortified. That yoga instructor never came back and didn't take the money for the three classes he did with me. Till then I never thought Vikram was the jealous type.'

The girls dissolved into laughter as they listened to each other's stories about their husbands and in-laws. At some level they knew it was chatter on the surface of things. The deeper, darker secrets were something one could never reveal. Natasha never said how Vikram had a foul temper and that she was quite scared of him. While she made a joke about the yoga teacher running away, she didn't mention how he had yelled at her afterwards for meeting another man. And Sarita didn't mention how she had started going to the gym only to please her husband for the acrobatics he was now trying in bed. She didn't know if her friends would look at her as a freak who now enjoyed only kinky sex.

Each of the women felt the other's life was better, and somehow wanted to protect herself from revealing the truth. They were all educated, smart and beautiful, yet somehow, they had lost their way through the course of marriage and children. But they didn't want to reveal how badly it affected them. They guarded their vulnerability with a shield of humour. All they knew was that they were grateful for each other. A simple fact that wouldn't even be there weeks from that moment.

Natasha bit her lip and looked towards the party hall. The meeting had finished. Vikram, who had attended it for the first time, was on his way out.

'I better go. The meeting's over,' Natasha said.

'We'll all go,' said Gita. 'We can't just sit here while the husbands are at home, anyway. It doesn't look nice. And I have to pick up the kids from Julie's place.'

'That American who leaves dirty notes for her boyfriend around the house?' asked Natasha.

'She does?' asked an incredulous Gita, giggling at Natasha's remark.

'Yup,' replied Natasha. 'My bai works for her house too, and one day she brought a note to me, thinking it was for me. What language!' She giggled, as did the others.

'It doesn't matter to me,' Gita said. 'She's an excellent piano teacher and my children love to hear her sing. It's the best one hour of the day for me. No husband. No children. No in-laws. Peace!' Gita got up and straightened her kurta.

Natasha shook her head and said, 'More classes, Gita!' While she knew that Gita was strict with her children, she wondered if she should have been as well. Her relationship with her daughter wasn't always smooth and she had no help from her family in bringing her up.

They all said their goodbyes and left the conversation hanging. They realized that they could continue talking about several topics, if given the opportunity. But Gita was in a hurry to get home. She needed to speak to Shailesh about joining swimming classes. She couldn't wait to start doing something for herself, now that she had some free time on her hands.

6

'Shailesh, I want to talk to you about something,' Gita said to her husband. 'Can you come into the room?' Shailesh was sitting at the breakfast table, where he had been for the last hour, nibbling at his food and reading the newspaper.

'Now?' he asked, extremely irritated about being bothered before he had to leave for work. Gita decided to let him be: she didn't want a fight in front of the children. She decided she would tell him about the swimming classes when he was going downstairs to the car. She went back to the kitchen as she pondered about her marriage. How she had forced herself to adjust to her husband and family. She had to work around his timings, learn to eat what he liked to eat, and ultimately, stopped cooking anything she liked to eat because she couldn't be bothered to do that extra bit of work. She also had to socialize, if he wanted her to, with his friends, even though she thought they were the biggest misogynists in the world. Yes, her journey as a housewife had so far been about adapting, adjusting, behaving properly and obeying, in a family that had, supposedly, welcomed her. And she had done it perfectly. Along the way, though, she had forgotten who she was. It suited Shailesh beautifully.

Shailesh's voice interrupted her thoughts; he announced he was leaving. Hurriedly, she put the flame to low and ran to catch him. She found him waiting in front of the elevator.

'Shailesh,' she said panting, 'I had to ask you something.'

'Gita, what are you doing!' Shailesh exclaimed, as he looked around in panic. 'People will see you in your nightgown. Go inside!'

No one else was around though. Gita looked down at her fully opaque half-sleeved kaftan that showed no part of her body, except the ends of her arms and her bobbing head on top. She shook her head, 'Shailesh, I wanted to ask you. Swimming classes are starting today for ladies.' The lift door opened and she held on to it as he got in, 'Can I please join?'

Shailesh was too busy with his mobile phone to bother listening intently to what she said. Without looking up he remarked, 'There's no need for you to swim, Gita. Who will manage the house? I have no time! Please remove these thoughts from your head.' Gita let the lift door shut without saying another word. She would have managed the house perfectly, she grumbled under her breath. Without him. Like she had been doing for so many years. What was the use? If her own husband hadn't seen her eagerness, why should she even bother learning swimming? What good would come of it? She went back into the house and saw the poha had burnt. Just like her heart. Yet again, Shailesh had left a searing hole and killed her hopes of doing something for herself.

She called the clubhouse and told them to cancel her name from the swimming class. The attendant tried to convince her, telling her again that the lessons were for free. But Gita refused. It wasn't about the money anymore. It was about her respect. Shailesh was behaving like the conservative men from the meeting. He didn't want his wife to wear a swimsuit or get into the pool. It irritated her to no end that he didn't understand that she wanted to do something for herself desperately. But he had never understood any of her wants. How did she even expect him to change now?

Gita served her in-laws some toast. Without waiting to hear their taunts of the simple breakfast she had made for them, she went into her room and locked the door. Every day she made elaborate breakfasts, lunches and dinners to keep them happy. Not once had they praised her for her cooking or for the fact that she took so much time and effort to make them happy. Shailesh barely noticed her cooking, gobbling up the food when he came home and not saying anything. When she asked him he would comment, 'The salt was too much.' He never seemed to be pleased with her, no matter how hard she tried. She took a long shower, silently absorbing her feelings as she had done for years. Adapt, adjust, mould, she told herself. This was her life now. There was no use in hoping for anything different.

In the early days of their marriage she would seek her parents' advice for every time Shailesh said no to a request from her. Her parents would always tell her she needed to 'adjust' to what her husband liked. Eventually, she stopped talking to them about anything important in her marital life. They would call and ask her how everything was, and she would simply say, 'Fine.' She didn't want to hurt their feelings and she never wanted to create strife in the house, too.

She sat on the edge of the bed, looking out of their flat, which was on the nineteenth floor. It had been a blessing to marry him and get away from her parent's tyranny. They never let her do anything and she was stifled. So when the 'rishta' came for her to get married, she jumped at the offer. A great set of in-laws, who gave her a gold chain at the engagement and a high-rise flat with her own room. She thought it was a wonderful way to get away from her parents and live in Mumbai. After all, people called this 'the city of dreams', didn't they?

What a farce that had been, she mused, as she looked through her closet to wear something that would cheer her up. In the early years her bedroom became the nursery, where she slept with the baby while Shailesh took the drawing-room. They barely touched each other, except for the monthly ritual when he usually finished before she could even take off all her clothing. She never enjoyed sex with him, and soon, she began to dread it. She gritted her teeth every time and treated it as another thing she needed to adjust to.

'Gita, chai,' asked her father-in-law from the other room for what she felt was the tenth time today. Gita sighed. Maybe she should buy a flask and keep several cups of tea in that. When she thought about it she realized that the number of times in a day she went into the kitchen just to make tea was staggering.

She looked at the clock. She had an hour before she needed to fetch Anu from her school, diagonally across the road to Sapphire Towers. Today was one of those days when she was mighty depressed. 'PMS,' she thought to herself, blaming her hormones. She hoped that her logic would make her feel better. But it didn't. Then the milk boiled over as she made tea, and she lost it. She started crying. Shailesh had destroyed her self-esteem and now Nature was teasing her with spilt milk?

She wiped her tears with her dupatta and served the tea silently to her father-in-law. Her mother-in-law had gone downstairs to chat with the other old ladies. Probably bitching about their daughters-in-law, she thought. They had a routine to chat every morning, while the younger women met in the evenings. It was a good arrangement since none of them had to bump into each other.

Gita sat in her room quietly for a bit and picked up the book she had started reading. But her mind was racing too fast. She went to the desktop that was in the corner of the room, for Renuka to practise her computer skills. It took forever to come on and showed some error. She had completely forgotten to call the computer engineer to fix it. Suddenly, Gita felt as if she was in a pressure cooker. She had to do everything in the house. Besides cooking and straightening up after the entire family, she was also calling people to constantly fix things that were broken: the plumber, electrician, the carpenter. She was also looking after her children constantly without the help of a maid. All they had was a cleaning woman who came in the morning and chopped the vegetables for Gita to cook. She also took her in-laws for doctor's appointments and took care of them when they were sick.

She remembered how two years ago her mother-in-law fell seriously ill and had to be taken to the hospital. Gita was running between the hospital and home, managing a two-year-old Anu and leaving Renuka with friends who were willing to look after her for a few hours post-school. Shailesh would come around eight in the evening after work and sit with his mother for a little while. His mother would soon tell him to go home as he was tired from work, so he would do that, leaving Gita to spend the night in the hospital too. She would quickly rush to the house early in the morning to make tiffin for the children and get them ready for school. Those were difficult days for Gita, and mostly, she was alone. Shailesh's sisters, both settled abroad, did not come to see their mother, much less take care of her. And yet after all that, once her mother-in-law was home again, Gita did not receive a single 'thank you' from anyone in the family.

And now that Gita was asking Shailesh for permission for this one little thing, he shot her down. It wasn't the first time, Gita realized. He had done it before when she had asked if she could take cooking classes; she even tried to convince him that it would benefit not just her but the entire family. But it would have meant travelling to Dadar thrice a week and finding someone to take Renu home from the bus-stop downstairs, something that she thought her mother-in-law could have done but she said it was too tiring to remember. Shailesh told her to drop the idea. Once, she asked him if she could take the kids to visit her parents every summer, and his reply was curt: 'Who will look after *my* parents then?' So her parents would come to visit them instead, staying in a hotel for a few days, while she shuttled between the house and taking her children to see their Nana and Nani.

Gita shut off the computer. She wore a kurta and jeans and looked at herself in the mirror. She felt extremely fat. Even though she was underweight for her age and height, today she felt bloated and uncomfortable. She hated that she had such small breasts. Even after two children they hadn't grown as Sarita claimed hers had. She changed into a long Anokhi skirt and a plain white kurti with 'mukaish', a present from her friends in the building for her birthday. She combed her dark, wavy hair slowly, hoping the time would pass by quickly before she had to pick up Anu. At least her children added laughter to her life, even though sometimes she wished she could get away from them as well. She had no clue why she was feeling conflicting emotions today. Her pre-menstrual symptoms seemed to be racing through her body, leaving her helpless and completely out of control with her emotions.

'I'm going out, Papa,' Gita began her daily dialogue, 'to pick up Anu. The maid is still here. So if you need anything, please let her know.' She shut the door behind her. The cleaning maid stayed until her mother-in-law came back from chatting with her friends downstairs in the lawns. Gita snorted as she thought they were hardly friends. Their common topic was who did what in the latest 'saas bahu' serials, and how they could torture their daughters-in-law in a similar fashion.

That day, as Gita stepped out of her flat, she felt defiant. She wanted to rebel. Just a little. Against a system that was suppressing her, a society that had constricted her, and a family that caged her. She was tired of her life. Being the perfect bahu, the perfect wife and the ideal mother. For once, she wanted to live her life on her own terms. How, she didn't yet know.

But the chance was just around the corner.

Little did she know that her outing for that day would lead her to take decisions she had never done before. For the first time in her life she would be hiding things from Shailesh and the rest of the world. And she would start moulding herself yet again.

7

Natasha sat in her drawing-room, sipping her coffee and looking at the photos that hung on her walls. The photos were all of hers, taken by her husband Vikram, a fashion photographer, when she first became a model at twenty-one. She had kept all the photos many years later. Maybe, now she thought, as a reminder of how wonderful Vikram had been in the beginning. He was the model boyfriend, the ideal husband, when they got married, the most amazing man she had ever met. He was kind, caring, loving, generous, thoughtful and understanding. *What more could a woman want?*

Natasha finished her coffee and walked back into the kitchen that resembled a village that had been hit by a tornado. Everywhere she looked were reminders of Vikram's early-morning tantrum: smashed pieces of plates on the floor, stains of masala on the wall, pieces of vegetables on the counter, broken eggs on the floor. He stormed off as soon as he finished his violent outburst, leaving her in tears and with a huge mess to clean up.

It was not the first time that Vikram had thrown a fit; and like those other times, this was no fault of hers, though he damn well made it seem so. She had found him in the kitchen making breakfast, and she remarked to him how sweet he was. He asked, 'What do you want in your eggs?' She said, 'Throw in as many veggies as you see. I want a healthy breakfast.' He put bread in the toaster and flipped an omelet in the pan. She noticed that he had used too much oil and she casually said, 'I think we should watch our oil, honey. We both have bad cholesterol.'

Snap! That was it. He took the ladle, picked up the eggs and threw them out of the window. He yelled, 'If you're the expert, then why don't you fucking make it?'

She was shocked, but he continued, 'What, bitch? You don't think I know how to cook? Here, let's see how you put vegetables in your food.' He took out the vegetable crisper from the fridge and dumped the contents all over the countertop.

'You want some pepper in it? Here, take the spices!' He picked up the masala dabba and hurled it against the wall.

Natasha tried to calm him down, 'Honey, it's okay. Whatever you made was perfect. Let me help you make some fresh eggs. Should I make them for you?'

'You don't like your eggs that way?' He took the eggs out of the fridge, holding two in each hand, and flung them on the floor. 'Cook that now!'

With that, he wiped his hands on the kitchen towel and walked out of the door, leaving Natasha extremely puzzled as to what she had said that was so wrong as to have triggered Vikram's rage. She began sobbing uncontrollably as she leaned against the refrigerator, praying for a solution to his anger. She let herself cry for some time, then composed herself and calmly made a cup of coffee. She sat down to ponder over what had happened and where her life had taken this drastic turn.

They started dating when she was very young and he was six years older. Her parents had disapproved, telling her to focus on her studies instead. But she was already making great money as a model and felt independent enough to make her own choices. Vikram took her side and encouraged her to continue with her career.

When he finally proposed she had been a model for eight long years and felt ready to be a wife. Two years of travel and a bagful of memories later, they decided to have a child. Natasha was then twenty-six and quite clueless about how she would raise Diya. Soon all her friends, who were still professional models and travelling across the globe, dropped out of her life. Diya was also proving to be a difficult baby, keeping her mother up all night and always preferring to cling to Natasha than be cared for by the nanny. Natasha's mother and mother-in-law both came, ostensibly to lend a hand, but they were hardly any help as they were old and needed caring themselves. Eventually, Natasha politely told them they could go, and it was back to just her and the baby, and rarely, the nanny.

In the early years of Diya's life Vikram was travelling constantly. In the rare times that he was at home he really wasn't there to help. His only preoccupation was taking photos of the child. Even in the smallest of activities, like burping the baby or taking her around the garden in the stroller, Vikram would call the nanny. When Natasha asked him why he couldn't do the basic child-rearing activities himself, pat came the reply, 'I'm paying for maids, anyway,' he told Natasha one day. 'Why are they there if I have to do everything myself?' Natasha resented it but let him be.

But before she was prepared to admit it, she was resenting the fact that Diya kept her bound to the house and she seemed to have lost her freedom. There would always be one or another reason why she couldn't do what she desired. When Diya began going to school, Natasha wanted to start something on her own, but Diya was always getting into trouble and Natasha couldn't concentrate on any of her projects. Vikram indulged his daughter in everything and he never denied her in the smallest of wants.

Natasha remembered once when Diya was five, she had prepared a regular, lovely dinner for the family. Vikram had come home from work and Diya had asked for pizza. Without another word he had ordered the pizza. When Natasha told him that dinner was already prepared and she had taken Diya to a birthday party just the previous day where she had pizza, Vikram had flared up and said, 'So what, Natasha? Can't the child have what she likes? My God!'

Natasha could only guess that this was why Diya turned out to be a brat as she grew older. Whether it was food and toys when she was small, or designer clothes and the latest mobile phones as she grew up, Vikram gave Diya everything.

Eventually, Diya learned that it was her father who always said yes, and Natasha's relevance to her life decreased until there was no respect left for her mother. The smallest issues in the household triggered nasty arguments with Vikram. He wanted her to still work but she just wasn't able to find any. It was only a matter of time before she needed to take antidepression pills.

Vikram's mood swings, meanwhile, became more extreme. He would go from being a happy soul, who would put on an old record and start dancing with Natasha and kissing her passionately, to a brooding, reserved, and even extremely upset man, who didn't want to touch her. Natasha would be very scared of him then, tiptoeing around him, serving him food and sitting quietly in one place until his mood lifted again.

No one knew about his dark side. She never told her friends, as she was sure they would advise her to leave him. And she couldn't. She didn't have enough reason. Nor the money. He had never hit her. Only raised his voice a few times, slammed a few drawers in front of her, and smashed things around to terrorize her. He succeeded, of course, but then shortly, he would start being nice again, even extra sweet. He would cook for her and buy her expensive presents. Then things would be fine for a month or two, before he erupted again.

Today's bout of rage in the kitchen had come after just two weeks of peace. Natasha wondered if this was going to be a regular pattern in her life and what she needed to do about it.

She sighed and picked up her phone to send a message to her friends on the Lovely Ladies Whatsapp group they had created for themselves, 'Want to come over for coffee?' She needed some female company and a bit of superficial banter to take her mind off her issues. She wasn't the kind of person who could confront problems head-on. She always asked people and Vikram for advice in her life. Her friends in the building were her soulmates. At the ripe old age of forty-one Natasha knew that she could no longer make new friends. It was too difficult to socialize with her old model friends and she hardly went anywhere to meet new people.

Sarita wrote back, 'Can't. At gym.'

Natasha was puzzled. What had gotten into Sarita that she was perpetually at the gym? Maybe she needed to start exercising as well, she thought. Vikram had earlier bought her a stationary cycle and told her to start using it. It was now being employed to hang towels when it rained. She did yoga three times a week at the local gym and it was good enough for her. She did it more for the breathing they taught that helped her calm her mind. What was the point of exercising beyond that? Her body was still toned and slim, but not skinny that was needed for the ramp. And with the new crop of models entering the market, as a mother, her options for work were, ironically, slim. Her days of self-starvation and working out were over. She sat at home and watched daily soaps, a bowl of popcorn in hand.

She saw two more messages on her phone, both from the Lovely Ladies group: Aarti was travelling, and Gita was helping Renuka with her homework. Natasha uttered a 'thank you' for the fact that Diya did most of her homework in school or went for tuitions where she completed her school assignments; she simply had no patience to sit and help with her child's homework.

Natasha decided to go to the mall. Diya wouldn't be back from school till five in the evening and it was only 11 o'clock. The twilight time of day for every housewife: when the children had left for school, the maids had finished their chores, and the husband had gone to work, there wasn't a single thing left to do. It was the time when housewives felt helpless, as if their lives were going nowhere. A dead period between hectic activity and lunch that made a woman question her choices in life. A time to ponder how an intelligent woman had such a deep sense of seclusion from the world, that no one understood her and she had nowhere to go. She wasn't alone, she guessed, and most housewives experienced such emptiness. So they sat and watched TV, or went to the gym, or tried to busy themselves in some work that would distract them from those two dreariest hours of the day.

But not today! Natasha needed a 'pick me up' today. Natasha wore her white denim pants, a short lemon top, some beads around her neck and beige wedge heels. She applied some light lipstick to boost her morale. She was in no mood to clean up the mess that Vikram had made. Today was going to be about her.

She grabbed her bag and checked her image in the hall mirror before stepping out. For a moment she saw a lonely-looking woman of forty-one, who had spent her entire life looking after her family and had got nothing to show for it. They hated her and she hated herself. She needed to change that. She desperately wanted a little laughter and some happiness in her life. She opened her heart to the universe and asked for a miracle.

8

Gita reminded herself that she had two lovely children who looked up to her, and that should be good enough. She counted life's blessings and let the argument with Shailesh be. She glanced at herself in the elevator mirrors and decided that she wasn't going to be annoyed any longer. Your worth cannot be measured by how important you are in someone else's life, Gita thought, it needs to be determined by your place in your own life.

The lift went down a few floors before it opened at the lobby. Sahil got in. He was surprised to see her. 'Arrey, where are you off to, lovely?' he said, bringing a smile to her face.

'Picking up Anu,' she replied, as she stepped out of the lift. He let the elevator go and remained standing where he was. 'Where are you coming from?' Gita asked. She tried not to stare at her brother-in-law's muscles that seemed to be rippling through his casual Tantra T-shirt and tight, dark blue jeans.

'Swimming,' he replied, as he showed her his gym bag that reminded her again of the fight with Shailesh this morning. 'I was actually going to get a shave now,' he said, running his hand over the hint of stubble on his face. Gita thought he looked even more handsome with that bit of facial hair. 'Unless you want me to keep it?' he teased Gita. She shrugged her shoulders, 'No no, do what you want. How does it matter?' She looked down at her shoes and hoped Sahil did not see her cheeks blushing. Sahil only teased her more, 'It doesn't matter because I look good either way?' Gita could swear he had a naughty twinkle in his eye.

She shook her head, unable to find the words to respond to what she felt was his overtly flirtatious gesture. She remembered when she had lunch with him and they had spoken about movies, his work, and her interest in poetry. They had ordered non-vegetarian Chinese food that she had eaten heartily along with a whole bottle of Coke, something she always had to share when her children or in-laws were around because they asked for 'just a sip' from it. It was a lovely post-birthday gesture and she had had so much fun.

'Come with me,' Sahil said.

'Where? To the barber shop?'

He shook his head, as the lift came to the ground floor and they both got out. 'I also need to pick up some groceries for the house,' he said. 'I've run out of butter and bread. Some other things, too.'

They stepped into the elevator, though Gita was hesitant. If anyone saw her shopping with her brother-in-law, tongues would wag. And then she wouldn't hear the end of it from her in-laws. And Shailesh, what would he think? He would have a royal fight with Sahil and that might result in friction in the family. Wives just didn't go shopping with other men! Even if they were brothers-in-law.

He pleaded, 'It'll only take a few minutes! Please? For me? I'm really bad at picking things up for the house and overspend on things I don't need.'

Her heart really wanted to spend a little more time with Sahil and it told her not to overthink. After all, she was a good daughter-in-law and, surely, there was no harm in helping him pick out some groceries.

'Okay,' she nodded. 'But maybe we should pick up Anu first?' She thought it would be wise to have a child around, in case they were seen by someone they knew.

Sahil looked at his watch, 'But school won't be done until another forty-five minutes or so. We can't keep waiting in front of the school till then. Come on, I promise not to bite you. Unless you want me to!' Sahil had disarmed her with his smile. The thought of Sahil putting his lips on her body sent shivers down her spine.

Gita took a moment to answer, but eventually, she nodded. They finished grocery shopping in exactly ten minutes, where she picked out everything for him and told them to deliver it in an hour. He then suggested they go have ice cream. This time she meant it when she said no, 'I can't, Sahil.' Surely someone would see them! Shailesh would be jealous and have a fit of rage. The thought actually made her feel nice. Maybe Shailesh would start taking more interest in her, do something nice and special for her? Then again, he could turn extremely mean and forbid her from leaving the house. She didn't know what to do.

But Sahil wouldn't take no for an answer. He dragged her along. They took an auto to a small place, close to the house, that had opened recently. It had home-made ice cream with many different toppings for a very reasonable price. He ordered a sundae for her and she laughed like a little girl. She had never had so many flavours all at once, always choosing to have a scoop at the most when her daughters insisted she eat with them.

'Sahil, this is crazy!' she said, while taking a bite. He reached across and wiped a small bit of ice cream from the corner of her mouth. It was the most innocuous gesture but he looked into her eyes deeply, speaking a language she at once knew. The language of love.

Suddenly, she felt a gush of deep attraction towards Sahil that just as quickly plunged her into depths of guilt.

She dropped her ice cream cup on the table. 'We should go now. Anu will be waiting.'

Sahil understood that he had crossed the line. 'But at least finish your ice cream? Five minutes?'

Gita finished her ice cream in haste and wiped her mouth. What was she doing? Why was she cavorting with her brother-in-law? This wasn't right!

'Now let's go.' Gita stood up and started walking out the door. Sahil jumped up from his seat, leaving his sundae half-finished. She hailed an auto and quickly got in.

It was a five-minute drive wrapped in an uncomfortable silence that had suddenly descended upon the two of them. When they reached the school building, Sahil said to Gita, 'Nothing happened. Don't get upset. Nothing's wrong. I'm home the whole day, if you want to just come and talk.' Gita didn't reply. How dare he think she wanted to talk to him? It was obvious he had romantic feelings for her and she now needed to keep a distance.

And what about your feelings, Gita? a tiny voice inside her head whispered. She thanked him for the ice cream and walked briskly across the road to Anu's playschool. A thousand thoughts raced through her mind. But the only one that lingered was the feel of Sahil's fingers caressing her lips.

9

Natasha got into an auto and told the driver to take her to a mall some distance away.

She noticed several buildings that had come up in such a short time, and remembered the time several years ago when she and Vikram had gone hunting for a house. That was the time when he had included her in many decisions. Now, nothing she said or did mattered, neither to him nor to Diya.

Vikram was clever enough to hide his anger for Natasha in front of Diya. Their daughter worshipped him and hated her. She suddenly had an idea: she wondered if it had anything to do with her post-partum depression that lasted several months after Diya was born. In hindsight she knew she should have seen a doctor about it and gone on some sort of medication, but there was no one to talk to about why she seemed to be so depressed all the time. Neither her mother nor her mother-in-law were great listeners, and she didn't want to burden them further with her post-partum depression.

To add to her woes, Diya was a colicky baby and she had bouts of crying when nothing shushed her except rocking her back and forth continuously or turning on some white noise like the static of the TV. The sleepless nights, fatigue, body changes, including cracked nipples, were enough to make Natasha severely depressed. Secretly, she hated Diya. It was a thought she never dared voice out loud. But it was so powerful that it transmitted itself through her bodily fluids. She wasn't surprised when the child began reciprocating the feeling as she grew up. Much later, when she visited a therapist, the doctor told her it was all hogwash. It was just stubbornness in Diya that made her who she was, and had nothing to do with Natasha or a post-partum depression. That was simply hormones. All women were allowed to experience post-partum depression, and maybe even hate their children at some point or another. It was a natural thing. It didn't mean anything. They would get over it and still love their children and look after them forever.

But Natasha, it seemed, didn't get over hers. Her post-partum period was traumatic. Vikram was of no help then. She used to be continuously hungry and he refused to give her more food. What was required for a model wasn't enough for a nursing mother. And he desperately wanted her to get her figure back as soon as she delivered. She couldn't care less then. She just wanted to stuff herself with cakes and chicken puffs and see if that would make her happy. She would stuff her drawers with biscuits and chips and eat them in the middle of the night when Vikram was asleep.

She felt even more miserable lying to Vikram about it, but he soon lost interest in her losing weight and started his temper tantrums over the smallest issues. 'Why were all the lights and fans on?' he would yell, when he entered the house. 'Why is there no milk for tea?' he would shout in the morning, when she had just about fallen asleep with Diya next to her.

Natasha was lost deep in her thoughts, and didn't realize that she had automatically got out of the auto, and walked inside the mall and reached Tea Leaf and Coffee Bean.

'Yes Ma'am,' the man behind the counter said. 'What would you like to have today?'

'Oh,' she shook off the daydreaming. 'A cappuccino please.' She added, 'And a chocolate chip muffin.' It had been a long time since she indulged herself in anything nice.

'Would you like chocolate sauce with that?' the young man asked, and she wanted to just bite off his head and say instead, 'Do you think my body needs chocolate sauce? I just want a little happiness in my life. Not everything has to have extra chocolate!'

But she just shook her head, 'No thank you.' She paid the amount and turned to find a table. Standing behind her in the queue was Sarita's son, Rahul.

'Arrey! Natasha Aunty!' he exclaimed. She cringed. How did she get from the eighteen-year-old Nuts, who was labelled that for being a wild child, to 'Natasha Aunty'?

'Just Natasha, Rahul,' she said and started walking.

He took a few steps and said, 'I'm so sorry if I offended you.'

'I'm not that much older than you,' she said. Of course, she was lying through her teeth.

He laughed. 'But what's wrong with being Aunty? I happen to like older women. They're far more mature and womanly than the girls around me!'

Was he flirting? Natasha wasn't sure. Maybe making polite conversation. Either way, he was her friend's son and she didn't want to encourage the chatter. 'They're waiting for your order. See you later, Rahul.' She walked away. He went back and stood in line.

She had just started on her cup of coffee when Rahul came over. 'Do you mind if I sit with you?'

'Why?' It was her first thought. Why would a young teenage boy want her company?

He sat down anyway. 'I'm alone. You're alone. We can be alone together.' It was typical teenage talk that actually made sense to Natasha.

'Have a seat,' she said, with a warm smile.

Seeing Rahul and hearing him talk brought back her modelling days, when everyone was free with each other.

Adolescents spoke openly without fear of consequences. Marriage bound you to think before you opened your mouth, as the repercussions could label you in a negative way. As a teenager she had spoken her mind, done what she wanted and lived a free life. As a married woman Natasha had kept her *bindaas* attitude in check and spoken only when needed.

Did marriage really change life's rules for women? Natasha wondered. She had always felt constricted by the concept of marriage and the rules that society imposed on married women. Who said she couldn't have coffee with her friend's son? It was a harmless five minutes. She needed a little bindaas in her life. She wanted to speak openly and freely, without fear of being judged as a bad wife or a terrible mother. She wanted to know how adolescents thought nowadays and if it had changed from her time.

She was actually delighted to listen to a teenager talk about his 'overly stressful' life. Somehow, Rahul opened up to her, sharing details about his life. She assumed it was because he needed a new perspective on his issues that no one else was able to give.

'I mean, I can't tell you the stress this woman has been giving me,' Rahul said, as he sipped his cappuccino. He spoke about his girlfriend as if Natasha was a close friend. 'And my parents and grandparents don't give me any money! How is a teenager supposed to live with no money? I can't buy things. So if I avoid the woman because I don't have any money, she gets bugged. How can I tell her that I can't take her for a movie because I have no money? And once when I asked her to pay for us, she said, 'Oh, you're so cheap. All boys are supposed to pay if they like a girl.' I mean, where the hell is women's lib? They're all down with equality and shit, but when it comes to paying for their own stuff or taking a dude out, they're all like, no, it's not chivalrous!'

Natasha burst into laughter, the first time in ages that a man had made her laugh. She suddenly realized, though, that he might not like it that she was laughing at his stories. 'I'm sorry,' she said, pushing her plate of muffins towards him. 'You want some?'

'You're making fun of me, aren't you?' he asked with a smile, and took a spoonful of chocolate-chip muffin. 'You know this cup of coffee is the only indulgence I have for myself once a week. My parents think teenagers shouldn't drink coffee. I mean, which world are they living in?'

'I agree. Everyone should be allowed a cup of coffee!' Natasha said, as they clinked their cups and took a sip. 'So where do you find the money for your weekly indulgence?' Natasha knew she meant that as a simple statement but Rahul took it as wicked twist and smiled provocatively at her.

'By indulging in a weekly ritual,' he said with a smile, and Natasha's eyes widened.

He laughed out loud. 'You should see your face. You look so shocked.'

She laughed, too.

'I work every weekend at a hobby class. I teach children drawing and painting.'

A boy of eighteen was teaching art classes? Incredible. 'How many children? Where? How do you know any drawing?' her questions came in quick succession, and it pleased him extremely.

'I used to sketch quite well. Took classes when I was in school and became quite good. So now I take classes for small children. Aged five to seven. Not too tough to show them how to colour in between the lines. And it gives me about ten grand a month. So I can afford to buy a coffee when I want, or a mobile if I save up. But not enough to take a girl out to expensive places twice a week,' he said, as he showed Natasha his iPhone. 'I would love to sketch you one day. You have very different features. You're not like the other aunties.'

Natasha smiled again and reprimanded him, 'Oh God! I always hated being an aunty. Never call me that again. And by the way, young man, I'm way too old for you to be flirting with me.'

'Arrey! I'm not flirting. But I can't tell you the truth or what? It seems like no one had paid you a compliment recently.'

Natasha realized that it was true; no one had said she was beautiful for a long time. Vikram had stopped noticing a long time ago. Sometimes she wished he would just tell her how to improve herself, as he used to. At least then, he was taking an interest in her. Now, he didn't bother. He gave her money whenever she wanted, and wasn't the least concerned about where she was going or what she was doing. He had become just an ATM in her life, without any emotional attachment or physical attraction. In a way it was good because she wasn't accountable to him anymore. But a wife somewhere likes to be accountable to her husband. Not all the time. But just once in a while, so she feels important in her husband's life.

'Okay, you can sketch me,' she said unexpectedly. 'But you can't show it to anyone.'

Rahul beamed, 'Give me your number. I'll come over tomorrow.'

'Not tomorrow,' Natasha laughed, 'but soon. I'll let you know.'

They exchanged numbers, and she said she was going to do some shopping and went off while he went in another direction. Natasha recognized a nice feeling in the pit of her stomach at that moment. He was young but he had a streak of independence that she admired. And he wasn't bad to look at, either.

Natasha bought herself a dress that day. She planned to wear it when sitting for her portrait. She wondered how teenagers were so misunderstood. Here was a boy who was earning his own money to manage his life. He didn't ask his parents at all. And there was her child Diya who constantly asked for more money and refused to do even basic chores in the house.

How different they both were. Yet their lives would be so intrinsically woven that it would lead to fatal decisions.

10

Finally, Sarita could wake up late. That was probably the only benefit of having your children become teenagers. They could wake themselves up, prepare their own breakfast and tiffin, and head off to school without you getting disturbed from your sleep. It was all about training. The family had to be taught right from the beginning that you weren't going to be their maid. Start the family with lowering their expectations and they wouldn't be disappointed later when you refused to comply. (She imagined Gita's family who relied on her for every small thing, and she shuddered.)

When Sarita finally emerged from her room at nine o'clock, she was fresh, happy to make them breakfast.

Sarita believed it was the little things she did that held her entire family together. It mattered, some days, that they wouldn't let her buy new things and kept handing clothes down from one generation to another. But on most days they didn't demand too much. And because she was so attentive towards her in-laws and asked them ten times whether they wanted another roti, her husband adored her. She took extra care of his parents and, in turn, he took extra care of her and made sure she was satisfied, even in bed!

She stretched her left arm to the side and heard a 'crick'. She needed to crease out the aches of the previous night before she got up. Her whole body was sore from the antics Jai had thrust on her. She must ask him where he was getting these kinky ideas but she was too scared he would take offence and stop. Alas, the dilemmas of a housewife!

She went to the washroom, came out and stood on the weighing scale, something she had recently bought for herself with the money she stole from Jai's wallet. She did that occasionally and he didn't even know about it. A few hundred here and there and she could save enough to buy a few things she really wanted, whenever the time arose.

Three kilos down! She squealed with joy. All the exercise she was getting on the treadmill and in bed had actually worked. She could feel her thunder-thighs already looking more toned. Her heart lifted. The happiest thing in the world was when you saw the weighing scale needle go towards the left. No, it wasn't the birth of your firstborn. It was weight loss: the topmost agenda on a woman's mind on most days.

'Ma, Papa,' she greeted her in-laws, as she came out of her room in her new dark blue kaftan from Elco Arcade. It covered her from head to toe with just her arms jutting out. Made her look like a sack of potatoes, but it was the best thing to wear in front of male members of your house, as it would never show you in a desirous light. 'What would you like for breakfast?'

Her father-in-law was reading the paper and her mother-in-law was watering the plants in the balcony. It was a tiny little balcony that was used to look into the houses of the million other buildings that were peering into your house. Her mother-in-law had covered the area with various plants and cared for them like little babies. Sarita smirked and thought, if she cared half as much for her grandkids, they wouldn't be out of the house so often.

This three-bedroom apartment had started feeling extremely small for the entire family. Rahul hated coming back home. A few times when she confronted him late at night he had slurred about 'life is so unfair', and gone to bed. She was sure he was drunk. Kids today loved their alcohol. It was an alcoholic generation. It was the era of drinking and partying. How could adults even think of stopping it? It would mean huge fights and tremendous fallouts. Sarita didn't want that. She just wanted her children to be happy.

'What will you make?' her father-in-law looked up from his newspaper.

'Poha, upma, eggs?'

Her in-laws made a face and she scowled. If they didn't like her food, why didn't they just make it themselves?

She held her tongue. 'There's also cornflakes. It's quite a healthy diet with some skimmed milk.'

'In our days we never needed skimmed milk!' snorted her father-in-law. 'We had full cream milk and we all lived to be a hundred years old.'

'Really Papa?' Sarita asked, her voice laced with saccharine. 'From today I will give you only full cream milk. I also want you to live to be a hundred.' She muttered to herself, 'If I didn't look after your cholesterol and diabetes, you would probably kick the bucket by New Year's Eve!'

She went into the kitchen while they called out to her to make them some eggs. Just then, she got a message on her Lovely Ladies group and checked who it was from. Gita. She was dying to have an egg. A simple egg. Sarita thought she could kill two birds with one stone and wrote back to Gita, 'Come over, please. I'm trying to figure out how to make an omelet in any case. So you crack an egg first, right?' Gita sent a smiley and wrote that she would be there in two minutes.

Gita came with a dozen eggs and a few other groceries in a bag. She greeted Sarita's in-laws. They had met a few times and adored Gita. Whenever she came over she whipped them up some extraordinary dishes and often brought her own supplies. She was a wonderful woman.

'What will you make for us today, Gita?' Sarita's mother-in-law said cheerfully. The father-in-law already had a twinkle in his eye. Sarita rolled hers. They were so excited to see her as if she'd got them a shiny car. Gita started whipping up some eggs, chopping up onions, put the microwave to an oven setting, popped in some toasts, took out some milk and sugar and pretty much made herself feel right at home in Sarita's kitchen. Sarita sat in one corner sipping her tea.

'I don't know how you can do so many things altogether Geets,' Sarita said, using her pet name, 'I'm so useless in all this.'

Gita smiled as she popped in a dish into the oven and stood for a minute, 'I love cooking. It comes easily. I've been doing it for years. Except I don't get to make any non-vegetarian food at home, and sometimes I really want to experiment with different dishes, you know?'

'No, actually I don't know,' Sarita said. 'I've never had the need to experiment with any dish!'

They both laughed as Gita flipped the French toast. Sarita told Gita that she had lost three kilos.

Gita was amazed. 'How did you do it?'

'A personal trainer,' Sarita winked.

Gita's jaw dropped, 'Your in-laws let you have a personal trainer?'

'No!' Sarita slapped her forehead dramatically. 'It's Jai.' And she winked again.

Gita looked even more surprised, so Sarita continued, 'Jai has been trying new things every night and it seems to have helped. Either that or the constant running on the treadmill!'

Gita took out the baked eggs with caramelized onions and sautéed tomatoes from the oven. She put the French toast with warm honey on a plate, and buttered the fresh, hot brown bread that had popped out of the toaster. She put the spicy, crisp potato cutlets in a bowl and said triumphantly, 'Come, let's eat! You're looking too thin!'

Sarita smiled as they sat at the dining-table. Sarita's in-laws ate heartily, barely speaking to the girls. 'This is all so good,' Sarita said. Gita was just glad that she could have her heart's fill of eggs. She hadn't seen Sahil since the day they had ice cream. It had been a week and she missed him terribly. There had been no conversation with Shailesh, as usual, and Gita missed the natural camaraderie she had with Sahil. Sometimes, no amount of female friendship could make up for the male attention that a woman needed.

If Sarita and Jai could have such a rocking marriage after so many years, the least she deserved was a little bit of happiness in her life as well. And she and Sahil could go back to being buddies. Yes, she decided that was exactly what she would do as soon as she left Sarita's apartment.

Gita finished and helped Sarita clear up.

'I want to know more about your personal training session later,' Gita whispered to Sarita, as they were putting away the dishes. They exchanged a secret giggle before the maid came in to clean, and Gita said she had to leave. And because of the lovely breakfast, courtesy Gita, Sarita's in-laws were jovial the entire morning.

Sarita went out for coffee in the evening with her gang of Lovely Ladies and chirped about how well the day had gone. Even when Rhea came back with a bad grade on her Science project, it hardly mattered to Sarita. Rahul was home in the evening and he spoke about some art school he wanted to go to. Sarita listened to him and wondered if he was gay. Which boy liked to do art? However, she didn't say a word. She decided to be supportive. All because of the lovely breakfast she had that morning.

In the evening, once she had finished serving her family their supper of rajma chawal, she cleared up the dishes and went inside her room. Jai followed. Sarita was willing to try anything today. It had been the perfect day. News of her weight loss, a great breakfast, a good chat with fabulous friends. Whatever Jai did now would be a piece of cake.

Jai took out what looked to be a contraption from the 1900s.

'What is that?' Sarita asked, in trepidation. This seemed so out of the blue.

'A swing!'

Sarita's face belied her shock. 'Relax,' he said, as he started hooking it up to the curtain rod. 'The man at Yari road told me how to do it.'

'Yari road? Andheri? Are you sure? Was he legitimate?'

'What have you got to do with whether he's legitimate or not? This is not drugs.'

'It's equally wild,' she muttered to herself.

He finished setting up and put his hands on his hips. 'Chal, climb!' It looked like a contraption between a hammock and a leather whip, neither of which Sarita felt was a comfortable proposition.

'Are you serious? *I'm* not climbing that.'

'This will be fun. Just open your mind and let your body free.'

'I like the freeing-the-mind part, but won't it open the body a little too much!?'

Jai pulled Sarita close. He wrapped his arms around her and slowly started gently massaging her neck. 'Release all the tension.' The stroking of his fingers sent pleasant jolts through her body. He caressed the length of her neck gently, kneading his fingers into her soft, supple skin. She threw her head back, enjoying the massage. He had such magical hands! He swivelled her around as he laid gentle kisses on the curve of her neck. He slipped his hands underneath her kurta and fondled her breasts. She let out a soft moan. He pressed his body against hers and she could feel the urge in his desire. She turned around, tossed her hands around his neck, and kissed him passionately. Their tongues explored the recesses of each other's mouths, as the kiss sent new spirals of ecstasy through her. After so many years the touch of his hands, his body next to hers and his deep kisses still meant they were so much in love. They slipped off their remaining clothes. He took a deep breath. He was all ready for this new venture.

Jai took the seat, the harness holding his chest and shoulders with a tight grip. Sarita moved slowly to sit on top of him. She put her legs through the harness that held her hips and waist in place. She settled on top of him as he moved the swing with his leg. And as the swing moved he slipped more and more into her. She felt waves of pleasure rolling through her body as the double movement aroused her more. Her anxiety left her as she felt more secure in the harness. She held on to the swing from the ropes that were hanging and let out a loud groan. Jai laughed out loud as he thrust himself deeper into her. It was an exhilarating feeling to know your wife loved this new form of lovemaking, the shapely beauty of her naked body bringing him to the edge of frenzied passion. Her breasts tingled against his hair-roughened chest. It was exhilarating. With each swing back and forth he pulled in and out of her body, leaving them both in pure ecstasy. She tossed her head back and arched her back in sheer pleasure. This was a wonderful new adventure.

If hindsight could be sold in the supermarket, it would become more popular than rice. Sarita knew she had done something wrong the minute she heard the crack.

Her movement made the tension on the rope tighter. It couldn't take the weight of her body. Jai's eyes popped out in fear as everything happened in slow motion. Suddenly, the harness broke.

Sarita saw it all again and again, as if it was a Hindi television serial. She looked up and saw the loop of the harness tear. She shouted for Jai to 'watch out!' Steadily, the harness broke from its loop. Before they could get out, he lay flat on his back with her on top of him. To break her fall she landed on her right hand, and she could feel an excruciating pain tear through her body. The fall, the fracture, the humiliation was too much for Sarita to bear. At that moment all she could think of was the dealer from Yari road who had sold the damn contraption to Jai. She knew she was going to find him and give him the thrashing of his life when she recovered from this shock.

Her in-laws were banging on the door. 'Beta, what fell? It sounded like the expensive painting you bought for your room. I hope it's not broken.' Sarita knew she would not only kill the Yari road dealer, but also her father-in-law one day.

'No, it's not the painting, Papa,' she said, as her face turned from a deep crimson of shame to a dark blue of pain. She muttered to Jai, 'Your stupid parents want to know if the painting has broken. What do we tell them?' She quickly got dressed, dismissing the fact that her right arm couldn't work. She didn't want her family to see Jai and her naked with a swing. How humiliating! Jai made some excuse, kept the harness away rapidly, and wore his clothes. He mumbled back, 'Stick to this story. We were trying to do yoga and you fell down.'

'Yoga?' she asked. 'Are you mad? No one does yoga after dinner!'

'It's new yoni yoga, Sarita. Stick to the goddam story!' He looked at her for a brief second and asked, 'Did you come though?'

Sarita answered with a smile, even though she was about to lie to her in-laws and head to the emergency room, 'Long time back, baby!' The pain suddenly returned for both of them. He nodded, happy he had pleasured his wife before giving her this pain, and desperately needing some ice for his groin. He had no words for his mortification when he opened their bedroom door and saw his children and parents standing there, wondering what was going on. Just then, Sarita grabbed her purse and said, 'We need to go.'

'Where?' Jai followed her.

She opened the front door. 'To the hospital. I think I broke my arm with the yoni yoga.'

11

'Sarita!' Aarti gasped dramatically, as Sarita stepped out of the lift and into the lawns to meet her friends. She had been off Whatsapp and her phone for the last two days, and the women had started to worry about her. When they saw her right arm in a bandage and a sling around her neck, they were shocked. 'What happened?' they asked in unison.

Sarita had decided that she would not tell her friends the whole truth about how she got a fracture in her arm. 'Nothing, yaar,' she said casually. 'A minor accident.'

But they insisted on knowing the whole story, so Sarita made one up. 'I got hurt in the gym. Was doing some weights and pulled a ligament. Kept going and it worsened.'

Natasha looked unconvinced but didn't say anything. Aarti sympathized immediately and said, 'You poor thing. How are you feeling now?'

'Was really painful for the last two days. Was on heavy painkillers that made me so drowsy I couldn't even message you guys.'

'Don't worry about that,' Gita said, and hugged Sarita. 'Tell us if you need any help. It looks really bad.'

'There is a silver lining to this entire scenario,' Sarita smiled. 'Now I can hire a cook! My husband has put his foot down with his parents and insisted we get a cook. I'm off kitchen duty! I hope I can twist his arm into keeping her for life.' She threw such a fit about it that her husband had to agree to all her terms and conditions. He also found himself agreeing to Sarita's demand that he would look for a separate house for his parents as well. She was mighty pleased with the situation. She didn't know whether he would carry out his promise but he had made her feel very good when she was upset.

The girls thought that it was quite brave of Sarita to remain so positive, despite such pain. Natasha, though, had something else in mind: there was something Sarita wasn't telling them, she was sure. She decided that she would ask Rahul for the real story behind his mother's fracture. She said to Sarita, 'I'll send you my cook. She's great. Try her out. My cleaning maid is terrible though. But I can't replace her. She's at least trustworthy.'

Aarti nodded, 'I've had the same cleaning woman for years. I can't even tell her what to do anymore because she gets upset.'

'These damn maids think that they own us,' Gita said, grinding her teeth.

'I know! It's the same thing with my maid!' Natasha chimed in. 'We can't live with them and we can't live without them.'

'I agree,' Sarita said. 'But guys, on another topic, don't you think the security in this building sucks?'

'Why? Did something happen?' Aarti asked, as she munched on a mini chocolate croissant that Gita was passing around.

Sarita's voice was hoarse with frustration. 'I was in the lift with Rhea yesterday, and a labourer entered. The way he looked up and down at my daughter! Bloody fool. Who are these people who are allowed to enter our lift? Why can't they use the servant's lift?'

Gita was horrified. 'Oh my God! What did you do?'

Sarita shrugged her shoulders and replied, 'What could I do? I never know in these times who will fall for whom. I told Rhea to hold her tongue and not say anything mean to him. That child could slap a person if she wanted to! Who knows if he will stalk her and God forbid, throw acid on her!'

Gita shrieked, 'Sarita! Don't even say these things!' She shivered at the thought. She had two daughters and was extremely worried.

Aarti who had a young son didn't seem too perplexed, 'Gita, these croissants are delicious,' she said. 'Where did you get them from?'

Gita looked at her and wondered how Aarti could make every conversation about only her. If she wasn't interested in the topic, she would soon change the direction of the conversation. Gita smiled, 'I made them.' Aarti really was vapid, Gita thought, but sweet in her own way.

Natasha's jaw dropped as she helped herself to another croissant. 'Seriously? These are superb! How did you even learn to cook like this?'

Gita was pleased. 'Well, I have plenty of time at home. And I love experimenting in the kitchen.'

'Seriously, Gita, you should have a catering service or open a restaurant or something,' gushed Aarti. 'These are too good for just friends and family!'

'Thanks, but I'm on a diet,' Sarita said, as Gita passed the box to her. She looked at the mini treats that everyone was raving about.

'Just have one, Sarita. What's with all this dieting now?' Natasha asked, looking very happy with chocolate in her mouth.

But Sarita was adamant. 'The best way to lose weight is to shake your head from left to right whenever offered anything good!' She shut her jaw tight to show her determination at not giving into temptation.

'And everything good is illegal, immoral, or fattening!' Aarti said cheekily. They all laughed and agreed.

Gita was pleased that her friends enjoyed her afternoon occupation. She had started speaking to Sahil again, under the pretence of cooking something new that he should try. Then he would come over and eat it and inevitably shower her with some praise. Those few words of appreciation and those moments of attention were enough to brighten Gita's day. She began to think that she really needed that in her life to be a better person and a calmer mother.

'Come on, Sarita, have a taste of my croissant.' Gita said.

Sarita gave in, took a piece, and rolled her eyes as she took one bite. 'Wow. These I could bust my diet for!'

'What are you going on a diet for anyway?' Natasha asked.

'I'm taking this quite seriously, guys. I'm doing research on different diets on the internet also.'

Aarti remarked, 'You? And the internet? How? You can't even send a Whatsapp message! Diet, internet. Where's our old Sarita gone?'

Hearing Aarti talk of Whatsapp reminded Natasha of Rahul. Her face flushed and she had to look down. Rahul had been sending her naughty jokes on Whatsapp and she had not been ignoring them at all. It had come to a phase where they looked forward to chatting with each other on a daily basis. He had asked her if he could come to her place this week to finally do that sketch of hers they had talked about that afternoon at the coffee shop. To that message she hadn't replied yet, as she was unsure if it was the right thing to do. She looked at Rahul's mother, sitting right next to her. She justified her behaviour by thinking that maybe she and Sarita weren't such great friends after all? Just then, Sarita said, 'We must all keep up with Natasha. Look at you! You're still so graceful and beautiful.' Sarita gave her such a warm smile that Natasha felt even worse that she was flirting with her son. No, she would forbid him from messaging her. She would tell him that she was a happily married woman and a great friend of his mother's!

'Listen to this joke,' Aarti said, as she read out from her phone. 'In an art gallery a couple saw a picture of a girl covered only by leaves. The husband stood watching. Finally, the wife said, "Should we go home or are you waiting for a breeze?"'

The girls dissolved into fits of laughter as they started exchanging a few more jokes. Then Natasha suggested, 'Hey, why don't we have a party?'

The idea excited all the girls. 'Totally,' chirped Sarita, 'We can call the husbands also.' The girls shoved her playfully. 'No husbands this time! Just us. We always have a party with them!'

'Remember the time when we all went to Goa?' said Aarti. 'What fun that was.' It had been quite some time now since the four of them travelled with their children.

'Of course I remember!' Gita said. It was probably the last time Shailesh had said anything nice to her. Anu wasn't yet born then. 'Sarita got us matching hats and we danced at the bonfire night, completely drunk!'

'What fun times those used to be. Let's have another party like that!' Natasha said.

They began to plan, but with everyone's erratic schedules, it seemed impossible to set anything concrete.

None of them had a clue that there would be a party though. And it would be the last time they would be together as friends. The good times they once had would dissolve into accusations and tempers flying, and it would lead to the biggest fallout amongst the group that would change their lives forever.

12

Aarti looked resplendent in the pink and green sari that her mother-in-law had bought for her. She had got a pink choli to match her outfit. She slipped on a pair of silver heels and added the last touch by wearing the diamond set her in-laws had given for her reception. When she stepped outside, her son Aryan remarked, 'Mama, you look beautiful!'

She gave him a big hug and looked at Amitabh who was admiring her, too. She asked him with her eyes what happened, and he replied, 'Nothing. Just that I haven't seen you in a sari for so long. And you really do look beautiful.' They smiled warmly at each other and left it at that, never displaying affection and physical love in front of the elders.

'Let's go. We're ready,' her father-in-law said. 'My, my, we should take a photo of all of us. We've never all dressed up to go somewhere together. Either I or your Dadi have been missing from the family group picture.' He took out his digital camera.

'Yes, we have, Dadu. Remember my birthday at the mall?' said Aryan, and they all laughed at his innocence and just because it was the right thing to do. Once they had finished clicking photos, Amitabh went to get the car ready while Aarti walked with her mother-in-law outside. Her father-in-law and son were walking together to the lift, chattering about rules and how they should not be broken. Aarti thought that this was her perfect life. Wonderful in-laws who looked after her son, a loving husband who admired her, and a fantastic career that allowed her to travel. This night was going to be perfect and she was planning to enjoy herself.

The reception was in full swing when Aarti and her family arrived. It was an elaborate wedding at a banquet hall of one of the three-star hotels in the city. The food wasn't great, but the DJ was playing the latest tracks and the dance floor was already filled. The bride and groom were on a podium, receiving guests. Aarti and her family waited for their turn and showered the newlyweds with their congratulations. Then they dispersed: her father-in-law started chatting with some relatives, and her mother-in-law sat with a few of her friends, while Aarti brought her a plate of food. Amitabh had found an old college friend, and Aryan played in the kids' zone where they played musical chairs.

She grabbed a cold drink and went to look for Amitabh. She found him chatting with a friend, and after a few pleasantries, excused herself to go to the powder-room. She had always hated weddings. They were the most boring functions on earth for everyone except the bride and groom's closest families. Distant relatives like Aarti's family had to always make an appearance, and an entire evening full of small talk commenced.

She found a seat close to where Aryan was playing and sat down. Suddenly, she heard a familiar voice. 'Is this seat taken?' She looked up and was quickly sucked into a vortex of nostalgia for a life that she lived a decade ago. She couldn't believe her eyes.

'Dhruv?' she asked dumbfounded, looking at her ex-boyfriend. He smiled and sat down next to her. She looked around to see if Amitabh had seen them. He hadn't. He was too far away.

'What are you doing here?' she asked. She realized she was uncomfortable with his presence.

'Relax. I'm a friend of the bride's,' he said. He took a Sprite from a waiter who passed by and gave her one as well.

'Like the friend you used to be with me?' she asked, suddenly jealous and curious at the same time.

He smiled. Aarti looked at him and her heart did a little flip. He still looked so good. It had been so many years and her heart suddenly pined for him once again. His dark wavy hair fell over his piercing brown eyes and he ran a hand through it to smoothen it out. His massive shoulders filled the dark grey suit he was wearing and the hint of a beard gave him an even more attractive aura. It took tremendous strength for her to not lean over and kiss him. Like she had all those years ago. First, she had stolen him from his girlfriend in college, and then that other time...

'Seven years, Aru,' Dhruv tried to remind her of the last time they met. But she didn't want to remember.

'Yes. A *very* long time ago.' She didn't want to be attracted to Dhruv again but it seemed like she was not in control over her feelings.

'Are you still with Vodafone?' he asked, making polite conversation.

'Yes, I am. I'm Asia Pacific Head of Sales.' She didn't know why she wanted to impress Dhruv but it seemed important to her.

'Wow! That's incredible, Aarti. I am super proud of you.'

'Thanks.'

They both took a sip of their drinks and didn't say more. Both feared the subject of what had happened when they had met last.

His square jaw tensed as he asked without looking at her, 'How's Amit?'

Nervously, she moistened her dry lips. This was wrong. Her feelings. This insane attraction she felt for him all over again.

She stood up. 'There's no need to make small talk, Dhruv. I'm glad to see you. I have to go now.'

He got up, grabbed hold of her hand, and yanked her towards him, holding her closely by the waist as she came close and caught a whiff of his freshly washed hair. He had a commanding manner that didn't allow her to leave. He whispered in her ear, 'Don't go. Please. Five minutes. If you're so glad to see me.' His burning eyes held her still and Aarti didn't know what compelled her to stay. In that minute if she had walked away, life would have been very different. But temptation is the mother of all evil. And Aarti had made friends with it.

She pulled away from him, sat down, and composed herself. He sat beside her and held her hands.

'I've missed you, Aarti,' he said, with a faint tremor in his voice.

Her tone was unapologetic. 'We decided that we wouldn't see each other again. It was a promise we needed to keep for our families.'

'Well, guess what,' he said with a hint of sarcasm. 'My wife and I aren't really getting along. We've separated. So I'm not breaking any promises here.'

Aarti was surprised, and more uncertain than ever. 'What!'

He nodded. 'I couldn't be with the woman I love, so God punished me with a woman I despise.'

'But what about Rohan?' Aarti asked. His son was just a little older than Aryan.

'He's with his mother and, thankfully, I can see him whenever I want. But Aarti, let me tell you, it's not easy.' His voice was filled with distress. 'I would love to see my son every day. I would love to take him to school. But I can't stand his mother. We've even stopped being cordial. I don't know what she fills in his mind. And she refuses to give me a divorce. She says I can live separately and have as many women as I want, as long as I never dissociate myself from our marriage. She just wants to remain Mrs Dhruv Khanna. I don't even know what that means if you've stopped loving and respecting each other.'

He took a deep breath as Aarti pondered over what he had just said. Was there love and respect in her own marriage?

He continued, 'All I want is freedom from this useless institution. All I ever wanted was a child. But Indian law never allows a man to adopt alone. And a marriage is the only way one can procreate and be a part of your offspring's life. What a useless system!'

Aarti merely stared, tongue-tied. There were so many things she needed to tell him. So many reasons they should have been together. She longed to reach out and hold him, tell him that she would always be there for him, that she should never have done what she did and that maybe this was a sign that they needed to be together. Instead, she clenched her fists tightly and closed her eyes. Maybe they both deserved to be unhappy in their marriages. Not even that would be enough to atone for the terrible sin they had committed.

'I really wish we had kept in touch,' he said. 'I know I wasn't good enough for you and that's why you chose Amit. I didn't give you a commitment when you asked for it.'

'No no, Dhruv.' She choked back a cry. 'I shouldn't have cheated on you with your best friend. It was all my fault. I never meant to hurt you. That's why I came to apologize that night...' Her voice trailed away as she recollected how she had pretended to be out of town but gone to meet Dhruv at a hotel. She had gone with the purpose of leaving her ghosts behind. And yet somehow, she had only created new ones. Ghosts that now stared her in the face.

'I forgave you long back, Aarti. You didn't have to come to me that night. But I'm glad you did. You gave me another lease in life. And here you are again, like a breath of fresh air. It's a sign.'

She looked at him, half in anticipation and half in dread. 'What?'

'I believe in signs now. A reason why you are here today. It's because something is about to happen. We just don't know it yet.' Aarti looked at him incredulously, wondering if he had gone mad and that was the reason why his wife didn't want to stay with him.

Before she could respond, Aarti saw from the corner of her eye that her son was looking for her. She wanted to find out more about Dhruv and his life but she knew that if she stayed, there would be disastrous consequences. She needed to leave quickly. She hastened the conversation by putting her hand on his arm softly and saying, 'You stay strong. I have to go. Amit will be looking for me. It was good to catch up with you Dhruv… Just adjust a little more in your life. You'll be fine. I wish I could chat. I need to go. Goodbye.'

Dhruv looked at her pleadingly, 'Goodbye, Aarti. Take care.'

Aarti walked towards her son who was calling out to her. She gathered him up in her arms and walked towards Amitabh. She was done with this wedding. She needed to leave immediately. Thankfully, Dhruv had got busy with someone else and didn't notice Aarti picking her son up and leaving. If he had, he would have realized that Aryan was a spitting image of himself.

13

Gita and Shailesh had sex once a month but Gita had not had an orgasm for years. Their sex was mechanical. He wouldn't even kiss her, he would do his business, roll off her, clean himself up, and fall asleep. A ritual she had learned to anticipate and dread at the same time. Her body felt cold and closed when he touched her and she would squeeze her eyes waiting for it to end soon. But she never complained. She believed it was the duty of a wife and she performed it to the best of her ability. Even though she had read somewhere that it could be called 'rape'. But who would listen to a wife who didn't want sex? Everyone would just tell her it was a domestic issue and they wouldn't get involved.

Some months would elapse because she would claim to have her menstrual cramps and he would let her be. Gita often wondered how a man could go without sex for so long. She had trained herself to not feel anything for him. Hence, not even desire sex. She hardly had anything to compare it to anyway. Shailesh and she had an arranged marriage and he was the first and only man she had ever slept with. And if this was what everyone was raving about, then she really didn't care for sex at all. It was something she could do without. She was happy being frigid. That's the term he had used one night on her and she had calmly accepted it.

It was one of those mornings following a night when they had sex. Everything seemed right with the world and everything felt wrong in her heart. Gita felt her life was going nowhere. All she did was cook, clean, manage a house, look after her in-laws, and sit at home. She had no ambition left. She had no desire within her. There was no reason to live besides bringing up her children. Gita sat in her room alone after the children and Shailesh had left for school and office. She wondered if this was what she had envisioned for her life. She was just a college graduate. Something that Shailesh had said to her once to put her in her place. And she had never retaliated. It was a fact.

She wondered if this world would ever give credit to a housewife. No matter how hard they work, it is presumed that a woman's *duty* is to look after an entirely new family and bear children for a man she has known for just a few years (or not at all). The woman's dreams, her ambitions, her choices are laid to rest as soon as she gets into wedlock. One fine day she needs 'permission' from her husband and her extra family to do the things she's dreamed of doing for so many years. It's a 'laxman rekha' that housewives need to adhere to suddenly. And no one can help them.

Gita sighed and looked at her watch. From today Anu was joining an extra class of music and would be staying another hour at school. This meant that Gita had more time to herself, and even more time with nothing to do. She found a joke on the internet and sent it to her friends on the Whatsapp group of Lovely Ladies. They all replied with a smiley. Then Natasha sent another joke back and it was her turn to reply with a smiley. But Gita didn't feel better. She couldn't spend her entire day, day after day, week after week, just sending jokes. She was getting claustrophobic! This didn't even feel like home. She missed Sahil. It had been a week since they last spoke. He was busy with work and she realized that she craved for a conversation with him.

She sent him a message asking what time he'll get home. He replied that he was working from home. Her heart skipped a beat as she asked him if she could meet him for a bit. He said,

'Okay.' She took a batch of fresh samosas she had made in the morning for the kids' tiffin as an excuse to meet him.

She decided to take the stairs instead of the lift. Somehow, she didn't want to encounter anyone and have to fend off questions where she was going. People's prying eyes had always made her feel uncomfortable. She never knew what to say to people when they asked her probing questions. Apparently, they mistook her sweet smile of acknowledgement anywhere as a start to a conversation. And all she wanted to do was avoid them to the best of her ability. She wasn't a great conversationalist. She didn't know big words like Shailesh and couldn't impress many people. Even though she had read so many books and was up-to-date with technology, she wasn't an expressive person. So it was difficult for her to mingle. It had been a godsend to have women who came and chatted with her everyday and pulled her into their crowd. And these three women were the closest she had to best friends. And yet, even with them, she couldn't share the deepest part of her life.

Sahil opened the door with a smile.

'You can't stay away from me, can you?' he asked with a mischievous smile.

'If you're going to be like that, then I'm leaving.' Gita glared at him but did not move an inch. She felt secretly happy that he could be his normal self around her. God knows what had got into her that day. Maybe there was nothing from his side and she had just imagined the entire scenario. She needed to stop reading all those romantic novels!

Sahil quickly said, 'I promise to behave properly, Madam.' And just as Gita glowered at him, he took the steel dabba from her hand and opened it. 'Wow, samosas. Home-made. Oh, how I missed your food. Even more than I missed you.' He popped one samosa into his mouth. Gita settled down on the sofa and looked at him. She could feel her heart expanding. *Did he say he had missed me?*

Watching him eat all the samosas made her laugh heartily. All of a sudden she knew there was still reason for her to live. 'Gita, these are amazing,' he said. 'You're really the best.' He wiped his mouth and looked at her warmly. 'So tell me, what have you been up to?'

Gita replied by telling him about the children and their homework. Sahil interrupted her and said, 'I didn't ask about the kids, Gita. I asked about you. I get to hear enough about the kids when I meet Mummy and Papa. And the kids talk to me plenty for me to know you're raising them very well. Renuka comes first in her class, and for a four-year-old, Anu is such a great singer. Obviously, it's all your hard work and dedication. I wanted to know what's new in your life?'

Gita sat quietly. She didn't know what to say. Sahil probably knew an assortment of women who had *happening* lives. She, meanwhile, was nothing of that; she was a simple housewife. What could she possibly tell him? She cleared her throat, 'Well, nothing really.'

'You know, we've known each other for some twelve or thirteen years since you got married. And we've never chatted about anything but Shailesh and the children. In fact, you've hardly spoken to me about anything else. I know it's partly my fault because I wasn't around so much and I didn't want to interfere in your life but now with both the babies grown up, you have time to just be and talk to me! So tell me about you.'

Gita nodded. 'All my life I've looked after everyone. I really had nothing to say. I don't have any hobbies. I'm not good at anything. And I'm a regular housewife. I've always seen you climbing in your career and mingling with so many different women. You're the one with the exciting life. You tell me about you.'

Sahil came over and sat next to her, and this time, Gita didn't move away. He said, 'Yes, I have had different women. It's been quite an interesting ride. But you know what, Gita, I've never really wanted a long-term relationship. So to make the kind of commitment that you and Shailesh have is quite commendable.'

Gita snorted and looked away. 'Commendable? Any fool can get married. But it takes commitment to stick to your career. Where am I today? Nowhere. When I was in college, I wanted to become a professional. And then I got engaged in my third year and got married. It was done so quickly that I had no say in it.'

Sahil looked at her quizzically.

She continued, 'Please don't get me wrong, Sahil.' She gently put a hand on his arm and pleaded, 'Please don't say anything to Mummy, Papa or Shailesh. Or my parents. They'll kill me. And I'll have no place to go!'

Sahil put his hand on top of Gita's. 'Relax, Gita. I'm not like that. I won't tell them. This is just between you and me. And you'll always have a place here, remember that.'

Gita was relieved. She leaned back on the sofa, her warm chestnut hair falling carelessly over her face and breasts. In her cream coloured kurta and clean face she looked far more beautiful than any woman in a fancy dress or make-up that Sahil had ever seen. She was petite and flower-like. Her smooth skin glowed with pale golden undertones and he could feel himself drawn to her pure, innocent beauty. No mother of two had ever been as attractive as Gita was, Sahil thought. He yearned to stroke her hair and tell her how special she was. Couldn't she see how important she was to the entire family? His world had changed since she walked into their house. His parents depended on her.

His brother would be a mess without her. And he, Sahil sighed and tried to control his beating heart, he desired her like nothing in this world. He wanted to give her so much love, knowing how she lacked that in her life. But all he could do was give her space to be who she wanted to be, and an ear to hear her whenever she needed to speak. Of course, he knew the food was just an excuse she was making to see him. If only he could make a thousand more to see her every minute of his day as well.

'Gita, talk to me. Tell me what you're thinking.' Sahil moved slightly away, giving her space to feel and speak.

And Gita finally spoke from her heart. Something that she had never done in so many years with anyone. It was as if a dam had burst.

'Girls from small towns aren't allowed to think. They don't know what they want. Until they realize that what they have isn't what they need. I could never find myself because before I even knew the world, I was married and pregnant. My parents hadn't told me about birth control. And when I started feeling sick I went with your cousin Nandini to the doctor, who asked me 'Do you want to keep it?' What could I have said? No? It was too soon? I've only had sex once? I didn't know what was the safe period and even how to raise a child. And here I was already with one.'

He put his hand on her shoulder as a comforting gesture, 'Oh Gita.' He didn't know she was a virgin till she got married. His stupid brother should have been more careful. How was this poor girl supposed to know about contraceptives when no one had told her? An abortion would have made her feel very guilty. Oh, how he wished he had been there for her in the early years of her marriage. But his instant attraction to her then just made him stay away. He plunged himself in work and women to camouflage his true feelings that were brimming for his brother's new wife.

Tears started flowing from her eyes. It was the first time that anyone had cared to ask her about her choices, her feelings, and truly listened to her without interrupting.

'There was a boy who used to chase me…when I got on a rickshaw after college. All the people saw it and told my father. That's when he set up this rishta. It was all done so fast, Sahil.' She took a long pause before continuing, 'I don't have any regrets. I am just saying that I wish I could be something more than someone's mother or someone's wife. I wish I had that chance. I've not been able to pursue any hobby. He didn't even allow…Shailesh and I…' Gita trailed off, unsure whether she should tell her husband's brother the gory details of how bad the sex life was, or how he had suppressed every desire in her to work or succeed in anything. A hot exultant tear rolled down her cheek.

'Shailesh and you what?' he asked. And she shook her head. She decided to just let it be. He need not know. She continued, 'I haven't seen the world. I haven't travelled anywhere. Shailesh doesn't care anymore. I don't know if he ever did or he just married me to make his parents happy.' Gita bawled her eyes out. Sahil stroked her back while she hunched over and cried. When she had finished, he gave her a handkerchief and she wiped away her tears. He smoothed her hair away from her face in a loving gesture and Gita looked at him with a feeble smile.

His gaze travelled over her face and studied her eyes. She was so beautiful, so pure and vulnerable. All she needed was love and attention. Sahil couldn't help himself anymore. He leaned over and gently, ever so softly, covered her mouth with his. The kiss sent the pit of her stomach into a wild swirl. This was wrong. So terribly wrong. But she closed her eyes and lost herself in him. He wrapped his arms around her midriff and pulled her closer to him as he kissed her again, softly caressing the corners of her mouth with his lips. Gita kissed him back with a hunger that belied her outward calm. Her heart felt such peace, while her mind raced in a thousand directions.

Suddenly, she pulled away and pushed him back. She sat up and straightened herself out. 'This is wrong, Sahil. We can't do this. What just happened?'

He looked at her as a man possessed with love. 'What just happened? Passion is what just happened. Something that you haven't had for years. It's not wrong, Gita. Don't stop your heart from finally being free.'

A flood of emotions went through her. This had never happened to her before. Not in a million years would she have thought that she would be disloyal to her husband, she who worshipped the institution of marriage, who had given everything to her family. Now she had become an adulteress!

She knew it wasn't his fault but she needed to blame someone for her infidelity. She stood up. 'What rubbish are you talking? You think you can take advantage of me because I told you my story? Because I shared something deep inside me? How could you?'

Sahil stood up and took her hand, 'I didn't take advantage of you, Gita. You're beautiful. I was just attracted to you. I'm sorry.' He didn't mention how ardently she had kissed him back.

Gita looked flustered and extremely nervous, 'What if someone finds out? Shit. What will happen?'

Sahil said calmly, 'No one is going to find out because we're not going to tell anyone. And nothing is going to happen. Just chill.'

But Gita wouldn't hear it. She didn't know what had come over her. Sahil made her sit down while he went and got her a glass of water. He knelt beside her as she gulped the whole glass down. He spoke to her calmly, 'Gita, I'm sorry. I'll never do that again. It's just that today you looked even more gorgeous than you generally do. I've always wanted to tell you how I admire you.'

'Admire me?' Gita looked at him with curiosity. How could a man who had lived completely on his own terms admire a housewife and mother who hadn't achieved anything?

Sahil nodded, 'You're incredible. And you don't even know it. And you have people around you who can't see it.' His vitality was compelling, his magnetism so potent that Gita felt drawn to him. But she knew that this conversation would lead to nothing good.

Finally, when she had composed herself, she stood up and walked towards the door. 'Please, Sahil, if you admire me, promise me something.'

'Anything.'

'You will never speak of this afternoon with anyone ever in your life.'

'Of course. Why would I…'

'And you will leave me alone. Forever.'

Without waiting for an answer, Gita walked out of the door. She couldn't accept the dull ache in her heart. She had been so lost in that kiss. She had finally felt free after so many years. Her mind told her that she needed to get as far away from Sahil as she possibly could to keep her family intact.

Her heart just refused to listen. Somewhere deep down she knew that even though he would keep his promise, she was unsure if she could listen to her mind for too long.

14

'But I want to go to Paris!' Diya screamed at her mother, while Natasha sat quietly, unrelenting at her daughter's nth temper tantrum.

'No, Diya, your grandparents are coming this summer and they want to spend time with you. I cannot send you with your class to Paris. Besides, Dad and I have already taken you to Paris just two years ago,' Natasha said, in a cool and rational tone.

'But I don't remember anything of it,' Diya pleaded. She felt that her mother was being extremely unreasonable.

'Well, maybe you shouldn't have been on the phone so much then messaging your friends back here who didn't have that opportunity.'

'You're a mean fucking woman. And I hate you!' Diya shouted at Natasha, and banged the door shut before Natasha could respond.

She was shocked to hear this kind of venom in her fourteen-year-old. She was becoming more and more difficult every day. She had to ask Sarita what she could do to make things easier; after all, Sarita always seemed to have control over her children. Which reminded her of Rahul. She had said no to his request of coming over that afternoon to do her portrait. Diya was home and she felt it wouldn't be right. In reply Rahul had sent a sad emoticon and she didn't change her mind. Let us stick to chatting for now, she thought. Although she never initiated any conversation, she looked forward to their chats. His opinions were so refreshing; she felt young and vibrant when she was with him, even virtually.

But she wondered, was he obsessed with her? He was confessing his ideas and life to her, and she had started giving him advice and enjoying their conversations that lasted for hours every day. She laughed out loud at the thought. Just thinking about him took her mind off Diya and the awful morning she had with Vikram. She had forgotten to remind him about the society bill they needed to pay. Now he had to pay some late fee and he was furious. He grabbed her wrist hard and twisted it. It had turned black and blue and Natasha tried desperately to cover it with some concealer. She wondered why lately she had been forgetting things. She was also becoming more frightened of Vikram. Diya was no help either. They had put her in the best school that cost them a pretty penny. While her peers went to average schools, Diya studied in the best premier institute in Mumbai. Yet instead of coming out extremely well groomed, she was turning out to be an adolescent little monster.

Natasha felt completely isolated and alone. When they got married, she and Vikram were very much in love. But Natasha was tired of being a model. Just because she was tall and had great features, it came naturally to her to enter that industry. But she was tired of competing. She didn't like the backbiting, the constant travel, and the perpetual diet she had to be on. Her breakfast was composed of fruit, her lunch a cup of coffee and her dinner of soup and salads. She was relieved to leave the industry and eat whatever she wanted.

After some time Vikram began to say, 'You've changed. I don't recognize you anymore. Where has all your ambition gone? I thought you wanted to be someone. Something more than just a plain housewife, like the rest of the women in this country.'

And she didn't know how to respond. She loved being a housewife in the beginning, taking her role diligently. She decorated her house the way she wanted to. She threw parties for his friends and clients and encouraged him to take several projects that furthered his career. He rose in his career as one of the country's best photographers because she encouraged him. It was because of her prodding and pushing that he became successful. Her love and support gave him the impetus to fly high. But he never saw that. His thinking had always been highly individualistic. Though he gave her money to keep a house, he stopped respecting her. He would come home late at night and not bother about her. He gave her too much of everything but himself. And that was what she needed most from her husband.

Natasha went into the bathroom and took a long, hot shower. When she came out, she rubbed lotion over her legs and added a little bronzer to give them some shine. She glanced at herself in the mirror, fully naked and smiled. She wasn't bad looking at all. Rahul thought she was attractive. Sure, she was slightly heavy on the hips but she liked her curves. She wished Vikram felt the same way but he was into thin women. Was he having an affair? She had hints but she had never confronted him. What would she do with the truth, anyway?

As she got dressed, her mind journeyed to the day Diya was born. He had been overjoyed. It was probably the last time they had kissed with passion. Soon after, she went through such a hard time and Vikram didn't even realize it. Once, she tried to explain that she was feeling sad but he simply told her to 'get a grip'.

Suddenly, she heard the bell ring and wondered who it could be. If it was a delivery boy, the security guard would have called on the intercom. She opened the door and found the last person she would have thought to see that day.

'Rahul!' she exclaimed, surprised but most receptive. She instinctively put a hand over her wrist to cover the inflamed, red mark.

'Hi, Natasha. Can I come in?' He used her first name, not Aunty or anything, as if he was already familiar with her, having had so many conversations on the phone. Before she could protest, he walked in. She noticed he had a large notebook and a box of pencils in his hands.

'What are you doing here? Didn't I tell you I was busy?' She hoped he would leave and not see her wrist.

'I just met Diya downstairs. She said you were home doing nothing,' he said with a smile.

Natasha inwardly grimaced at her daughter. She wondered if Diya had any sense at all. Parenting was tough. People made it look easy but it was the toughest job in the world. How was Natasha supposed to understand it all?

'So where should I set up?'

'For what?'

He ignored her question as he walked about the room, and finally kept all his equipment near a window, stretched out his hands, and joined his thumb as if to make a 'frame' for a picture. 'Sit here,' he ordered. She was caught off guard by the sudden vibrancy of his voice.

'I don't think this is such a good idea. Maybe some other day.'

'I won't take too long,' he smiled. 'I have to submit this tomorrow for my art class. And you've been dilly-dallying for so long now. Please, I beg of you. Just sit for half an hour. The light is perfect. Pretend I'm not here.' He folded his hands, a hopeful glint in his eyes. 'I really need your help. Please do this for me?'

Natasha shrugged. 'Okay, let me get you some coffee and cookies then.' She walked to the kitchen and made two mugs of coffee. He set up his equipment and waited until she emerged. He thanked her as she gave him a cup of coffee and laid down cookies, sandwiches and some chips.

'You're feeding the poor, aren't you?'

Natasha blushed, unable to understand how she could be fumbling around a nineteen-year-old. She sat down with her cup of coffee and listened to instructions as he told her to look this way or that. He shook his head impatiently as if he wasn't getting the right posture and walked up to her, pushed tendrils of hair from her cheek and cupped her chin with his hand while trying to find the correct angle. She inclined her head in compliance and smiled warmly at the artist in front of her. A pensively sensuous light passed between them.

His hand lingered on her face a second longer than necessary. He gazed down her body and admired her gorgeous features. 'Be natural. You'll sit still, I hope.' He moved back to his canvas and started sketching her.

Natasha could not stifle a giggle. 'I've never got my portrait sketched. Photographed when I was younger, yes, but not pencilled. And yes, I can keep a pose for hours. I was a model. There would be so many people around me getting the lights right, the make-up, the bikini tightened, while I had to stick one leg out and look up at the sun at Mauritius or the Andamans, or when it was freezing in Iceland. So I'm not fidgety. Take as long as you like.' She turned her face away from him and sipped her coffee.

He stared at her. An electrifying shudder reverberated through her. 'What?' she asked.

'The thought of you in a bikini just blew my mind away.' He looked away, blushing.

She laughed despite herself for the first time. She had stripped for so many people when she was a model and never realized that 'bikini' was a word you just didn't say aloud as a housewife.

'Are you making fun of me?'

'I would never do that, Rahul.'

A part of her revelled in his open admiration for her. She wanted more. He seemed so sure of himself for someone so young. She noticed his features more carefully as the sun shone through the window. He was tall, raw boned, clean shaven, with an ingenuously appealing face. He was handsome with dark eyes and an expression that said he was hiding some sort of secret. Natasha wanted to be part of that. She was curious about him.

'I thought you taught art to children. You never told me you took an art class as well.'

'Oh, didn't I? I thought I told you over coffee that day. Yes, I'm doing an online course with Tisch School of Art in New York. But I really just want to study there. I've always wanted to live abroad for some time. There's something about being in a foreign land that opens up your mind, frees your soul and just gives you more from life. I'm sure you've experienced that. Unfortunately, my parents are never going to agree. If they can't buy me a phone, I doubt if they'll spend thousands of dollars for me to learn art.' His lips parted in a dazzling display of straight and white teeth and she found it impossible not to return his disarming smile.

'You could ask them, you know.'

'Not a chance. I know them. But not to worry, I'm going to save up enough and go with my own money!' His brows drew together in a concentrated expression as he sketched rapidly while talking.

Natasha was impressed with his determination but she knew that it would take too long for his dream to come true if he let his ego take over and didn't ask his parents for help. 'I think you have great parents.' She realized she was defending her friend Sarita.

He shook his head. 'For them, getting into an IIM is important and they'll give me money only for that. Art and design is just random shit. They think that teenagers just go through different phases in their life and that it's best not to indulge any of them.'

'That's not true. I indulge Diya in everything she wants.'

'Well, maybe you shouldn't.'

'What did you say?'

Rahul didn't reply until he finished his sketch. For several minutes he worked furiously, trying to make up for the blunder of commenting on Natasha's parenting. He didn't want to upset her. He really liked her. She was so different from all of his mother's friends. Hell, she was unlike any of the women her age. She looked kind, sweet and extremely beautiful. He was blown away by her grace and charm. She was confident of herself, a generous parent, from what Rahul could see. He had noticed the black and blue mark on her wrist that could only have been made by a large man who she had allowed to hold her like that. He knew he had no business telling her anything about her marriage, but he suddenly wanted to be older than he was, be with her and protect her, be the one to make her happy.

'You can move now. Not that you were very still to begin with, Ms Model.' He stepped away from his canvas. Natasha stood up. She walked over to him and looked at the sketch. It was a brilliant rendition of her. The shadows on her face, the curves of her body, and a look that she hadn't seen before. A frown between the eyes and a soft determination on her lips. She was startled to see how he had captured her inner feelings so well. No photographer had ever achieved that, not even Vikram.

'I thought it was just going to be my face. You're so good!'

He shrugged his shoulders. 'Your legs were so great that they were begging to be drawn!'

She lightly punched him on his shoulders and felt his taut, hard body underneath his shirt. She was wearing tiny yellow shorts with a white blouse, a pair of diamond earrings and silver thong slippers. An outfit that she felt was most unglamorous for a sketch. But when she saw the portrait, she was caught off-guard by its simple beauty.

'It's really beautiful.' She was honestly impressed.

He was pleased that he had made her happy. Her thick dark hair hung in long graceful curves over her shoulder, and her lips were full and round, making her look like a Greek goddess. He desired her, something he had never felt for anyone before. Not even while he watched porn quietly in the privacy of a bathroom.

He whispered softly in her ear, 'You *are* beautiful.' She stared at him. Suddenly, Rahul seemed older than nineteen. Or maybe she felt eighteen all over again. A girl who hadn't been touched, who desperately wanted to be wrapped in a man's arms. Natasha felt a curious pull.

She looked away. What was she thinking? She couldn't take this relationship any further. He was her friend's son, for chrissakes. What was going on, midlife crisis? Subconsciously aware of the dull ache that had started in her heart, she turned away and went to the kitchen to get herself a glass of water.

This time Rahul followed her. She stood over the counter pouring herself a glass of water as he came and stood behind her. Without turning around she spoke clearly, 'I think you should leave.'

But he did the exact opposite. He leaned his body forward and put one arm on either side of her, holding the counter and pinning her slightly more to it. He breathed in the soft lemony smell of her hair and gently ran his face along the side of her long neck. A vivid scarlet rose up her neck and cheeks. She could feel the bulge of his desire as he gently pressed himself against her back. He spoke softly into her ear, 'I want you, Natasha.'

She knew she wanted him, too. Age didn't matter. She hardly bothered that he was her friend's son. All she wanted was to give in to him. To realize that there was someone out there who could make her feel special. That there was hope for her empty heart. That love, passion and desire were natural emotions and needed an equal place in her life as duty and loyalty. 'Wife', 'mother' and 'friend' were just nouns that society bestowed upon her. It seemed too big a burden for her to carry. They had no place in her life but she was doomed to live with them.

Natasha turned and stared at him. Today could not be the day when she gave in. There would be too much guilt. She needed to stay strong. She focused on Sarita's face in her head. She couldn't lose her friendship, not over these raw, unfathomable desires. She said, more firmly and confidently this time, 'Go.'

Rahul backed away, 'I'm sorry.' He went back to the drawing-room. She heard him gather his things and leave, shutting the door behind him. Only then she emerged from the kitchen, afraid to encounter him and the space that had propelled their friendship into an incomprehensible relationship.

She saw her portrait lying there, a gift from him to her. But wasn't this a project he needed to submit the next day? She picked it up, admired it again, and saw the note he had written on the back: 'I can always sketch something else to submit. But we will never get this wonderful afternoon together again. Thank you for letting me into your house and heart. You're the most captivating woman I've met. I'm sorry if I crossed the boundary. Will never trouble you again.'

Natasha released the sketch from her hands as the tears started flowing from her eyes, a heaviness centred in her chest. She knew that Rahul had changed her life forever, leaving her with an inexplicable sense of emptiness that she knew now only he could fill. It wasn't as if it was morality that was weighing down on her that stopped her from going further. It was the magnitude of her desire for him. She knew it could only lead to their worlds exploding, with no conclusion, and nothing good coming out of it.

15

'Where is Rahul?' Sarita asked, as she checked her watch. They had finished dinner and Rahul was still not home.

'He's a teenager. Let him be,' said Jai, picking his teeth.

Sarita wondered what was wrong with Rahul. Was he becoming a recluse? It had been days since he had been in the house. He would come in late at night and immediately go to sleep. He would wake up late the next morning, take a quick shower and leave. Something was troubling that boy and she didn't know what. He had also started drinking a lot of alcohol. Sarita was beginning to worry. All he did nowadays was sketch and carry his folder around everywhere. He had even stopped going to the gym. He refused to talk to his parents too.

Sarita sighed. This so-called 'motherhood crisis', would it ever let up? You couldn't understand your children completely at any given stage of their lives. No wonder parents wanted to get them married off as soon as possible. So that's why all these matrimonial sites existed, for harrowed parents who wanted to kick their children out of the house so someone else could look after them, or they could finally be responsible enough to look after themselves.

When she asked Rahul what was wrong, he replied, 'Life has endless problems, Mom. Love used to be the solution. Now that's also gone away.' What did he mean? Who knew what these adolescents were thinking? It was all a daze to her.

She had her own problems to think about. Jai had been acting very strangely. Ever since the accident, he had refused to come close to her. He came home late and barely noticed her even when she was wearing new lingerie. She wondered if it was because she wanted something simple and regular in bed. When she suggested that they ease off for a bit on the kinky sex because they were a simple middle-class Gujarati family, after all, and she wasn't used to such raunchy things, he got offended. Now it had been two weeks since he last touched her. He would act like he was extremely tired and go off to bed. This was so unlike him. She was beginning to get suspicious.

She finished her food and went inside her bedroom to use the attached master bathroom. As she stepped out, she saw his mobile phone, buzzing, He had left it for charging on the side table. She picked it up and was about to give it to Jai when she saw who was calling. It was a woman's name, Shefali, and it had a photo attached. The woman was wearing a short sundress. The photo was taken on a beach with her hair blowing around her; she looked like a supermodel. She cut the call and decided to check his messages. She knew she was getting into dangerous territory but instinct told her she had to invade her husband's privacy and check his phone.

There it was, their exchange of messages. Shefali's were more direct, saying how she missed him. His was a simple, 'When is the meeting?'

She sat down and took a deep breath. Her husband was having an affair! She couldn't deny it. She didn't know what to do. Should she confront him?

She glanced at herself in the mirror. Her face was well modelled and feminine. There was both delicacy and strength in her face that she hadn't noticed before. Her skin was smooth and glowing with high cheek bones and almond eyes. She had shoulder-length straight jet black hair that she maintained through regular oiling. Among her peers she had the best breasts and she was proud to say that no store in the city carried her 36

DD bra size and she had to hunt very hard for it. Her features were a stunning combination and she didn't look a day above twenty-five. Because of her accident she hadn't been able to go to the gym and gained three kilos back. It had been the most depressing two weeks of her life. She had lost her husband to another woman and gained back the weight on her hips.

She didn't know how to handle the situation tonight. What would her parents say? That she couldn't keep her husband to herself! She wasn't good enough in the kitchen or the bedroom to hold her man at home. Parents could be an unsupportive lot.

What would her friends say? Should she tell them? All she knew was that she was going to investigate this affair. She wouldn't be a woman to take this nonsense lying down. She would confront him and ask him to choose. Either her or that bitch Shefali.

But what if Jai chose Shefali? She shuddered. This society was cruel towards single women and they hadn't opened their minds to divorced women yet. At best, people viewed divorced women with sympathy: Oh, the poor thing needs help. Or else they looked at them with disdain: she must have been an overly aggressive female who couldn't adjust and, hence, stay in a marriage. There were no shades of grey in Indian society. The man was always given a longer rope than the woman. He was allowed to stray or work long hours, and not care if the wife had any needs, physical or emotional. He was even allowed to abuse the wife sometimes. She had heard old aunts say, 'Kabhi kabhi ek do thapar mil jata hai, but that's no reason to give up a marriage that you've worked so hard to build.' Her own mother used to say, 'Men are biologically like that.' She used to be shocked to hear such statements, unable to convince them otherwise. And as much as she saw things changing around her, it was because of her uprbringing that still made her believe in this. Sarita believed that the divorced, independent woman who could manage life on her own and was proud of her decisions was still looked at, even if for a brief moment, as a person who had failed her marriage. That was the truth. No matter how many times her friends refuted the idea.

Sarita knew she needed answers. But she didn't know how to go about finding them. And if she did, what she would do. Would she want to save her marriage? Or would she walk out with her head held high? On the one hand, she didn't know what was happening with Rahul, and on the other, she didn't know what was going on with her husband. For the first time in her life, Sarita felt confused and all alone. All she could do now was wait till sleep took over to rest her racing mind.

16

'I am never buying lingerie again,' Sarita complained to her friends as they sat around chatting one evening.

Aarti burst into laughter. 'Why, darling? Don't you need something to uplift the masses?'

Gita guffawed, 'Are you planning to go commando?'

It was one of those evenings when they all needed to talk about inane things rather than what was actually happening at home. They had decided to go for a walk around the three buildings and take a stroll in the lawns.

'I definitely need to buy a better sports bra,' Natasha said, as she increased her pace to keep up with the girls.

'Well, don't go to the guy on Hill road in Bandra,' Sarita said, shaking her head in alarm.

'Why? Did he make a pass at you?' Natasha asked.

'No, but he said I would look *sexy* in a five-piece.'

The girls giggled and continued walking. 'What's a five-piece?' Gita asked. 'Is that even lingerie? Don't we all only wear two things?'

They had covered the entire walking track for the first time in their life. It was a beautiful landscape that went around the lawns, the yoga room and the swimming pool that Sapphire Towers was proud of. After sitting in one spot for years, they had finally decided that they would start walking and talking and that way could get healthier, since Gita was now bringing some snack or the other every alternate day and the calories were beginning to sit on their hips.

'A five-piece is little items of clothing including a sheer, slip, robe, I think. Even I don't know, it's all very confusing. But that's not the point!' Sarita said.

Gita still didn't get it and looked at Aarti for help. Aarti replied, 'Leave it.'

But Sarita insisted, 'How did he say I would look sexy? That's just shocking! Was he looking me up and down?'

Aarti dismissed the idea. 'There are only male salesmen for lingerie now. It's very embarrassing. Wherever I go, they ask me, what size do I want? Why should I tell them? Even my husband doesn't know!'

Natasha added, 'I hate how they look you up and down and say, you must be an A cup. Bastard! I'm completely a B!'

The girls burst into laughter.

Aarti suddenly said, with characteristic drama, 'Oh my God! I have some gossip for you.'

'What?' the girls said in unison.

'Apparently, the society members are going to meet this afternoon to discuss whether to light up all the refuge floors. Some chairman caught his daughter making out with a boy in one of them.'

Natasha gasped. She hoped it wasn't Diya.

'What's a refuge floor?' asked Gita.

Aarti replied, 'The floors that connect all the three towers.'

'There is such a thing?' Gita was clueless. 'An entire floor?'

'Well,' Aarti explained, 'There are apartments on the floor but instead of three, there are only two, and the third is an area that leads to the other building. All the buildings are connected through these refuge floors. There are four or five of them, I think, on the 3rd, 8th, 12th and 15th floors. It's a safety precaution that multi-storey buildings have in case a fire breaks out.'

'So who got caught?' Sarita asked.

'Srivastav's child.'

'Really?' Gita said. 'But she's just fifteen years old, isn't she?'

Natasha scoffed. 'These children start early. I wouldn't be surprised if Diya also has a boyfriend. Kids nowadays hide everything from us.'

'Reminds me of Shivani's son,' Sarita said. 'That one is so spoilt. He doesn't say please or thank you. He is five and already so rude! Not only to strangers, mind you, but even to his parents! He speaks badly to the servants, I tell you.' How are women raising their children these days? Sarita thought to herself.

Gita gritted her teeth. 'That's one thing I won't tolerate, being discourteous. If Renu or Anu spoke back to me or the servants, I will slap them. Thankfully, it's not happened yet.'

Natasha stayed quiet. Diya had often behaved badly with her and thought nothing of speaking coarsely to the maid. She had reprimanded her but Vikram had taken Diya's side, as always. The maid had then quit, leaving Natasha scurrying around to do all the housework. It seemed the maid issues never ended. She decided to ask for help this time. She couldn't keep things bottled up. Diya was getting out of hand. If her friends couldn't help her, then who else could?

She said, 'When Diya told the maid off, the maid left. I just didn't know what to do then. I don't know how to raise that child. I've tried being her friend, being firm, indulging her, being around for her. Nothing works.'

'That's terrible,' Sarita said, adding in jest, 'I would rather have my maid stay with me than my kids. The maid is indispensable.'

The girls again burst into laughter and decided to sit down. They had done enough walking for the day.

'You've got to be firm with Diya,' Gita said to Natasha. 'What you allow will continue. Be strong and stop the things you don't like. The sooner the better.'

'I've done that. But she still likes throwing a tantrum,' Natasha said.

Sarita replied, 'Stick to it then, Natty. You can't be firm one minute and give in the next. You're sending out mixed signals to your children. If they don't like your decision, tell them to do it themselves.'

Aarti chimed in, 'I read in a magazine that the only way to get through your teenage kids is to use social media. Like friend them on Facebook and start liking their posts so they think you're on their side. Then discuss if they want to talk about something specific when they're around. If they're really troubling you, send them an email about how you felt about their behaviour and what you want to do to reach out and understand them better. Aryan is turning eight soon, so I'm keeping all this in mind. It might help, darling.'

'Thanks, you guys,' Natasaha said. 'Great suggestions.'

'About another thing,' Gita said. 'I've been thinking about the catering service idea that you all have been encouraging me about. Do you really think I should try it?'

'Yes!' they all said. Gita was a great cook and they were sure she could make a profession out of it. Aarti said she would ask Amit to help, and they could sit together to take the idea forward. Sarita offered to go around the building to distribute pamphlets. They started making a plan on what she should include in the 'dabba' service.

'So what name should we call it?' Natasha asked.

They came up with a few suggestions but Gita didn't like any of them. 'I like Gita's Kitchen,' she said, and everyone agreed it was a nice name. Natasha almost blurted out that she would ask Rahul to come up with a logo for it, but she knew Sarita would ask how she knew that her son could draw.

While the women discussed Gita's business, Natasha plotted how to talk to Rahul again. A thought that made her smile.

17

Motherhood was overrated, Natasha was convinced. They told you having a child was something that changed you, made you complete and whole, made you a woman that no other experience ever could. Those were all lies. They didn't tell you that it could also destroy you if you weren't ready for it. And that you would be stuck with a child for the rest of your life and not know how to raise it, no matter how many books you read and how much advice you followed.

She sat in her tiny balcony and sipped her wine as she pondered motherhood, marriage, and how she so desperately wanted to change her destiny by making new choices in her life. She was glad to have the house to herself for a change. Diya had gone to spend the night at a friend's house and Vikram was out of town for a shoot. Natasha felt relieved to be alone.

The faint voices of Simon and Garfunkel came through the wall from a neighbour's CD player. 'Hello darkness, my old friend…I've come to talk with you again.'

Natasha hummed along. She took a large gulp of her wine and realized something: she was a loner. She enjoyed solitude. She enjoyed the peace of an empty house. She looked up at the twinkling stars as a wave of calm washed over her body. She embraced loneliness. Her life wasn't meant to be lived with other people. It didn't matter how old or young she was. She didn't need a companion. She didn't need to prove to society that she could be the perfect mother or a wonderful wife. She didn't need to prove anything to anyone. She could just be herself. And that was best done when alone.

Just as she was gloating in this new revelation about herself, the bell rang. She cursed whoever was at the door. The incessant bells from the courier man to the ironing guy and the milkman gave her a headache every day. The minutiae of daily domesticity, and that too, dictated by society, were such a burden! She wished she could be in a place without any of this.

She opened the door and saw Rahul. Staring straight at her and smiling, confident and looking rakish.

She was speechless for a few seconds, before asking, 'Rahul? What are you doing here?' She felt confused, elated and shocked at the same time. Even though he had interrupted her enjoyment of being alone, she was glad to see him. It had been quite a while since that afternoon and she just didn't know how to approach him again. She was pleased that he had taken the initiative. They had started chatting again through messages, and this time, it had gone into flirtatious territory. Seeing him again made her pulse quicken. She knew such a mutual attraction would be perilous.

Rahul entered without being invited. 'I got your message about designing some logos for Gita. I've come up with some stuff. I wanted to show you.' He placed his art books on the table and surveyed the atmosphere.

She took a quick breath of utter astonishment as she closed the door behind him. 'You could have just emailed them to me.'

Rahul glanced at the half-empty bottle of wine lying on the table and a glass kept in the balcony and figured he was doing the right thing. A woman sitting by herself could only mean she was wallowing in self-pity. He could sense that she needed company. His eyes studied her with curious intensity before he spoke with genuine concern, 'Then I wouldn't be able to see how much you like them! Come, sit. Let me show you what I've made.'

Rahul laughed easily and Natasha said, 'Get yourself a glass and join me.' Her eyes were pools of appeal that he could see himself drown in. They sat on the dining-table discussing his ideas. Natasha was enthralled by this young man. He spoke animatedly with his eyes lighting up with each design, his brows drawing together with her suggestions, and a slow secret smile that they shared every time she poured him more wine. By the end of the hour, they were both quite intoxicated.

Suddenly, Rahul came closer to her. His voice had an infinite compassionate tone, 'I have a good idea.' His nearness was overwhelming. Her heart pounded an erratic rhythm. Natasha wondered if he was going to make a move on her again. But he didn't. He grabbed another bottle of wine from the table and picked up her house keys that were lying on the centre table and stuffed it into his jeans pocket. 'Come with me.' She felt the electricity of his touch as he took her hand.

Natasha asked with trepidation and a bit too loudly for midnight in a hallway, 'Where are we going? I'm not dressed to go out!' She looked down at her red polka dot chiffon blouse and black cropped trousers. His eyes raked boldly over her body.

Rahul kept his fingers on his lips requesting her to stay quiet. Instead of pressing the down button for the elevator, he pressed the second highest floor in the building.

'Why are we going up?' Natasha wondered, and Rahul just shushed her and looked around. He didn't want anyone to hear them. She took a frank and admiring look at him. In her intoxicated haze she could see that he was actually very handsome. Where had he got his good looks from? Not his mother, she thought. He stepped out of the lift at some floor, turned left and walked through a door. Natasha walked behind him as she let him hold her hand. His grasp was warm and firm.

'What is this place?' Natasha asked, as she looked around an open space that was covered only from the top and one side. The front view opened up to the bright lights of the tops of buildings in the western suburbs of Mumbai, all the way down to the inky black sea that was barely noticeable.

'Welcome to the refuge floor!' Rahul said. 'Come, sit down here.' He walked towards the edge of the floor where there was a balcony with a glass front that overlooked the entire neighbouring areas. She sat down on the cool marble floor and leisurely stretched her legs to look at the twinkling lights of the apartment buildings around her. Rahul disappeared for a minute and came back with a small rug and two cushions.

'Where did you...' Natasha didn't complete the sentence as Rahul smiled. He set it down next to her, as she moved her body on top of it, and dropped down beside her to face her.

'I wouldn't want your beautiful ass to get cold,' he said, and she giggled. He suddenly put his hand on her mouth and looked deep into her eyes. 'Try and be quiet,' he said, more sure of himself than he had ever been in his life.

She wrinkled her nose and nodded as he removed his hand. He poured some more wine into her glass and poured himself a little bit as well. She inclined her head in a small gesture of thanks. She looked at him, half drunk, and inquired a little too late in the day, 'Are you old enough to drink?'

Rahul dismissed the thought, 'If I'm old enough to vote, I'm old enough to drink.'

Natasha figured he had his own logic and hers was quite blurry, in any case. But she added as a precaution, 'You know you shouldn't drink so much.'

'I promise to not drink so much if it makes you happy, Natasha,' he said sincerely, as she hardly discerned anything but the view.

'This is beautiful, Rahul. But are we allowed up here?' she asked. She vaguely remembered someone saying something about getting caught on a refuge floor.

'No.' He sipped his wine. 'That's half the fun of it.'

Her eyes widened. He noticed how gentle and childlike she could be. Someone needed to take care of her. She deserved someone who loved her and wanted to look after her. Natasha's hormones raged like a burning fire. She had not done anything this exciting since she started dating Vikram. And the fact that they kept their relationship secret was thrilling enough for her to stick with him, even when her parents said she shouldn't marry him. She sighed and wondered how something so great deteriorated into something so horrible?

'Hey.' Rahul's gentle nudge brought her back from her daydreams. 'What are you thinking about?' An easy smile played at the corners of his mouth.

Natasha's tight expression relaxed into a grin. 'Nothing. Old days, the past.'

Rahul shook his head. 'I'm with you now. Think about the new days.' He came slightly closer to her as she looked around. Every time his gaze met hers, her heart turned over.

'Are you sure no one comes here?'

Rahul leaned back on the rug. 'Nope. It's the middle of the night. Most families have gone to sleep. Others, even if they need to cross the building, will go on the lower floors. And anyone who does want to do this isn't smart enough to know there is a refuge floor right next to the roof. They would still go up on the roof. So yes, we're all alone, Natasha.' His voice was velvet edged and sure. She noticed his set face, his square jaw and sparkling eyes. How could he be so young? He looked far older than his years. A boy blossoming into a man. A butterfly ready to be released from his cocoon. He only needed the impetus to fly.

Natasha finished her glass and took a deep breath. Tilting her head back she peered at his face. It was time to face the truth. There was no running away from the moment that demanded answers. 'What do you want from me, Rahul?' she decided to be blunt as she didn't want to misread his signs. She didn't want to be his 'friend', and she definitely didn't want to venture into anything that was not reciprocated.

She could feel his muscles tense as he moved closer to her. He licked his lips nervously, 'I'm open to suggestions.' The underlying sensuality of his words captivated her. His eyes filled with a primal desire waiting to be unleashed, hungry for an adventure and longing to be set free.

Her eyes shone bright in the pale light of the moon. She had an air of calm that made her immensely likeable. Natasha's past, her present and her fierce determination for her future made her even more attractive. Rahul was amazed at Natasha's inner beauty. He had never met a woman like her. She wasn't a typical 'aunty' and she was nothing like the girls who hung around him. She was ethereal. He had spent nights thinking about her. He had daydreamed in class about how to take a step forward without offending her. And he had hoped that she would just let herself go in the moment and be with him.

Natasha closed her mind to logic and opened her heart to love. As if she had heard Rahul's thoughts she moved towards him, impelled involuntarily by her own passion and a desire that had started burning deep within her. She kept her mouth within millimetres of his face and whispered, 'I have an idea.' The scent of her hair, the shadows of light falling on the curves of her body, the touch of her fingertips on his face, and the caress of her lips near his mouth made Rahul impatient to please her. He could wait no longer. He covered her mouth hungrily with his, devouring her. She answered back, eager and excited to be in this dangerous situation with a man half her age and a space that was open to invasion.

Natasha lost herself in that kiss, the moment, the tidal wave of lust that overflowed between them. She felt a bottomless peace and satisfaction, as if her heart had been lifted from long years of suppression. He held her around the small of her waist, kissing her passionately as she let out a soft moan. He broke away for a brief moment, hesitant to continue. He didn't know if she had liked his kiss, his enthusiasm. This was all new with a woman who was twice his age. Suddenly, he was shy, insecure about how the woman of his dreams would respond to him.

'Why did you stop?' Natasha asked, with a faint tremor in her voice. Had she gone too far? Had he not liked her initiating the kiss? Was it too much for him?

'I...' Rahul stuttered. 'I'm not sure if you really want me. Whether I'm man enough for you. Whether...If...I can match your expectations?'

A powerful relief filled her. At this point she was beyond logic. She was filled with lust, a primal longing that tore through her body like a wild beast. She felt like a breathless girl of eighteen all over again. Not a mother and definitely not a housewife. Just a woman with a craving that was pleading to be satisfied. Because it was juicy, forbidden, and bordered on being deliciously wicked, she knew what to do. She would teach him. She would show him what her expectations were and how to match them. She would give him the ride of his life. A night he would never forget. And she would enjoy this control over him. Because though Natasha didn't know what it was like to be a mother, the one thing she did know was how to be a lover.

She slowly moved her body over his, shifted him slightly on the rug. 'Be comfortable. I wouldn't want your beautiful ass to get cold.'

In the refuge floor of Sapphire Towers overlooking the expanse of buildings glowing in the distance, and the perverse pleasure of someone walking in on them, Natasha played a game of voyeuristic pleasure that cut through the boundaries of anything she had ever done before.

She straddled his hips with her thighs as she removed her blouse, revealing her black lace bra. The twinkling lights from the neighbouring buildings faded as more people went to sleep while Natasha went to bed with Rahul. The sexual desire she had for him heated her in the way of a fever that no man had ever done before. She slowly took off his clothes and started circling his nipples with her tongue. She moved gently across the length of his torso to take his hard, warm flesh into her mouth. Slowly. Gently. Firmly. Moving faster, holding him with her hands, stroking him with her tongue, caressing him with her fingers. His tormented groan was a heady invitation as she rubbed her shapely breasts over his body in long, gentle movements. Discarding her clothes, she stood naked defiantly against the moonlight. His impatience grew to explosive proportions as she relented and finally, gently eased herself onto him, tucking her curves neatly into his own contours. He groaned with delight.

'Try and be quiet,' she whispered.

Lying on the cool marble floor of Sapphire Towers, Rahul never imagined in his entire life that he would lose his virginity to a hot, older woman, who took charge of his body and, control of the night. A night that he would remember forever, even after she went away from his life and left him to find a girl of his own age.

18

The guilt was killing Aarti. She had met her ex-boyfriend and still not told Amitabh about it.

'Please fasten your seat belts, pull the window shades up, and put your chair in upright position. The use of lavatory is no longer permitted till the seat belt sign has been taken off. We're ready for take-off. Thank you,' said the steward over the aircraft's PA system.

Aarti looked out of the window, lost in her thoughts, ready for take-off. She had two hours to prepare herself for a very important pitch for a client, and all she could think about was the moment that Amitabh would realize that Aryan was not his son. What would she do then? What would he say?

'Ma'am,' the steward spoke, as Aarti was suddenly brought back to the present. 'Can I put your purse up for you?' Aarti realized she had been holding on to her purse so tightly that her knuckles had turned white. She nodded and handed her purse to the attendant. Aarti held her hands and looked out of the window.

'Are you nervous?' asked a fellow passenger next to her.

Aarti turned to look at who was sitting in the aisle seat in her row. Thankfully, the middle seat was empty and she had a little more room to rest her arm. This constant flying was taking a toll on her. She had been thinking she would quit and spend more time at home. But then again, what would she do at home? Aryan went to school from morning till afternoon and then had soccer, music and maths classes till late in the evening. If she sat at home she'd go completely mad. And the only thing she would think about was that she and her husband never had sex.

She shook her head at the elderly woman, 'No, I'm good.'

The elderly woman seemed to take that as the start of a conversation. 'Well, I am, a bit. This is my first flight alone.'

Aarti nodded. She didn't want to chat. She wanted to go back to staring out of the window. But the old lady continued, 'My husband and I used to travel together. But he passed away last year. I'm going to see my grandchildren in Delhi this time. They've been coming and seeing me for so long that I needed to go see them now.'

Now Aarti was interested. She was amazed. 'You live alone in Mumbai? Isn't it unsafe? Wouldn't you want to be with your family in Delhi?'

The woman shook her head, 'My whole life has been in Mumbai. This is where I met my husband, had children, and lived a full life. I have so many friends here. I don't want to go to Delhi and be a burden on my daughter and her family.'

'I'm sure they wouldn't think of you as a burden.'

'No, they wouldn't. But I would. I've lived so long for someone else. It's time I learn to live for myself.'

The grandmother captivated Aarti and they spoke more about her life. Later, as the old woman took a nap, Aarti pondered whether she had been unfair to herself and her family. Had she only lived for herself? But she had done everything for them. Her whole life was about them. And even though she worked like mad, it was to look after them. Not many housewives understood that. She wanted to make Aryan proud of her. A working mother meant that later in life, he would understand if his wife wanted to work, too. Having a nurturing, caring relationship that she had with Amitabh and her in-laws would prove to Aryan how she could get along with everyone and how important it was to keep peace and respect in the house. All these values were important for a child.

She had seen how Natasha and her husband had raised Diya. She got everything she wanted and now Natasha was having problems with her. Aarti had noticed also how Rahul would go out drinking every night and come back late. Once, she had caught him in the elevator with alcohol on his breath, wearing a T-shirt that said, 'My mother is mental.' She had reprimanded him for it but he had answered back with something like, 'You don't know what it's like to be a teenager. Don't give me your gyaan.'

She didn't want Aryan to grow up and become like them. Even though she travelled often, she always came back and spent enough time with him. And with Amitabh. She thought about it for a few seconds and wondered if that was being honest to herself. Maybe she hadn't spent enough time with Amitabh. She was just doing her duty towards him by staying married to him. Even though he was the one with the problem.

Her mind raced back to a night in her college days. She had been dating Dhruv for some time and it had been going well. But there was a sense of complacency that had set in. He loved her and she enjoyed being with him but she needed more. She knew that he would propose one day and she would be stuck to him for the rest of her life. She needed one more excitement. One more fling. She needed someone else to want her, desire her, and if nothing else, at least kiss her.

She had been hanging out with Dhruv's best friend quite often. Amitabh was the complete opposite of Dhruv. While Dhruv was tall, tough and a complete athlete, Amitabh was a tad short, wiry, with glasses and a wit that was as dry as Chardonnay. Amitabh had never dated anyone. Aarti always felt he was shy with the way he looked. All the girls used to flock to Dhruv and leave Amitabh aside. Aarti used to feel bad for him. She even set him up with a few girls, and after the date, he would come back and tell Aarti exactly what was wrong with her friend.

'She has the intelligence of a baboon,' he would say, making Aarti laugh out loud. Or he would comment, 'My God, I can't believe you and she are friends. She's so hung up on her favourite yesteryear stars that she dresses like them. I cannot date Sridevi from *Chandani!*' Aarti would guffaw at his vitriolic remarks, and eventually stopped setting him up.

One day, Aarti had been waiting for Dhruv to come back from cricket practice when Amitabh landed up at her place instead. He said that Dhruv wouldn't be able to see her that day, and since her landline phone was out, he had come all the way to give her the message. Aarti had stood watching him, half drenched from the pouring rain in the wild monsoon of Mumbai, and realized that either he was such a loyal friend to Dhruv or he really cared about Aarti.

She invited him in and introduced him to her parents. They immediately asked her to get a towel and her father gave him a spare shirt. Amitabh had food with her parents and they quickly took a liking to him. He regaled them with his funny stories, sharp intellect, and homely attitude. He cleared the dinner dishes and was about to leave when he asked if he could take Aarti for coffee. The parents agreed readily since the closest CCD was a stone's throw away.

Aarti knew he was up to something but she didn't say anything then. She just followed him to CCD where her worst fears came true.

'I love you, Aarti,' he blurted out, even before they got their cappuccinos.

Aarti was shocked. 'Amit, I'm dating your best friend. Do you know what you're saying?'

He looked down in deep remorse. 'Aarti, I know Dhruv. He can never look after you. I mean, he's always in cricket practice, or in tuitions, or running on a treadmill. That man is doing so many things he might forget to do you! You want to spend the rest of your life with someone like that?'

Aarti smiled at his joke and felt a warm feeling through her body that was equally dangerous and strong. Their coffees came and Aarti put a packet of brown sugar into her cappuccino without replying. Amitabh went on, 'Just once, I want to be with you. Hold you. Feel like you're mine. I promise you, I won't be on the treadmill. Hell, I don't even need tuitions. I have all the time in the world to give to you. And I don't want to be with anyone else. Why do you think I didn't make it with anyone else?'

Aarti looked up at him then, dreadfully afraid of what she was going to hear. And he said exactly those words, 'Because all I've ever wanted is you.'

She had thought about that for some time and realized that all his actions did point to that but she had been too blind to see. She had always thought of him as a friend. And it had been great fun to be with him. He made her laugh like Dhruv never could. He pampered her when Dhruv wasn't around. And it was Amit who bought her favourite CDs.

She didn't know what would happen if anything went further with Amitabh. A part of her wanted to know what that would feel like. She promised in her heart that she would be faithful to Dhruv for the rest of her life, if she just gave in this last time. What harm would one kiss do anyway?

They finished their coffee and he walked her home. 'You haven't said anything, Aarti,' he said, as they got closer to the entrance of her building. 'Please tell me you want to be with me as much as I want to be with you.' And Aarti turned around to reply. A reply that would change her life forever. That would set into action a course of events that would make her question if she had truly been honest to herself that day.

'Ma'am,' the steward said to Aarti, and she realized she had fallen asleep. 'Please put your seat back up.' Aarti did as she was told and asked for a glass of water. Her dream had suddenly brought back the choices she had made. The conversation between the elderly woman and her lingered between them as the plane landed at the Indira Gandhi National Airport.

Aarti didn't know what she was going to do next. If she truly had to be honest with herself, she would have to tell Amitabh the truth. And, finally, confront Dhruv of a past that she thought she had buried a long time ago.

19

Love doesn't die overnight; it dies over time, and in small ways. An expectation not met, a hug not returned, nonchalance rather than excitement about something new, a look turned sour or even affection that is spurned. It takes a toll on the relationship. Finally, when there is only depression—that the other person is not responding, the lonely nights are endless, conversation is absent—and a feeling that nothing is going right with your life, do you turn to someone else. That's how a fling starts.

Gita never expected to be attracted to Sahil. But she was. For a while he stopped coming to her house, saying he was busy with work. Truth is, he didn't want to see her and make her uncomfortable after what had happened last time. But soon, her in-laws missed him and demanded that he see them more often, and so the visits started again. Gita realized that the time and space away from him had done nothing to stop her feelings. She longed even more for him to notice her. A woman knows when a man loves her. It's an inner instinct that cannot be explained. A flicker in the eye that sets the look apart from any other that she has ever seen. She saw that in Sahil. He still looked at her in the same way as he had when he had kissed her.

Thankfully, no one else noticed.

Gita no longer knew how to deny her feelings. She started talking to Sahil again and he responded. At first, it was harmless, 'Will you have some more vegetables?' when he came over for meals. Soon they were laughing with each other as they watched TV while the kids and parents slept. Before she knew it, she was again alone with Sahil, this time in his house eating mutton roganjosh and parathas one afternoon.

Gita polished off a second helping. 'This is what I missed the most when we weren't talking, Sahil.'

'Mutton? What about me?'

'Of course you, too. But mutton for sure!'

Sahil laughed and cleared the plates. 'This is the first time you've cooked non-vegetarian food and it's turned out brilliant. You have a gift, Gita. You should start a catering service.'

'You know, my friends have been telling me the same thing.'

'I agree with them. I could help you with funds if you want to start it.'

'But what will Shailesh and your parents say?' She was aware of these unwritten rules and didn't want to upset the household.

'Balls to them!' Sahil spoke defiantly. Gita laughed. He was quite cocky, a trait she admired. She was thankful to have him by her side. 'You make whatever orders you get, and from that you serve your family. No special requests from them anymore. Only from people who pay you!'

And with a certain smile he added, 'You have to pay me for helping you though, Gita. In kind.' Slowly and seductively his gaze slid downwards.

Gita continued washing her hands in the sink. 'Well, I like cooking for you. I'll repay you with dessert.'

Sahil leaned casually against the frame of the door as he studied her. His presence gave her such joy. She was ecstatic to have this entire afternoon to spend with him. With her girls at Julie's learning piano, her in-laws visiting their relatives and Shailesh out of town, Gita was free. Sahil had asked her to come over while they cooked together. She had jumped at the chance.

Sahil wiped his hands on the towel after taking his turn at the basin. They smiled at each other. She reached out and took

Sahil's hand. Was it the cooking together? Spending time? She wasn't sure what made her do it. She knew though that love was never planned; it just happens. It only takes a moment to reach out to someone, and the connection is made.

As they held each other's hands, an unmistakable, instant spark erupted between them. She wanted him desperately. She felt a primal need to put an end to all these years of being a simple housewife.

He gently tugged her closer to him. She took a step forward, not holding back. The smouldering flame she saw in his eyes startled her: he had always wanted her. She could hold back no longer. His breath, softly caressing the sides of her neck, felt warm and gentle as she looked down. He moved a few inches away, allowing her to reconsider her choices. It was the most important decision of her life. She looked into his soulful eyes. Her heart began to hammer in her chest. She gave a slow nod. She was sure, more sure than she had ever been in her entire life.

He wrapped his arms around her midriff, closed his eyes and pulled her closer. She knew what was going to happen. She surrendered to the ache in her heart.

He saw she was ready. He kissed her gently, breathing in the aroma of her body as he covered her mouth with his. She responded eagerly, passionately, surrendering herself to the moment. She leaned further in and wrapped her fingers around the back of his hair, drawing him closer, wanting more, hoping the moment never ended. They locked themselves in a passionate embrace, as his kiss sang through her veins and opened her up like a bird freed from a cage.

She let out a soft moan, 'Sahil.' He turned and whispered into her ear, 'Gita, should I stop?' He moved his mouth over hers, devouring her softness and praying she wouldn't get upset with his desire mounting for her. She drank in the sweetness of his kisses and whispered back, 'Don't stop, Sahil. Don't stop.'

They walked to the bedroom. He started removing the hooks from her blouse. She let the pallu of her sari fall; along with it fell her inhibitions and released the woman within. He ran his lips over her porcelain skin as a brief shiver rippled through her body.

She hungrily tore at his shirt, not wanting to lose the moment or have any sense of logic enter her body. He deftly removed all her clothing and admired her. 'God, Gita, you're beautiful.' Gita blushed in response to his words, his touch, and his desire.

She felt a wave of love sweep through her body. Finally, a man wanted her desperately. After years of hating being touched, she wanted nothing more but to have Sahil in her arms.

He lay her gently on the bed and started kissing her along the lines of her neck and stomach, gently touching her with the tips of his fingers on the side of her breasts, as her heartbeat skyrocketed. His hand slid across her silken belly and she shivered with delight, wanting more. His hands moved magically over her smooth breasts and paused to circle her swollen nipples. No one had ever touched her like that before. Shailesh had no patience for any of this. This was new. An obsession. This was heaven.

Sahil parted her legs and she looked at him quizzically. 'No one has done this?' She shook her head.

'Lie back then and let me do this.' Sahil gently rolled his tongue over her navel while caressing her breasts with the tips of his fingers. He moved down slowly, gracefully, and moved his fingers around her thighs. He rolled his tongue on the tips of her soft spots as she took a deep breath in, soaking in the newness of the feeling. His breath was warm and moist against her body and he took in her juices as she writhed in profound pleasure, eager to have him inside her. But he was not done and he made her soar through the sky, higher and higher. Gita felt as if she was floating. So this was what they called an orgasm. She had never felt this way before and she finally understood what it meant to have one. She bit her lip to stifle an outcry of delight and Sahil smiled. 'Don't hold back, Gita.'

Then he slid into her, moving slowly and finding a rhythm with her body. A primal desire swept deep within her as she arched her back to meet his yearning. His raw sensuousness carried her to great heights, as he moved faster and deeper within her. Their breaths synchronized, flesh against flesh, energy that had been set free after years of being hidden. They were one. Their desire, their love, their need. They moved into each other, their hearts beating in sync. He looked into her eyes and she looked into his.

With that, she felt waves of ecstasy pour through her as she experienced multiple orgasms that made her scream in pure pleasure. Spent, tired, and overwhelmed, he lay next to her. She almost moved to get up, as she did with Shailesh, when Sahil held her back, holding her softly and whispering, 'What's your hurry?' He smelled her skin against his face, the sweet perfume of a woman who had just been pleasured. Love flowed in her like warm honey. His touch made her fall back into bed and snuggle against his chest.

This was not wrong. How can it be? A woman was made to be loved. And if she married wrongly, then destiny had to give her a way to find that love. Society could not hold back a need. A marriage should never let a woman be caged. A relationship was meant to free you, to make you be desired, loved, touched and needed. Gita knew that Sahil had given her back more than her womanhood that afternoon. He had given back her confidence. She was not frigid, after all. And she was no longer afraid. She had just had a bad lover in Shailesh, a man who had broken her over the years.

'I love you, Gita,' Sahil said softly, as he laid his cheek against the contours of her body. She smiled and replied, 'I need to get up, Sahil. I have to get back to my motherly duties.' He snuggled her closer to himself and replied, 'Five more minutes. Please.'

And Gita lay there. She didn't know when this moment would come back. She didn't want it to end. All she knew was that she had started something that would now be extremely difficult to stop. And in the end she would have to make a choice. A choice that could split the family apart for the man she loved.

20

Aarti was sleeping late on a Saturday afternoon when she became vaguely aware of voices. They seemed to be shouting at each other. Was she dreaming? She had come in late the previous night and wanted a weekend of peace and quiet. She realized the voices belonged to her boys. 'Shut up, please!' she yelled, but no one listened. She dragged herself out of bed and walked outside to find Aryan and Amitabh racing their remote-controlled toy cars.

'Vroom-vroom! I beat you, Daddy!' Aryan was screaming at the top of his voice. Amitabh gave him a high five as they marched around the drawing-room. Amitabh made a trumpet with his hands and made sounds and shouted, 'The victor Aryan Aggarwal takes a victory lap. Everyone applaud for him!'

Suddenly, they stopped as they saw Aarti with her hands on her hips and a frown on her face. 'Seriously, guys, why can't you go down and play in the lobby?'

'Mummy!' Aryan ran to his mother and she took him in her arms.

'You're a big boy now, Aru. Mama can't pick you up anymore like this,' Aarti said, as she slowly walked towards the sofa and sat down.

'Dad can't pick me up either. He has no muscles!' Aryan said.

Amitabh laughed. 'I don't need muscles here,' he said, as he pointed to his biceps. 'I just need this muscle to work.' He pointed to his temple. 'That's the biggest muscle we need in order to succeed!' He tickled Aryan and asked, 'Am I right? Am I right?' Aryan giggled.

Aarti said, 'I agree too. Now can you keep it down so I can sleep? I get one Sunday off and this is what I get…' Her voice trailed off as the boys went back to playing and turned deaf to her whining.

Suddenly, Amit said, 'I have a surprise for everyone.'

Aarti was curious. Aryan squealed with delight and ran to his father, 'What? What, Daddy? Tell me!'

'Everyone has to follow me downstairs.'

Aryan quickly started wearing his shoes, as Aarti said, 'Downstairs? Oh God!'

Aryan tugged her hand and led her to the door. 'Okay, Okay, Aryan. Let me wear my robe first. And call Mum and Papa also. They must be awake. Let me brush my teeth. Amitabh, you're just too much!' Aarti smiled faintly at her husband as she walked back into their room to the adjoining bathroom. Aryan opened his door and jumped up to ring the bell of the adjoining house to wake up his grandparents. Aarti changed into a pair of jeans and a shirt. It wasn't proper to be roaming around in the society's public spaces in your pajamas. There were cameras everywhere that captured everything.

The grandparents came out, dragged by Aryan holding both their hands. He pleaded with them to hurry up.

'What's all the excitement about?' Aarti's mother-in-law asked. Amitabh had already gone downstairs. As they stepped outside the gate they heard the roar of an engine and Amitabh calling out from the driver's seat of a brand-new car, 'Hi guys!'

It was a Renault Duster. She knew that Amitabh's passion for cars was unlimited but she didn't know he was this mad!

'Amit, this would have cost a fortune!' she said, as her in-laws shook their heads and smiled at their son. Aryan was too excited and bounced around.

'I sold the other two cars. And took it on EMI. Relax. Get in. We'll all go for a spin,' he said nonchalantly.

Aarti got into the passenger seat as Aryan and her in-laws climbed in at the back. She whispered to him, 'At least you could have consulted me first. And if you've sold my car, how will I go anywhere?'

Amitabh didn't have a reply. 'Let's go, Daddy!' Aryan said from the back seat. Amitabh took them for a long drive, showing them all the features of his new car. His parents kept commenting how proud they were of their son that he was doing well in his career and could afford such an expensive car.

Aarti smiled at them and remarked how it was nice for all of them to enjoy a new car together. She knew her husband wanted to surprise her and make her happy but this wasn't the way to do it. Now she didn't have her Maruti to take her anywhere she wanted.

But she remembered how Amitabh had always been fascinated with cars. He had taken car decisions for the family all on his own. Over the years he had bought a Maruti Wagon R that she had kept for herself, a Maruti SX4, a Honda City, a Skoda, and now he had sold everything and bought a Renault. He loved cars more than anything. At first Aarti had thought it was just a craze. His mad obsession with Formula 1, him presenting race-cars to his son, purchasing cars for the family and selling them off for better ones. But this was the ultimate. The entire family always seemed happy with his crazy hobby. They went on long drives and enjoyed the smell of a new car.

Somehow, today she couldn't share in the joy. She felt left out of his life. She felt slighted. She was tired. There was such a pretence to the entire situation. A happy family. Content with life. A new car to show for their satisfaction in life. But today, Aarti felt extremely discontented with life and terribly unhappy with the new purchase that seemed to cover up what was really going on between Amitabh and her.

They got back home and Aarti started with the household chores. She told the cook what to make and gave Aryan a bath. Amitabh wandered into her room while she was putting away the ironed clothes. He said, 'Is there something bothering you? You didn't seem happy on the drive.'

Aarti didn't reply. 'Tell me?' he insisted, He sat on the bed.

Aarti turned to face him. 'I wish you had told me. Buying and selling cars. Financial investments. Our joint accounts. You handle all of it. And I don't say a word. I want to know. Your wife needs to be involved in all this, Amit.'

He stayed quiet while she took a deep breath. 'Look, I know you manage our finances well, but I just want to know what's going on. Give me that much respect that I'll understand. I'm in a Sales job for chrissakes. I know numbers, too.'

'But you've never asked me before,' he said, puzzled with her behaviour.

'Yes, I know,' Aarti said with quiet desperation, hoping he would understand what was really going on in her head. 'But I want to know from now on.'

Amitabh stretched his legs casually before him. 'Sure. From now on, I'll tell you. And I was thinking I'd hire a driver. He'll drop me to work and then you can keep the car for the rest of the day. I have fixed timings in office in any case. You might as well roam around in the Duster.'

'It's not about the damn car!' Aarti sighed. The tensing of her jaw betrayed her frustrations and deep exasperation.

Amitabh stayed quiet for several minutes before he spoke again, 'It's about us not having sex, isn't it?'

This time Aarti couldn't say anything. Amitabh spoke in a tense, clipped voice that forbade any questions. 'I went to a doctor. Nothing happened. We tried naturopathy. Nothing happened. I've tried meditation. Nothing happened! I even tried alcohol after you told me it helped us conceive. But that only gave me six months of a hangover. And still nothing happened. Now I'm happy with my cars, my son, and my comic books. I've let it go. The sexual urge. And till now I thought you had too. You're just reminding me of my shortcomings. You never see the good in everything else I've done. I gave you a choice then. I'll give it to you again. You're free to take it.'

Amitabh didn't wait for Aarti to reply before he stood up and disappeared from the room. He thundered across the hall and said he was going out for some work before slamming the door shut. His parents and Aryan were puzzled.

Aarti locked herself in the bathroom. She remembered when she had seen the hope in Amitabh's eyes the last time. When he had told her he loved her.

They had walked slowly back from their coffee date. Aarti had never wanted to hurt anyone. She had just wanted to see what Amit's kiss was like. At twenty-three she had been stupid and young and vulnerable. An inner torment had began to gnaw at her.

'Well, Aarti,' Amit had said. 'We're here in front of your gate. If you go in without saying a word, I'll never trouble you again. But if you do care about me, I want to know right now if the answer is yes. Do you love me too, Aarti?' He looked up at her with anticipation.

She moved toward him, impelled involuntarily by her own passion. She nodded and whispered in his ear, 'Yes. I love you too.'

Amitabh couldn't contain his joy. He pulled her gently towards him and gave her a kiss on her lips. She closed her eyes and took in the sweet sensation of another man's lips on hers. For so long it had only been Dhruv. This one was so wicked, so delicious, so sinfully good that she lost herself in Amitabh's smell, his arms, his overwhelming need for her. And only when they had pulled away from each other did they realize that Dhruv was standing right behind them, waiting for Aarti to return home.

Dhruv was pained and burning in anger. A glazed look of despair began to spread over Aarti's face. A raw and primitive grief besieged her as she realized what she had done. If only she could take back that moment and not have said 'Yes' to Amitabh or let him kiss her. She should have stayed strong.

But it had happened, and Dhruv then walked past both of them, shouting at his best friend and girlfriend, 'You're both dead to me!' He had turned and looked pointedly at Aarti. 'One day you'll regret this and come back to me.'

For several weeks after that Aarti had tried to apologize to Dhruv but he had refused to take her calls. Even Amitabh tried calling him to explain that he didn't mean to hurt his friend but Dhruv refused to acknowledge either of them. Eventually, they stopped calling him and became closer to each other, not knowing any other way to be. Although Aarti had said she loved Amitabh, it was Dhruv who she missed. How she really wanted both the men in her life. Her heart was split in two.

Aarti still missed Dhruv but eventually she became used to Amitabh around her, showing her his latest comic book or going for drives in cars from different showrooms. It was a new adventure she started enjoying. He truly loved her and she thought that maybe one person's love was good enough for both of them. He was attentive and caring. And she gave back by doing everything he wanted. Soon she began to forget about Dhruv and fell truly in love with Amitabh.

When Amitabh finally asked her to marry him, she readily agreed. Her parents had seen him court her for three years and they loved him. He had a job in equity trading with a multinational firm. His parents loved Aarti and even encouraged her to continue with her job. What more could Aarti's parents ask for in a son-in-law and his family? They readily agreed, and Aarti and Amitabh wed. Dhruv didn't attend the wedding but he was thought of on the wedding night.

When Amitabh and Aarti first tried to make love, she realized that he had a problem. He had been saying he wanted to 'save himself' for his wedding night. But it only meant he wanted to save the secret until he was finally wed. Amitabh was *impotent!*

Aarti realized that she would never have sex again. Dhruv had placed this curse on her. And in that brief moment when she looked at Amitabh in despair, he said, 'Maybe you should have married Dhruv.' Then he gave her the choice that he brought up again that afternoon, 'You're free to leave me, Aarti. This is my burden to carry. I'll understand if you want an annulment.'

In that moment Aarti's world collapsed.

21

'Oh my God!' Natasha exclaimed, as Gita giggled with her news. It was early evening and the friends were sitting in the lawns.

'Yes! The maid walked in on Julie and Michael having sex! She ran out in tears and came to my place. She didn't know if she should quit or keep the job since she needed the money.' Julie and Michael were their American neighbours who were quite famous for not being able to blend in.

'Some people are so progressive!' Sarita said, as she blushed a little, recalling the outlandish sex positions her husband had made her do only a month ago. Her hand had healed completely but her heart was still heavy. She had followed Jai to his office and realized that Shefali was just his subordinate who he didn't interact with at all. She had stalked him and read all his phone messages. She now knew where he went and what he did at all times of the day. And in the end, all she could gather from this intensive private detective role she had embraced was that her husband was really boring at work. Shefali had been flirting with him but he never responded. And he immediately came home to her post-work. So if he loved her so much, why wouldn't he still make love to her? She had even cuddled and said that she was ready to do things but he had pushed her away replying that he wasn't. Now her mind had been racing. Did he only want kinky sex? Would they ever go back to even missionary? Or worse, would they just stop having sex altogether? While her thoughts took her to Jai, her friends gossiped about their American neighbours.

'But what time did she enter the house? No bai works at night!' Aarti asked.

'It was the middle of the afternoon. Julie gave the bai a key. But she forgot to tell her they had returned from their vacation. So as usual she went in at two in the afternoon to clean up, and there they were, completely naked on the bed, and Ursula screamed and ran out of there.' Gita dramatically retold the maid's story.

'Then?' Aarti asked. She had always loved drama.

'Then what?' Gita said with a sly smile. 'You know what happens after that na, Aarti?' All the girls burst into peals of shy laughter, not wanting to admit any details from their own marital lives.

'Are you still going to send the girls for their music to Julie's house now?' Sarita asked Gita.

'Of course! I'm sure they won't be at it in front of my children. Julie's an excellent music teacher. You should send Rhea to her.'

Sarita shook her head. 'Nah baba nah! I'm not sending my children anywhere. You don't know how they can get corrupted and from where!'

Natasha bit her tongue. The memory of that night of having sex with Rahul came flooding into her brain. It had been nothing like she had ever experienced before. She didn't know how she was still sitting here with Rahul's mother, having a normal conversation. She dreaded to think what would happen if Sarita found out. She would surely lose her as a friend. But what was more worrying was if she lost Rahul as a lover!

'I must tell you about Guddi.' Natasha wanted to steer the topic away from children and possibly Rahul.

They all looked at her with bated breath. 'Her husband has come back to her!'

Aarti's hands flew to her mouth as Gita's jaw dropped. Only Sarita asked, 'Who's Guddi again?'

Natasha looked at her. 'Guddi is the Delhi housewife who lives next door to me in C wing. Her husband left her to go back to his first wife in Dubai. But she gave him an ultimatum. She said she would only wait until he returned! In the meantime she looks after their two cats and a million plants as if they're the best thing that ever happened to her.' Natasha reminded Sarita as Gita giggled at her description. Natasha always had a way with words. Being a part of the erudite culture Gita looked up to Natasha as the one who had everything; a glamorous life, foreign trips, a loving husband, and complete freedom.

Sarita asked, 'And now he's back?'

'She happily took him back, no questions asked.' Natasha said. 'Talk about unending support, no matter what!'

This put the girls in a pensive mood. They all thought the same question: Would they take their husbands back after he had an affair?

'It's not easy being a single or a divorced woman in this society,' Gita said. 'I guess that's why we forgive our husbands for their trespasses.'

'That's because we're all so afraid of being honest with ourselves,' Aarti remarked, and they all waited for her to continue. Aarti remembered her conversation with the old woman on her recent flight. 'We are the ones who are stronger. We've gone through childbirth and raised our children by ourselves. We're the ones who change for our family and children. And even after that, we don't give ourselves credit.'

'So true,' Natasha said. 'If a man cheated on me, I don't think I would forgive him.'

'What if it's the woman who cheated?' Sarita asked. 'Will that be forgivable?' She looked at everyone but Natasha thought, maybe because of guilt, that Sarita's gaze lasted longer on her. Had Rahul said anything to Sarita, Natasha wondered. She must ask him.

'Cheating only happens when there's no other way,' Gita said. 'Women should give other women some leeway. We're always pulling each other down. Look at how strong the male species is. They're always supporting each other, no matter what they do. They'll be there for each other, even if they have to go out of their way. And we women? We're not ready to help each other, even if it's not out of the way.'

Aarti shook her head. 'I don't think so, Gita. Look at us. We've always been there for each other. Women do support their friends. But yes, maybe we're quick to judge and lazy to help. But if you really needed me, I would be there for you.'

Gita looked at Aarti warmly. Would she really be there for her if she learned about her and Sahil? She was an adulteress. How would her friends respond to that, she wondered. 'Thank you so much, Aarti. That means a lot,' Gita said.

'But why haven't you brought something for us to eat?' Aarti teased.

Natasha echoed her, 'Yeah, Gita. Now we've grown used to your savoury snacks. Hey, you should call your catering service that!'

Gita laughed. 'I'm calling it Gita's Kitchen. And I'm making a menu to figure out what to do next. I still haven't asked Shailesh what he thinks about the idea. I'll need tremendous support to do this…' Her voice trailed off as she knew that she couldn't expect any support and her dream might die yet again.

She remembered that for years after Renu was born, she couldn't even go in for a shower till she finished all her household duties. She would prepare an entire breakfast for her in-laws and request them to feed it to the two-year-old child while she went to the bathroom. When she would emerge a half-hour later, the child would be at the table with no food, while her mother-in-law would be watching television, claiming to have forgotten!

When Renu was older at five, Gita hoped the in-laws would help her with managing their grandchild. But when Gita would return from her grocery shopping, she would see Renu in the kitchen in the knife drawer looking for her crayons, while her in-laws were drinking tea at the dining-table. And instead of Gita reprimanding them for not keeping an eye out for her child, her mother-in-law would complain that she had to make the tea because 'who knows where Gita had been roaming around'.

Now, Gita had two daughters. She had to look after both of them. Her in-laws didn't change then and they wouldn't change now. She couldn't start a business and still manage a house all the time. It was well for Aarti to do so because she had such great help. But Gita had no option. She sighed. She knew the idea was now churning but she didn't know how to take it forward.

'We'll support you!' Natasha said. 'We'll look after the kids when you need us to. Don't worry. You just start with birthday parties. Lots of money to be made in children's birthdays!'

'I agree!' Gita said, suddenly buoyed by her friends' words. 'Just the other day I went to one where there were elephant rides for the kids. And the return-presents were Nokia phones, can you believe that?'

'That's ridiculous!' Natasha exclaimed. 'But I've also taken Diya to birthday parties where the themes were so elaborate that they would put weddings to shame. Once, she got invited to a party with the Cirque du Soleil, you guys know that, right? The circus show from Europe?' They nodded. 'So anyway,' she continued. 'After that party she also started demanding she wanted Michael Jackson at her parties. Thankfully, I stopped it, otherwise Vikram would have sold our house to get that for her! Now we just give her money on her birthday. And let me tell you, that's not cheap either!'

Gita was incredulous. What was Natasha talking about, giving money to young children? She would never do that. And theme parties? She took her children to McDonald's till now and everyone had a good time.

Sarita said, 'I don't throw parties. My in-laws refuse to spend money on their own grandchildren. You think they'll spend on other people's grandchildren? Ha! Unlikely. All their life, Rahul and Rhea have attended parties but we've all just gone to Pizza Hut on their birthday as a family.'

Aarti smiled at Sarita. She was so simple-minded. Aarti thought of her only son, whom she indulged. She organized grand theme parties for him. She thought that if she could afford it, she should give him the best. She wondered why Natasha was so rigid with Diya. But she didn't want to sound arrogant in front of them. She said, 'It's a quid pro quo, isn't it? If you attend a pool party at a hotel, then you have to throw an equally expensive party for your child, otherwise, there's tremendous pressure on him from his peers.'

Sarita waved her hands in the air. 'That'll never end then. How big can you go? How much money can you spend? And the child in the end hardly cares. They just want to eat the same pizza and have a good time with a few close friends.'

Aarti thought of her son's parties, where she would call her entire family and all his friends from school and the building. She did a jungle theme once, a pirate theme another time, and a Disney theme with actual bumper cars in hired lawns in the suburbs. She had spent lakhs on each birthday party, and she knew that he enjoyed it, as did everyone who had come.

She didn't think she had gone overboard. Birthdays for her only child came just once a year. And what was the point of earning so much as a family if they couldn't spend it on some fun.

'I think it's ridiculous,' Gita sighed. 'There's so much pressure on the parents! A child will want more, a parent can't give it, the child will feel alienated, then blame the parents. So either the parents keep up with the pressure of elaborate birthday parties, or not send the child or refuse to give in. I don't see us winning this war.' Gita realized that she had two children and a lifetime of parties to attend and throw for them.

Sarita put a hand on her shoulder. 'It gets better as they grow up. They have fewer friends and don't really care for parties. Rahul at age ten said he wanted to buy some paints rather than go out. Rhea stopped going to parties. On her birthday she just calls a few friends over to the home and I make an elaborate meal for them. Then they cut cake.'

Gita didn't feel assured. She wasn't like Sarita in the least bit. She wanted her children to have a social life and become outgoing, something she never had in her childhood and which led her to be a naive bride at a young age. She wanted them to experience the world and enjoy themselves. But she didn't know where to put a stop to the madness of birthday parties.

'It's a racket,' Natasha said. 'The best we can do is teach our children that this is all we can afford. And they shouldn't compare themselves to others and feel they need to throw elaborate parties because everyone else does. Those friends are not worth it because they don't treasure them for who they are. They only like them for their money.'

The women looked at Natasha as if she was an alien. Having said these wise words, it seemed impossible that Diya was her child. The teenager demanded everything and often received it. Natasha looked at them and as if reading their thoughts said,

'Hey, this is how I have tried to bring up Diya but it's all her father's fault for spoiling her!'

The girls nodded their heads in sympathy. A woman had no say when a father had the last word. After all, he brought in the money and always got the final say. That's why it was important to earn as well. Aarti knew how important that was.

'Forget about their parties, let's all go back to my place and have some tea,' Natasha said.

'I'll bring dhoklas!' Gita said, and they shut her down.

'What a Gujju you are. You can't think of anything but dhoklas? You don't need to bring anything. I'll just make tea and order some snacks,' Natasha said.

'As long as it's non-vegetarian,' Gita said. Aarti and Natasha were amazed at this revelation, even though Sarita already knew about it. They all agreed and trooped up to Natasha's house for some tea and chatter, wondering how Gita managed to remain a strict vegetarian in her house for so many years.

It was the first of their secrets that was to come out.

22

Sarita knew she needed to confront Jai about their lack of intimacy. Her hand was much better, and she wanted to have sex with him again. But Jai was behaving like she was covered with warts. Well, this had to stop.

One midnight after everyone had gone to bed and they were alone in the room, she woke him up gently. 'Jai,' she whispered. 'Jai, wake up. I want to talk to you.' Jai awoke groggily, wondering what was going on.

'What? What happened? Are mummy papa okay?'

'They're fine. I'm not. I want to talk about us.'

Jai groaned, 'Can't this wait till the morning?'

Sarita yanked the covers off him. 'No, it can't. Because everyone is awake in the morning and you leave for work again.'

Jai rubbed his eyes. 'Okay. Tell me.'

'Are you having an affair?' She made a sad face.

Now Jai was fully awake. 'Are you crazy?'

'Yes or no?'

'No. Of course not. Why would you think that?'

'Because we haven't had sex in a month. And it's been bothering me. Do you not find me attractive anymore?'

'I do find you attractive, Sarita. But I've held back because I don't want you to get hurt again.'

Sarita sighed with relief. 'But I'm fine now.'

'I know but…it's just that the last time you got hurt and I thought you don't want to do it anymore.'

Sarita finally had to ask about all the kinky sex. 'What's with all those handcuffs and harnesses, by the way?'

'I heard some women talking about a book called *shades of grey* or something. They were saying how it had turned them on. So I bought it and realized that maybe this was something you would like to do. So I did more research and checked out that the longer you are married, the more effort you need to put into your relationship. So I figured it was something you would like. But I guess it backfired and you hated it.' Jai said, his voice turning into a whisper in the end.

Sarita took his face in her hands. 'Jai, I loved it. I love plain old sex and I love kinky sex. I love any sex, as long as it's with you. Best of all I love that we have such attraction towards each other after so many years.'

Jai was pleased. 'But what about the harness? It broke your hand. You cursed me and hated me for that stunt.'

'Jai,' Sarita said plainly. 'I cursed you when I was giving birth too. But it didn't mean I didn't love you for giving me two children or a wonderful life.'

'So you want to go back to the plain old sex we used to have and just be us?'

'No. I want to get back on that harness. But I can't do it with your parents outside. I want us to try handcuffs and blindfolds again. But I want to be able to scream in pleasure without worrying about the after-effects at the breakfast table.'

'So what are you suggesting?'

'Let's start doing what we both want to do at that moment. If it's plain missionary, so be it. If it's swinging from the treetops naked, by God, I'm all for it. But don't run away the next morning when your parents give me sly looks. At least, kiss me and leave.'

Jai understood. 'You know what, I think it's time for my parents to shift to another house. This place is too small for all of us. You and I need more space. What am I earning so much money for? Why do we have so many houses if we can't live comfortably?'

Sarita was delighted. She couldn't believe that Jai had said something she had wanted for so many years. She felt she could do anything for him at that moment.

Jai kissed her gently. 'I'm ready now.'

Sarita laughed out loud. 'I am, too.'

Jai pulled back. 'But I want you to take initiative, too. Tell me what you like and show me what you love. A marriage is kept alive by both people trying to surprise the other person with love. So show me also sometimes.'

'I will. Starting right now.'

Jai smiled as Sarita pulled her clothes off her head and climbed on top of Jai. He lay back as she took control. And for the first time in a while, Sarita was unafraid to do so.

23

Infidelity isn't really the absence of loyalty, Aarti thought. It is the need for physical intimacy when there's no love to be had. Take her, for instance. She had gone seven years without having sex. Seven. Years.

It wasn't because she didn't want it. It was because she could never get it. She made a decision to be with a man who couldn't give it. For years later she would wonder why she stuck to a marriage for the sake of fidelity. Why did she stay, when she craved human touch? When she desired to have an orgasm with a man rather than by pleasuring herself in the bathroom. Sure, she had perfected the art of touching herself. But that was only because she did not have any alternative. No alternative, dammit! And even though Amit had tried several times in the beginning to be a good lover every other way, he wasn't very good at it. All Aarti wanted was plain, normal penetrative sex. Which he was unable to do. And soon he stopped any form of lovemaking or even touching each other.

She took a drag of a cigarette while sitting in her car in the basement and pondered her alternatives. She had felt such deep guilt at kissing Amitabh that day. Guilt that had made her body freeze. She could never look at another man again. Her flirtatious side came to a grinding halt. Her 'one more fling' was the kiss she had. Amitabh truly thought that she loved him at the moment. But the love came later. When there was no alternative.

It wasn't a bad love. They had a good life. But Amitabh couldn't give Aarti the one thing a woman needed: sex.

And the guilt kept her in the marriage. She knew she had betrayed Dhruv. She felt that was a burden she had to live with. Yes, Amitabh had been dishonest, not telling her that he was impotent. She could have immediately got an annulment. But she chose to stay and help him. They did go to counsellors and he did take several pills for many months. But there was no improvement. He needed surgery, something he hadn't been willing to undergo. So she suffered. Alone. Through the nights. And days. And when people spoke about romance and their explosive sex lives, she reached for a cigarette in the quiet solitude of her car park in the basement where no one came to disturb her.

Two years into the marriage, Aarti got a Facebook request from Dhruv. He was married and wanted to make amends. She desperately wanted to leave the past behind. They met. Instead of having coffee, they checked into a hotel room, told each other they were forgiven, and had sex.

That was the night Aarti conceived Aryan. As soon as Dhruv got off her, she knew they had made a baby. And Aarti wanted to keep it. She was ready to be a mother and she knew she never would be with Amit. She got her husband drunk the next night at their favourite pub and went home. She pretended to make love to him and the next morning when he awoke and saw both of them lying naked under the sheets, he realized he could do it while he was drunk. He tried alcohol several times after that to initiate sex but it didn't end up well. In six weeks' time Aarti told him she was pregnant and the sex stopped anyway. He didn't bother after the birth of Aryan and Aarti didn't push him. She also never told Dhruv. It wasn't his place to be a part of her life again. He had a wife and child of his own and she couldn't wreck that home.

So she kept her terrible secret. Another layer of guilt piled up. Because there was no alternative.

Now that baby, Aryan, was seven years old. She wondered how long she could hold on to the secret, and her guilt. When would she be free of this burden?

She looked around and realized that there were portions of the basement that were quite dark. It was only reserved for guest parking and no one came down there. It was her place to smoke. The occasional cigarette that was really a bad habit. But in comparison to her life, it seemed as if it was not a vice at all. She decided that she couldn't continue like this anymore. She needed to give up this habit of smoking, as she needed to give up the pattern of feeling like there was no alternative.

There was a reason she met Dhruv again at the wedding. It was a sign. She was a woman with needs. It was time she acted on what she wanted from her life instead of just living a lie. Dhruv had sent her a few messages about catching up again over coffee. But she needed to feel something more in her life. She didn't need him for a conversation, she knew exactly what she wanted him for.

Aarti went upstairs to greet Aryan who had just come back from school. Her in-laws had given him a glass of milk and he was telling them about his day. He was overjoyed to see his mother. Aarti's mother-in-law said she wanted to go to her own house and lie down in bed. Aarti said she would take Aryan for his tennis practice after he finished his milk.

She looked at Aryan as he spoke about his day at school. He had the same features as Dhruv but his mannerisms were very like Amitabh's. The same excitement at discovering a new thing, the same way he winked at Aarti when he told a joke. Aarti smiled at Aryan. He was definitely Amitabh's son. If she hadn't had him through a lie, they would have gone for a donor sperm and IVF treatment to have children, one at least.

Suddenly, Aarti felt like a rock had been lifted from her shoulders. Of course, that was it. Aarti assimilated the thought that had popped into her head. Amitabh never expected to have a child. But he married Aarti and she gave him the greatest gift in the world. An heir. A son. A child that he could call his own. And if he knew he was impotent, he would have agreed to any terms and conditions for Aarti to get pregnant in any case. They would have gone for a donor sperm to have a child. But she didn't need to. She had redeemed him of any consequences of his actions. She had protected his impotency from the family. And she would carry his secret to her deathbed. She would never tell Aryan about his biological father. But she needed to tell Amitabh what she wanted.

She was afraid it was not something that Amitabh would like. But there was one thing she needed to do before she took her final step. One more piece to fit in this entire jigsaw puzzle before she could be sure of her decision.

She picked up the phone and dialed a number.

She spoke softly, 'Hi Dhruv. This is Aarti. Can we meet?'

24

Kismet. A word with Turkish roots, loosely translated to Destiny. Something that was predetermined for some, and a choice for others. Kismet is a word used a lot in India. For housewives the word is embraced at least once in their lives. 'Hai! meri kismet,' one might say, their fate was completely against them. Or, 'Leave it to kismet,' another would exclaim, hoping that things would improve if they said their prayers. There is also the expression, 'Kismet can change anytime,' implying that some aspects of their life had improved but since they were so pessimistic, they didn't believe it would last too long.

Then there were still some who didn't believe in kismet at all. For them destiny was something you chose yourself and kismet was just a point when opportunity met preparation. It was a choice you made when you were pushed against the wall. Or in Natasha's case, literally, against an elevator.

Natasha had decided to go swimming late one evening and had happily discovered that there wasn't anyone in the pool except Rahul and a lifeguard. The instructor was on the phone and not too bothered about them since both Rahul and Natasha were excellent swimmers. All of a sudden, the instructor came up to Natasha and asked, 'If you don't mind, madam, can I close the pool early. I need to leave. My mother has been admitted into the ICU.'

Rahul and Natasha were doing laps and she said, 'Sure. We'll come out. But you can leave if you want to. We'll just finish and go in another five minutes. We don't need to use the steam and shower here.'

'Thank you, Madam. Thank you, Sir,' the coach said. He locked all the premises and left. Only the pool was open and Natasha and Rahul were taking laps, racing against each other. It was late at night and many of the people in the building had already gone to sleep. Natasha loved how Rahul kept her on the edge. She pushed her body harder to compete. Rahul marvelled at the speed of a woman who was in her forties. He could barely keep up.

She had beat him yet again. She said, 'This is too easy.'

Rahul laughed. 'Let's make a bet then.' She quickly agreed. 'The loser has to remove one item of clothing.'

Natasha smiled, realizing she was wearing a two-piece bikini while he was in his swimming trunks.

'You're on. Those shorts are coming off!'

'On your mark,' Rahul said, wondering which part he would ask her to remove. He was quite tempted for both of them to lose their lower half item of clothing. She completed the sentence as he went off in a daze, 'Get set, GO!'

Natasha raced ahead, her strokes hard and fast with her breath clear and strong. She was an excellent swimmer, with long legs and lithe arms. But Rahul chose to hold his breath a little longer and pull ahead. His long arms stretched farther and pulled him inches ahead of Natasha. And as they drew close to the finishing line, Natasha gave it one last leap of strength. But she was no match for Rahul who touched the tile seconds before her. They started panting, swallowing large gulps of air and laughing at the same time. When they had finally caught their breath Rahul said, 'Alright now, a bet's a bet.' His gaze roved and lazily appraised her body underneath the water.

Amusement flickered in the eyes that met hers. She threw back her head and let out a great peal of laughter. How was it so easy to be around Rahul? With his disarming smile and easy-going ways, she felt as if she had no worries in her life. He made her feel whole and complete. 'Alright mister. Here you go.' She said as she shimmied out of her bikini top and swam away with a twinkle in her eye.

With the water being pitch black, he couldn't see her bare body. And he ached to feel her breasts against his in the cool waters of the night. 'Come back!' he said, as he began to swim after her. But she was too quick for him this time, stopping only for a brief second to turn around and lightly graze her naked breasts against his chest, before she moved away once again. She turned her back to him and climbed up the stairs, leaving him to see just a side glimpse of her magnificent breasts as she covered herself with a towel. She laughed triumphantly. 'I'm going home now. I'm hungry.' She didn't miss his approval of her body.

Rahul's hormones raged. He came out of the pool and stood close to her, in the shadows of the covered area of the pool. No one could see them. He walked forward, stopping in front of her, with water dripping along his hair and bare chest. She leaned in close and wiped away his wet neck, reaching down slowly to feel the length of his tight abdomen. As a sliver of light fell between them, she noticed how his eyes were magnetic and compelling. He surveyed her with intense desire, a primal need gnawing away at his insides. Her heart jolted and her pulse pounded. He swept her weightless into his arms and buried his mouth on her burning lips. They writhed against each other's bodies, kissing passionately, till her towel fell and her breasts lay bare on his chest. He moved back to suckle them fondly as she let out a soft moan. She looked around and was suddenly aware of her surroundings. 'Not here,' she whispered softly to him, picking up her bikini top and wearing it. She covered herself with a robe, picked up her towel and headed towards the elevator to go home. Rahul wiped himself with his towel, covered himself with a shirt and followed her.

He followed her into the service lift of the C wing. And just as they were about to reach her floor, Rahul stopped the lift by pressing the button in between floors. He grabbed her hard and kissed her passionately. He yanked open her robe and let it slip from her shoulders. He untied her bikini and clutched her breasts. Her breasts surged at the intimacy of his touch. She fell back against him, powerless in his arms, with desire mounting in every inch of her body. His hands began a lust-arousing exploration of her soft flesh. Her emotions whirled and skidded as he kissed her softly along the length of her bare back. He turned her around as she held on to his neck while he devoured her with a fiery kiss. His tongue made a path down her nipples to her stomach, as his hands searched for the pleasure points in her body. He moved her bikini bottom aside as he slid two fingers deep inside her and started making small, circular motions. She let out a groan and lifted her leg to let it sit along his other arm that he had stretched out. His body imprisoned hers in a web of growing arousal.

He untied her bottom as it fell to her ankles. He removed his shorts and kicked them aside. He lifted her leg and let it lie on his arms as he entered her slowly, standing against the back wall of the elevator. He picked her up as she wrapped her legs around him, supporting herself against the wall as he moved deeper inside her. His strong arms held her close against him as she held him closer to her body. Passion pounded the blood through her heart, chest and head. Together they found their rhythm. He didn't stop, keeping up his rhythm, until they both reached orgasm. An electric shock scorched through their bodies.

It was probably kismet that pushed them to make love in the elevator. But it wasn't kismet that revealed to everyone what they did. Someone was watching. And they would soon tell everyone.

25

Gita was supremely excited about her catering venture. She had taken the counsel of her friends about the menu, the design of the pamphlets, what name to keep. She had also spent many afternoons with Sahil discussing how much help she would need and how to break it to Shailesh. Sahil had given her unconditional support and Gita had been grateful. Sometimes, Gita felt that it would have been so much easier if Sahil had been her husband. But life has a way of not giving you everything you want. Only things you need.

'Shailesh, can you come to the room for a moment? I want to speak to you,' Gita said. She didn't want her in-laws or the children interrupting them. It was a warm and pleasant Saturday and Shailesh was lounging and reading, while the children played with some new game that Sahil had brought them.

'Now?' He didn't look up from his paper as he gave his usual reply when Gita summoned him.

Gita let him be. She went to the kitchen and finished preparing another round of tea for everyone before she sat down for her breakfast. She would speak to Shailesh after his tea and when he had finished his newspaper. Renuka, their ten-year-old, came to her with her homework. Gita examined it.

'The last two are wrong, Renu,' Gita said. 'But it's okay. Don't worry about it.' She smiled as she handed the notebook back to her daughter.

'What? Why should Renu get any wrong? She's a smart girl,' thundered Shailesh. Gita knew he wanted to be loud so he could make his point in front of the whole family. His parents looked at him with approval and Renu cowered down close to her mother without saying a word. 'Give me the notebook,' Shailesh said. 'I will check.'

Renu went to him with her copy. 'Renu, you know this,' Shailesh said. 'Come on beta, I know you can do better!' He handed the copy back to Renu and he got up to go to the bathroom.

Gita followed him with a look of disdain. Renu had tears in her eyes. Gita felt extremely guilty that she had pointed out Renu's mistakes in front of this family who didn't appreciate Renu's work or Gita's way of bringing up her daughters. She took Renu to the kitchen and spoke to her. 'I know, my darling, that these maths sums are far more difficult than the rest of the class. Ms Ritu told me you're doing very well.'

A hot tear rolled down Renu's cheek. Gita continued, 'It's okay to get some things wrong if you're trying to attempt something difficult. Because then, through practice, that will make you better.'

'But Papa isn't proud of me,' sobbed Renu openly, as Gita gathered her in her arms. And for the first time Renu said what was in her heart. 'They wanted a boy, didn't they? That's why they try to make me as one. I've joined basketball so Papa will be happy. I've cut my hair short to look like a boy. They even call me beta instead of beti. I don't like Maths but since boys are good at it, I'm trying, Mama.' Gita bent down and held Renu tightly in her arms. Renu sobbed into her mother's shoulder as Gita felt a range of emotions. She couldn't believe that her silence for so many years had led Renu to change herself for the family. It was not her fault that the grandparents wanted a male child. Anger boiled inside Gita. She was furious! She should have taken action a long time ago but she didn't. Today, she would.

She spoke again, 'Darling, listen to me. First of all, beta is something grown-ups say for all kids, whether a boy or a girl. Don't think they say it because they want you to be a boy. I want you to be exactly who you want to be. Because then, you are the best thing I've done with my life. Don't let me down by being someone else. You don't like basketball? Leave it. You don't want to do so much maths? It's alright! I will still love you and Papa will still love you. He's just encouraging you to do your best.'

'But Mama, if I fail, he won't love me,' Renu said between gulps of air and tears still flowing.

'Of course he will. I will tell him not to say such bad things to my Renu wenu,' Gita said, speaking in the baby language she used when her child was younger. It still made Renu feel better. 'I want you to grow your hair. I want you to be the best *girl* out there, the way you want to be. We'll go shopping tomorrow and buy a lovely new dress for you.'

Renu started feeling a little better. 'I can put nail polish?'

Gita nodded as if a stone had been lifted from her heart, 'Yes, my baby. Whatever you want to do, I'll help you do them. And you don't worry at all about Dada, Dadi or Papa. Ignore them. We can't change who they are. We can't always make everyone happy. It's best to just make ourselves happy at least, na?'

Renu nodded, not completely understanding what Gita just said but knowing that she had her mother's support. That was good enough for now. Gita stood up. 'Now you run along and watch TV. I'm going to bake you some cupcakes. And you can come and add some pink frosting later. Would you like that?'

Renu nodded, smiling for the first time that morning. Gita gave her a kiss as she pranced out of the kitchen. Gita clutched the edge of the marble top and took in large gulps of air. To suppress her was one thing. But how can a mindset of a family suppress a child? Children should be allowed to do what they wanted and grow up as they liked. Discipline was essential in their life but to tell a child that they were inadequate because they weren't what the parents or the grandparents expected was just wrong. What had the poor child done? One could not take out one's own frustration on an innocent child. Children picked up on conversations, actions, behaviour, and buried them deep within themselves. These things would manifest much later, and parents would have no clue why the child was behaving in that manner when it was their fault.

Gita realized that if she didn't talk to Shailesh about his and his parents' behaviour soon, Anu would also start feeling the way Renu was. They would both become a version of themselves they hated, and eventually, blame their family for bringing them up that way. She had to also start taking strict action in the house and change the mindset instead of maintaining peace and letting things wash over her. But she didn't know how. For so long she had kept her mouth shut. She didn't know how everyone would react if she suddenly started answering back. Gita went about preparing to bake cupcakes while contemplating what to do next.

Gita's needs were put aside once again with her children's needs placed on priority. It had been that way for several years. Family always came first. After all, once you became a mother, you were no longer just a woman. You were the epitome of nurturing and you needed to live up to that ideal. It didn't matter if you were lonely, depressed, anxious, or desperate, you first had to deal with your children's issues before you could get to yours. And every mother knew that children's issues never ended. But that was the beauty of motherhood. It helped you become a better person, too.

Gita put a batch of cupcakes in the oven and went outside to see Anu and Renu playing with some Barbies. Her mother-in-law, who was watching TV, couldn't resist making a comment, 'Look at this, Gita. This is how you're bringing them up. Instead of studying when she's got her sums wrong, Renu is combing a silly doll's hair.'

Gita turned around, looked squarely at her mother-in-law, and spoke loudly for her father-in-law and her children to hear, 'I would much rather she comb a doll's hair right now and be happy than do sums that make her miserable.' Her mother-in-law was stunned. Gita herself was surprised. She didn't know where the strength came from. Maybe it had been building up over the years. Maybe all it needed was a push.

But her mother-in-law would not let up. She continued, 'Well, then she'll be nothing compared to the boys in her class who will get ahead, and we'll have to collect dowry and just get her married off.'

It was too much for Gita and her rage boiled over. She could finally see what her children had been subjected to for all these years. She had thought that cooking for her family and looking after the house *and* raising her children would be enough. But she was wrong. She needed to prove to her children that girls needed to stand up for themselves. Against anybody. Even if it meant going against their family's orthodox views. She went and picked up a Barbie and started combing the doll's hair when Shailesh came out of the room. She responded so that he could hear her as well, 'Renu and Anu are free to do what they want with their lives. They will never be forced to get married if they don't want it. And there will be no talk of dowry. Ever!'

Her mother-in-law took a sharp breath in as Shailesh raised his voice, 'Gita! What are you saying?'

Gita looked at Shailesh as she set the doll down and stood up. She knew that if she didn't say what she needed to then, she would never have the courage for the rest of her life. And somewhere deep down, there was a fire that had been raging for a long time. All she needed was an opportunity, and seeing Renu cry was all it took. 'What I'm saying, Shailesh,' she said, with emphasis on his name, 'is that I would like to raise my daughters my way, without getting any lip from your parents. And I want you to be proud of the fact that they are GIRLS! So stop telling me or them what to do to make them boys. They're not. Do you understand?'

Shailesh was shocked. He had never heard her speak this way, and his father almost butted in. Gita shot him a look to tell him to mind his own business.

'Come on, girls. Let's go buy some dresses,' she said, as she went to the kitchen and shut off the oven. The cupcakes were a beautiful golden brown.

'But you don't have any money,' Shailesh said, with a visible smirk.

'Yes, I do,' she replied. 'Oh, I don't think you know. I've started a catering business. Maybe if you cared enough to listen to your wife once in a while, you would have heard me.'

Renu smiled at her mother as Gita looked at her. For the first time Gita felt she had done something right. The catering business had not started yet but she needed to let everyone know that she was capable of managing a career and her children. And the money she had squirreled away for a rainy day was going to be spent on things her daughters wanted. She needed them to know that there was one adult in the world who stood by them, no matter what. That was what motherhood was about. To understand that your dreams could not be imposed on a child. And the best thing you could do was to let them soar on their own.

26

A society may be defined as a group of extremely judgemental people, who make social and moral laws for a large population without knowing what the real lives of those individuals are. Everyone is most concerned about 'Society', even though they make the individual's life difficult as hell. 'What will society think?' 'Society will not accept it.' 'Your reputation in society will go down.' It is fear, the kind that binds housewives to stereotypes.

Gita was convinced that most women would be happier if they stopped thinking about society and its norms, and instead, did what was best for them.

She still didn't know what had come over her when she had told her husband and in-laws off. For once, she cared less about what society would say if she answered back, and more about how she needed to. It was liberating! Maybe it was the encouragement that Sahil had given for her work or the way he praised her? Or her deep sense of frustration? All she knew was that when she came back with the girls, they were both happy and that was all that mattered. Life had gone back to the same grind after that evening but people around her began to realize that this small step by her was a giant leap for society.

The thing about society was that everyone seemed more concerned about it than they were for you. But the minute you stopped caring about it or giving it much thought, it would dissipate into nothingness. Hence 'society' was nothing but a fear that was created to keep people in check. The fear that lived deep within you that only you could release from your life.

When Gita took that step against her in-laws and husband in order to stand up for her children, she released a part of that fear. It wasn't completely gone, though. It would take years to understand it and then finally let it go. Society had conditioned women with such power that even if they wanted to not bother about it, they would think twice.

Her in-laws had been deeply upset, as was Shailesh. He didn't speak to her that night as she made dinner and set the table. The entire family ignored her. She didn't know if she should apologize for her behaviour but a sense told her not to. So she stayed quiet as they all went into their rooms after dinner and she tidied up.

When she went downstairs the next evening to tell her girlfriends, they seemed extremely pleased.

'I'm so proud of you, Gita,' Aarti exclaimed, giving her a hug. 'I didn't know you lived with this pressure for so long.'

Gita nodded. 'I didn't want to tell anyone because, you know, it's not nice to wash your dirty linen in public.'

'It's not dirty linen, Gita,' Natasha said. 'We're friends. We need to help each other. We need to talk about what's actually happening so we can support one another.' Natasha wanted to tell them about her own problems, too.

'That's right,' Aarti said. 'Women bottle up too much of their life because they think it's not good to talk about it. But sometimes, we carry too heavy a burden that it is important for us to talk to each other. We need an outlet. And if we're not there for each other, then how will anything change for any of us?' She secretly hoped to reveal her own secret to her friends.

Sarita nodded. Should I speak about our bedroom antics? She decided to try. 'I have a confession to make.'

Everyone looked at her. 'I didn't get the fracture at the gym.'

Sarita cleared her throat. 'I got it in bed. I kind of fell on Jai and twisted my arm while balancing on a harness.'

'Harness!' Aarti's eyes widened. She had never figured Sarita to be the wild kind. It was a complete shock.

Gita giggled. 'That's amazing, Sari. You and your husband have such an amazing sex life.'

Natasha was also stunned. 'Seriously? You're not making this up?'

Sarita looked at her in mock anger. 'Why would I make this up? It just makes me look like a fool anyway, but I thought I should share something with my closest friends. Now the problem is that Jai wants me to take the initiative and I don't know what to do. We've had such a normal life for so long that I don't know what new things are out there that would excite a man.'

Natasha laughed. 'There's nothing new, babe. It's the same old thing. But you can try it in different ways. Use whipped cream, chocolate sauce, silk handkerchiefs, lace lingerie.'

'Or sex toys,' Aarti said.

'I know. You get them on Yari road,' Sarita said, and the girls dissolved into peals of laughter. Suddenly, Sarita felt better. 'You have no idea how relieved I am that I've told you. You guys don't think I'm a freak, do you?'

The girls shook their head as Aarti gave her a hug.

Gita said, 'I didn't know there were such things at all. By God! I've learnt something new today!' The girls laughed harder.

'Oh, by the way,' Natasha said. 'Is anyone going for swimming after they've put up the massive wall to protect our dignity?'

Gita replied, 'Children have their swimming classes. The men are still peeping from their houses to see the women but now, I don't think anyone cares. As long as a wall is there the men seem to have done their *duty* to protect us.' Gita was seriously considering joining swimming and not telling Shailesh this time. What he didn't know wouldn't hurt him. Somehow, her outburst the previous day had given her confidence to do things her way. She wondered, though, when she would get the time, as she was starting her catering business this week. She and Sahil were planning to spend the next few days taking orders.

'Oh!' Natasha suddenly remembered. 'Have you all been added to the society email group?'

Gita nodded. 'I did get a mail. There was a link to join and add our email ids. I've done mine.'

'I'm useless at these things,' Sarita admitted. 'Show me please?'

Aarti opened her phone and saw the email and added herself. She showed Sarita what to do.

'There, so now we're all on the Sapphire Towers Google email group?' Natasha said.

'How does it work?' Sarita asked.

'Well there have already been several complaints that some members have written about to the society group,' Aarti said.

'Like what?' Sarita asked.

Aarti scrolled through her inbox. 'Like the lifts in C wing not working. The parking attendants unavailable at their posts and engrossed in chattering, the security guards are sleeping through the night. Also, the gym is looking extremely shabby. The floorboards are creaking and no one seems to be doing anything about it.'

'What a great idea this email group is,' Sarita said. 'Now we can all air our grievances.'

Little did they know the role that the email group would play on their friendship.

27

For Aarti, Facebook was a tool to make ex-boyfriends jealous. After all, isn't that what everyone did? Women she knew kept changing their profile photo to show how hot they had become and what their exes were missing. They tagged themselves in photos taken at parties to prove they had a more interesting social life than that loser they had once been with. Facebook was also the space to send messages to each other that no one else could see. With her mobile phone, Aarti's messages might be read by someone else, including her husband, and lead to suspicions. Facebook was a safe space. And it was exactly how Dhruv connected with Aarti after they drifted apart.

Dhruv was careful enough not to 'Like' anything she posted but he did stalk her page. Finally, he got the courage to send her a private message, asking her if she wanted to meet up. Aarti was hesitant and replied that she didn't have time, too busy that she was, raising a child. But soon, she started responding. If she posted a photo of herself with friends, he would ask her how the party was. She would tell him, and even include little details.

It wasn't as if she couldn't tell Amitabh these things. It was rather that Dhruv always seemed to be the first to comment, wanting to know more. Amitabh would ask general questions about where she was going, when she would be back and whether she needed the driver. He would forget to ask her how her day was, and when she reminded him he would say, 'Sure, tell me about it.' Lately, he seemed even more disinterested in her life.

Dhruv, however, had been present continuously. She was the one who had chosen to ignore him. But now she was speaking to him regularly. He would even appear jealous if she had her arms around a man in a photo. He would send her love emoticons when she wore a pretty dress. He noticed. He admired. He commented. What more did a woman want?

So when Aarti picked up the phone and asked to meet him, he was thrilled and eager. Dhruv offered to pick Aarti up and she agreed.

For the remainder of the week Aarti wondered if she should tell Amitabh. Would he be offended? Would he reprimand her? Would he stop her from going? She thought it was best to be honest. Her husband had to know about her life and she couldn't lie. She had done it once and had lived with the secret for seven years. She didn't want to tell more lies.

On Friday morning as Amitabh was leaving for work, Aarti said she needed to talk to him. They were alone as Aryan had already left for school and her in-laws were in their own house.

'I'm going out with Dhruv for dinner,' Aarti said.

Amitabh was surprised. 'I didn't know you were in touch with him?'

Aarti shrugged. 'We just connected recently on Facebook.' She didn't lie; she just did not reveal any more details than necessary.

He picked up the car keys. 'Sure. I'll be back by 7:30 tonight. You can leave Aryan with Mom and Dad if you're leaving before that.'

He stepped out of the house, and left the topic at that.

He's not jealous? Aarti wondered. Either he had no bone of jealousy in him or he was extremely sure his wife wouldn't stray. Now Aarti felt bothered that he wasn't bothered! She decided to have a fantastic time with Dhruv. She needed to go out, seek an outlet for her frustrations. She would go with the flow.

Dhruv picked her up on time. As they drove to their

destination they complained about the potholes, made small talk about his work as a sports coach in a college and hers as a sales agent who traveled a lot, and spoke about common friends, too. They successfully avoided the subject of their meeting seven years ago: bumping into each other at an airport, both frustrated with delayed flights, checking into a hotel, making love through the night, and leaving for their respective homes without having breakfast. It was a night that left them both so ridden with guilt that they chose not to keep in touch after that. And while Dhruv had desperately wanted to reconnect as his marriage began turning sour, he knew that Aarti would shut him down because she had a baby to look after and a loving husband who she had chosen to spend the rest of her life with.

And tonight they sat opposite each other in this newly opened restaurant called Jelly Place, in a small suburb close to Aarti's place.

'Try the pasta,' Aarti said, as she gave him a spoon of her fettuccini.

With three glasses of wine down and halfway through their meal, Aarti was feeling more relaxed. They spoke of old times and ribbed each other as if they were nothing but long-lost friends. Aarti felt completely comfortable and so did he. He admired her body, not missing her cleavage, which she had carefully bronzed for the occasion. She was stunning in a buttoned down red top with a short and tight silver skirt and sky high silver stilettos. Her dark wavy hair cascaded down her back and shimmered in the light as she tossed her hair back to clip it.

He longed to touch her but he knew that if he made a move, he might lose her forever. They had just started becoming friends and it would be a long time before she trusted him again. But once she gave him a naughty signal with her toes gently caressing his shin, he was most interested in reliving what they had seven years ago. They were having such a great time that he tried his luck. Halfway through dinner he held up two fingers at Aarti and smiled.

'What?' She didn't understand the sign.

He looked around before leaning in and whispering to her, 'Two buttons.' Aarti was still confused.

'Take off two of your blouse buttons,' he said. 'Undo one after the waiter asks you for your dessert, and one more when he brings it. He'll see just a little. I'll enjoy watching him squirm.'

You want to play? Aarti thought, sure. She nodded naughtily to Dhruv. Soon the waiter came and she seductively opened her topmost button, while asking, 'Is the tiramisu any good? We'll have one of that please.' Dhruv watched as she looked into the waiter's eyes as she passed the menu back to him, letting it brush against her cleavage. Dhruv's breath raced faster. She bent forward to reach for her glass of water, carelessly spilling a few drops on her exposed bosom. The waiter was quickly back by then. Aarti unclasped another button and exposed a hint of her plump breasts and her lacy black bra. The waiter clenched his jaw and looked towards the lights above to avoid seeing more. Dhruv immediately got a hard-on which he covered with a napkin over his pants. Aarti took a spoon and leaned over to scoop up a bite of the tiramisu and licked it slowly. 'Yummmm,' she whispered, closing her eyes, acting out some erotic scene for Dhruv's sake. She could tell how aroused Dhruv was, and her heart hammered in her ear. This was fun. She had never done this with her husband. She felt like a woman on the edge of something extraordinary. She cleared her throat, pretending not to be affected, as he summoned a waiter and asked for the coffee menu.

As the waiter stood next to them and Dhruv pored over the menu, Aarti took off her right shoe and slowly moved her toes up his leg. It was with immense control that Dhruv didn't cry out in sheer pleasure as Aarti's toes inched farther and farther up his thigh.

And that was how they played out the entire dinner. Aarti had never felt more alive.

It was way past midnight when they finished their meal. He called for the check, she offered to pay but he ribbed her about being a working woman who wanted to prove she was independent. She laughed, mindful of his chivalry. Amitabh cared for her deeply but he didn't desire her. Unfortunately, sometimes the only man a woman wants is the one who doesn't even know she exists. That's why the attention from Dhruv felt sinfully good.

'Let me drop you home,' Dhruv said, as they walked out of the restaurant.

'Should we take a cab?' Aarti asked, to be on the safe side as soon as the valet brought his car.

He shook his head as he gave the valet a tip and sat in the car. Aarti decided to go with her instinct and let him drop her home. It was a full-moon night. The radio played the latest romantic numbers from Bollywood. They both hummed along. Dhruv was an excellent singer. She turned her head and looked at him through the shadows that fell while he drove. *How can he be sexy in whatever he did?!*

'I didn't know you liked Bollywood music?' she teased him with a sly smile.

'Started only recently,' he replied. He smiled back as he stared at her eminently gorgeous face. They had always had such great chemistry, an easy, natural camaraderie that had obviously never gone away. Maybe some people truly lived in each other. Maybe distance, space and time never allowed them to meet but when they did, it was as if a part of them was awakened.

That's what Dhruv felt like for Aarti. Wherever he would go and whatever he would do, she would remain with him and he with her. They didn't need to meet, or marry or talk. They were passing friends in the train of life, who shared a compartment every now and then because luck allowed them.

They got to her apartment building, and as usual, all the guards were asleep. She told him to turn off his car lights and proceed to the basement. He looked at her with curiosity. She wanted just a few more moments with him. Before real life took over once again.

'Please,' she whispered, holding his arm, 'No one comes to the basement. And not all the lights work.'

He looked at her strangely. 'How do you know this?'

Aarti took out a pack of Marlboro Lights from her purse and said, 'I go there to have a smoke occasionally.' Dhruv's eyes widened.

'Relax,' she said, 'I'm not having any.'

'I didn't know you were such a bad girl,' he said with a naughty grin.

'You have no idea...'

He drove down to the basement without anyone noticing and parked in a spot where there was no light. No one could see that there was someone in the car even if they walked past.

Once he shut off the engine, he unbuckled his seat belt and turned to face her. Jauntily he cocked his head to one side and challenged Aarti with a look of faint amusement, 'Prove it!'

Aarti lifted her hips, slid her green lace thong down her hips, down her legs and over the high heels. Then she parted her legs ever so briefly to flash him before she crossed it and faced him, throwing her arm around his seat languorously. She stared directly into his eyes, 'I'm bad ass.'

She looked at him for approval and saw his erection. Aarti leaned in close and brushed her lips against the corners of his mouth. He kissed her back with a fervent ardour and Aarti moaned at the touch of a man, something she had not had for so long. Her hands flattened against his chest and she leaned in further, brushing her hardened nipples across his torso. He broke the kiss to pull the car seat back and moved in closer to her before resuming. He stopped very briefly and asked, 'Are you sure?'

Was Aarti sure? She didn't know. She had played too many games in her life. With too many men. She had led with her heart and not her brain. In all these years, she still wasn't sure. All she knew was that she had longed for this. She needed it desperately. Her body ached for a man's touch. And she had been faithful to an impotent man for so long that her brain didn't react if she was sure.

She simply nodded. He leaned her car seat back and parted her legs with his hand. He reached in slowly, gently to find the soft, warm spot within her. He used just his two fingers and thumb to caress her, moving in gentle circular motions that drew her to the edge of ecstasy. Aarti threw her head back and groaned in pleasure. He stoked a gentle growing fire. He used the small confines of space deftly to give her maximum pleasure. She unzipped his pants and found the length of his arousal. She was well aware of the strength and warmth of his flesh. A sense of urgency drove her. She bent down to kiss him. She moved her mouth over the tip of his arousal. Slower at first, and then faster. Harder. Hearing Dhruv moan encouraged Aarti and she continued to lick him, twirling her tongue around his tip, teasing him with her lips. Dhruv's breath began to get faster and Aarti knew she had still not lost her touch. She savoured the feeling of satisfaction she left him. She stopped and turned, breathing in unison, ready for more.

She turned and climbed on top of him. He kissed her passionately on her neck, leaving small marks on her shoulder. Aarti ran her fingers through his hair as she licked and teased his ear, finding his erogenous spots easily. He eased her off her dress halfway to expose her nipples, raw and hard, waiting to be captured in his mouth. Her heart fluttered. The warmth of his arms around her made her relax, sinking into the contours of his body. His tongue devoured her breasts as she let out a soft groan. Aarti's back arched as his hand cupped and squeezed her breasts. She braced her hands on the roof of the car as he continued to tease her, their hips rocking in slow motion. His hands gripped her ass and brought her down on his hardness as he kissed her with the strength of a man unleashed from the confines of decorum.

They moved together, their bodies throbbing against each other, desperate for the moment to last. Heat rippled under her skin as she recognized the flush of sexual desire she hadn't felt for seven years. She had killed that urge. She had slain the hope of ever having a man again. She had buried any hope of having a man inside her. And here she was, wrapped around a man who needed her as much as she needed him. She yielded to this searing obsession which had brewed for so long. She surrendered completely to his masterful seduction. Unlike last time, Arti was careful. She knew it was the safe time of her month and they could continue without any fear. As he finally climaxed, she felt a wave of ecstasy wash over her and a deep sense of peace.

They sat, panting, waiting for their breaths to normalize as they straightened up their clothes. Aarti had never had such an experience before. An itch that was clawed out through a restricted space and lack of time. She couldn't believe herself. She had loved every minute of this but there was something wrong. She couldn't do it again and again. It was cheating. She was not a cheater. She was a good wife.

'Thank you for a wonderful evening, Dhruv.' She kissed him gently on his lips and opened the car door. 'Goodbye.'

She knew that would be the last time she would see him again. It was a promise she made to herself. She also knew that she would need to tell Amitabh the truth. And she had no idea how it would affect him. The thought left Aarti extremely troubled.

But telling Amitabh would be the least of her troubles. What Aarti didn't know was that someone was filming their tryst. A trouble-monger who was out for revenge.

28

Gita was aware that love comes with conditions, no matter that people say otherwise. Marriage, too, comes with conditions. No matter what your parents tell you. And an extramarital affair? That one has consequences.

Gita sat and wondered about the conditions she had expected from her husband. Love, yes. Not in the beginning, but eventually maybe. A little support. A bond that would go beyond parenting but just as a couple. An emotional attachment. A desire for her as a person. Respect. Appreciation. Acknowledgement in his circle of friends. A little romance even. It was the basic conditions that Gita thought her husband should give.

She replayed the conversation she had with Shailesh. She hadn't decided whether to be honest with him or not about her act of infidelity. She just wanted to understand what his conditions were from her in this marriage.

'Shailesh, do you love me?' she had asked one morning, as he was wearing his tie in front of the mirror in their bedroom.

He looked at her strangely. 'After so many years, why do you ask?'

'I need to know. Do you love me?' She just wanted to hear him say, Yes, I love you, Gita. Then maybe she would give up everything else and go back to being his faithful wife.

He sighed deeply. 'I'm attached to you, Gita.'

'You're attached to me,' Gita repeated. 'What do you mean?'

'Well, we've had an arranged marriage...' He walked towards the door as his voice trailed off, and Gita did not understand what he meant. He continued, 'If I had a dog for thirteen years, I would eventually get attached to the dog.' He went his way.

Gita was stunned. She was being likened to a dog? Was she just a duty he needed to fulfil for his parents because they had pressurized him to get married? Was she just furniture in the house that he needed around for a comfortable life? A black cloud sat on her shoulders. She had a nagging feeling it wasn't over.

She was aware that he had never been proud of her. She had asked him often enough to invite his office friends over so she could cook for them, and maybe, she hoped, he would like that; but he never did. All these years he had refused to give her his office number, telling her to use his mobile if she needed to call him. She had begged for him to take her out to eat in a restaurant alone, just the two of them, but he would rather take the entire family saying it was important to bond with them as well. He never thought it important for the two of them to take time out as a couple, to keep some amount of romance in their life, even if they began with an arranged marriage. She wanted to tell him that if he had conditions for her as a wife, she had her own conditions as well. Time alone with him every now and then, for instance. But husbands thought that housewives' lives were inextricably joined to them or their children. They had no life, or dreams or opinions other than the family. So they never asked their wives what she was really thinking or how she was really feeling.

But now, she heard it clearly. If given a choice, he would leave her in a heartbeat if he found someone else who was not just a dog to grow attached to eventually, but really love. He would leave her when his children grew up or his parents died. She didn't figure in the scheme of his life at all. He had never loved her, he never would.

How she wished she had taken up a career earlier in her life. At least, she would have had the courage to walk out. She knew she needed to start immediately.

She wiped her tears and sent Sahil a message asking to see him. He was in the office, he said, but would go home if she needed him. 'If it's not too inconvenient,' she replied. He told her he would be home in an hour.

Why Shailesh couldn't be more like his brother, she didn't know. Had they really come from the same womb?

She had finished her chores by the time Sahil sent a message to say he was waiting for her downstairs. She gathered the children, on holiday from school that day, and dropped them off at Julie's next door. She walked to the lift but got impatient that it took too long. She decided to take the stairs.

'Natasha!' Gita was a little too surprised, bumping into Natasha one flight down. 'What are you doing?'

'All the elliptical trainers are occupied in the gym, so I thought I would walk up and down the stairs instead,' Natasha said, panting with the climb. 'You?'

'I was on my way to the market actually. Needed to buy a few things and the lift was taking too long.'

'Okay, see you,' said Natasha. 'I need to burn these calories!' They said their goodbyes.

Gita found Sahil sitting with his laptop. She sat down next to him and, for the first time since that morning, an easy smile formed on her lips.

'What's up, cookie, feeling like eating mutton today?' he said, as he turned off his laptop.

Gita told him about her conversation with Shailesh that morning, how he had likened being with her to having a pet. 'I'm nothing in his life, Sahil. I know he's your brother but why the hell did he marry me if he didn't want to? All these years I had thought that there was something between us, that he was just busy and that's why he always came home late. I had thought that even if he wasn't attracted to me, love was there. But now I know that there has never been love. It was all his duty.' She was disgusted with Shailesh.

Sahil seemed as shocked as Gita was. He didn't know how to console her. He didn't even think that she was still in love with his brother. Why couldn't she just leave Shailesh and be with him instead? He realized that he and Shailesh were like chalk and cheese. Sahil was a super confident child and didn't care that all the love of their parents was being showered on his brother. He had plenty of friends and freedom. He couldn't believe that his brother would behave so badly with the woman he loved.

Before he could say anything, Gita said, 'You have to help me set up my catering company. I need to do this right away. I want to earn for a change. I want to stand on my own two feet and never have to rely on Shailesh again.'

He nodded and turned on his laptop, 'Okay. Let's write this down. Gita's Kitchen. Logistics. What do you want to cook? How many dabbas will you make in a day? How much will you spend on the raw materials? How much on advertising? Who do you want to reach out to? What ideas do you have for special occasions?'

She had all the answers, her ideas flowed easily. He admired her more, seeing the excitement on her face as she spoke. He typed as fast as she spoke, and soon enough, they had covered several sheets of the Excel document discussing possibilities of what she could do.

'Wow,' he said, looking at their efforts, 'You really are fired up. Have a look at what we've written while I make us some tea. It'll probably be the last time I will be able to enter my kitchen, since you're taking it over for your company from tomorrow!'

'Thanks for all your help, really. I appreciate it.' She planted a soft kiss on his lips effortlessly. Without any doubt, without any guilt. He kissed her back and went to the kitchen. She recognized what was between them and hoped she wasn't wrong: more than the passion, there was love. There was also appreciation and support.

He came out with their tea.

'Are you sure you're okay with me taking over your kitchen for a few hours everyday?' Gita asked.

'Oh absolutely. I hardly use it in any case. I often confuse the oven for the washing machine and throw my clothes in there. Once I couldn't find my black shorts for a week and found them in the oven!'

They both laughed. 'I wish I had you around more often,' Sahil said.

'Me too.'

They finished their tea and biscuits in the same happy spirit.

Soon, Sahil said he needed to go back to his office. 'Are you hanging around here, darling?'

'No, I'll go home.' She went to keep the tray in the kitchen and Sahil followed. He wrapped his arms around her waist. 'I have another idea that we can use the kitchen for.'

'Show me,' Gita whispered back, unabashedly. Her body responded easily to Sahil's signals.

They kissed passionately. Their desire was fuelled by the urgency of his departure. She removed his shirt while kissing him along the length of his neck. She felt a lurch of excitement within her. He tugged at her kurta and it tore. He was horrified but Gita assured him, 'It's okay. I'll cover it up with the dupatta.' He liked her eagerness. She loosened the clip from her hair and let it lie around her. She wrapped her arms around his head and looked deep into his eyes. They locked themselves in an endless embrace, never wanting to let each other go. She whispered, 'But you have to go back to the office.'

'I have five minutes.'

He removed her churidar and slid his hands along the roundness of her posterior. He parted her legs and massaged her inner thighs gently, using all his fingers to give her incredible pleasure. He then slowly removed her panties. He hoisted her up on the kitchen counter as she wrapped her arms around him. He quickly opened a kitchen drawer and found a condom to slip on. Slowly and gently he entered her as she wrapped her legs around him to bring him closer. The window was open and the thought of someone seeing them gave Gita more pleasure. She grinded against him. As their movement became faster and harder, she closed her eyes as her world spun around her.

When they finished she cleaned up and checked her phone. There were a few calls and messages from Julie saying Anu was crying and wanted her mother. Gita shouted out to Sahil, 'I've got to run. Anu needs me.' She left hurriedly.

Without thinking she took the stairs and there, again, bumped into Natasha who was still doing her workout. This time Gita couldn't lie, because Natasha knew exactly how a woman looked, post-coitus: Gita was panting, her kurta was torn and crumpled and her hair was out of place. Natasha guessed, correctly that Gita had just had sex.

'Gita!' Natasha stared hard at her.

Right at the same time another voice called out, 'Gita!' Sahil had run out with her dupatta. *How could I have forgotten my dupatta!* She cursed herself and took the dupatta from him. 'Oh thanks. Ya, I forgot it while I was cooking,' she said to Sahil, and gave him a look to leave right away. She looked at Natasha. 'My cylinder had finished so I was cooking at my brother-in-law's place. Anyway, I gotta go. Anu needs me. Talk to you later?' Gita didn't wait for Natasha to say anything.

Stupid me! Gita knew that Natasha knew. She hoped that Natasha would keep the incident to herself.

29

'There has to be a fixed rate, otherwise, everything will go through the roof!' shouted Roshni, a housewife from the B wing of Sapphire Towers. The women along with their in-laws and husbands were attending an emergency society meeting to discuss the salaries of their maids and drivers.

Apparently, a few households had been pirating other families' maids by offering double the money.

'She herself wanted a bigger salary,' Shivangi, the one who manipulated the maid, said in a sarcastic tone. They stood on two sides of the large party hall facing a desk with society elected representatives who would mediate and settle the issue at hand.

'Fifteen grand for a full-timer is just bloody too much!' Roshni said.

'Now, now, Roshni,' spoke the chairman, Raj Deolekar. 'Let's not use bad words. We have elderly people amongst us.'

'Bloody' is a bad word? Roshni thought to herself and decided to stay quiet. She was dying to use real cuss words on this woman who took her maid away.

The chairman asked Shivangi, 'Why did you give her triple her salary?'

Shivangi spoke softly, 'I hope you understand, chairman, I have been looking after my two small children for three years now. I live in a nuclear family and I don't have in-laws to help. I needed someone desperately. She met me downstairs and offered to help with my children. She herself said she was doing too much work at Roshni's house and wanted to leave.'

'Oye, chup kar!' Roshni shouted. 'You went to her in the play area and offered her fifteen grand. She didn't approach you.'

'Now, now, Roshni,' the chairman spoke. Roshni felt like throwing her shoe at him every time he began his sentences with 'Now, now…' Why was the chairman taking this woman's side? Was it her fault that she was managing her house well, with the help of the maid that she had found first? Maybe it was the boobs; Shivangi definitely had better boobs than Roshni. That's why the bloody chairman was taking her side.

'The maid sleeps half the day, Mr Chairman,' Roshni reasoned. I have a cleaning bai and a dog-walker. If I start giving fifteen grand to each of them, what will my family eat? Onion now costs eighty rupees a kilo!'

Roshni only had to say that and she captured the hearts of the society members. Talk about food prices! Everyone could relate to that!

Even Gita and her friends, until then sitting at the back row, uninterested, suddenly engaged.

'I agree with Roshni,' Sarita said, and stood up. 'If we keep increasing the salaries and poaching each other's maids, what security do we have? Just because one family can afford it, and another cannot, doesn't mean the rest of us have to manage without maids.'

'What about the drivers?' Amitabh chimed in. 'Do we fire the driver who was caught smoking weed? Then what happens to the person who needs a driver? He'll have to look from the lot that is already there. Obviously by giving him a bigger salary.'

The secretary said, 'We've already removed Ramu from the building. Anybody who had employed him please submit your names. We shall try and find you a replacement. He had been harassing flat owners in the A wing about giving him more money and had even threatened to harm them.'

They were shocked. Though a few men snorted because the society had not found them a replacement. They also secretly held a grudge against the family in A-1602; they were sure they were simply making up stories about Ramu who was to them a faithful driver.

'Could we please go back to the issue of maids?' Shivangi asked. She didn't know what she would do if the maid was forced to go back to Roshni's house. She could afford the fifteen grand and was extremely happy with the maid's services.

The chairman cleared his throat. 'I think we need to fix the cap at five hundred rupees for every task. Jhadu pocha is one, bartan is another, dusting, cleaning windows, fans, etc., etc. all as five hundred. All in agreement raise their hands?'

Several hands went up.

'All in opposition raise their hands,' said the secretary.

Many members showed their vote.

The meeting then turned into a market, as the members haggled over a hundred rupees here and there.

'All right then,' said the chairman. 'Let's fix it at three hundred and fifty. Okay?'

He didn't get any objections.

'Great!'

'And the full-timers?' Roshni asked. She was desperate to get her maid back. She had invested in that bai, she repeated to herself: trained her, given her old clothes, given her days off when she was sick and an entire month recently to go to her native village to visit her ailing mother.

'Full-timers have to be settled at individual salaries and work around the house,' Raj said. 'The cap can be at ten grand.' It stirred a lot of twittering. 'Roshni and Shivangi, I would suggest that you both sit down with the maid and tell her that both households will offer just ten grand. Then let her decide.'

Both thought it was a fair deal.

On that note the meeting was adjourned and everyone retreated to the lawns for some samosas and chai. Most of the members then left to go their separate ways, while Gita and her friends stayed back.

'I'm starting my catering service from next week!' Gita shrieked. 'Instead of a cook coming every day, you can order an entire package meal for four for lunch and dinner, and even breakfast. The dabba will come to your home with piping-hot home-cooked meals!'

'We're so impressed, Gita!' said Aarti. They wrapped her in a tight embrace.

'So what name have you decided on?' Natasha asked.

'Gita's Kitchen.'

'Great,' said Natasha. 'I'll send you a few logos. I have some ideas.'

'That would be nice, thanks.' She still hadn't been able to make eye contact with Natasha, after that afternoon when she caught her in the staircase after having sex with Sahil. But she sure could use her friends' help. She also wanted to figure out a way to do some profit-sharing with them if they helped her market it well.

'Hey, come over for some karaoke tonight?' Aarti said. 'Bring the husbands. It's Amitabh's birthday tomorrow. I'll get him a cake and we can *sing in* his birthday.'

'That's a great idea!' Gita said. 'But I don't think Shailesh will come.'

'Just come alone then,' Aarti said.

'But I can't sing,' Natasha said.

'Who cares?' Aarti said. 'Even I can't. We'll just all bray together!' They all laughed. 'It'll be a surprise for Amitabh.'

The girls were excited. They always looked forward to their gatherings, whether with simple tea and snacks or something more fancy. Last weekend they had a chowmein and dosa party on the refuge floor, for no particular reason at all. Birthdays are a given, they celebrate each other's, apart from festivals like Holi and Diwali. That Saturday they had nothing, but called a local caterer for some fresh noodles and dosas and they partied on the refuge floor.

These women were bonded in their affection for each other. Friends became family, and family became stronger because of their friendship. Somehow, it didn't matter if all was not right with the world, as long as they had each other. And they felt special living in Sapphire Towers; the society had given them a sense of belonging. Their friendship was solid.

30

' A woman who loves her husband's brother is no better than a woman who desires a friend's son,' began the email, sent anonymously to the email group shared by members of the Sapphire Towers Society. 'Lust knows no bounds. That's why some women use the basement or the lifts to do their thing. Faithful wives and devoted mothers. I know who you all are. And I'm not afraid to tell.'

The email caused tongues to wag as soon as it flooded the inbox of everyone in the email group. Hushed whispers spread like wildfire.

Aarti freaked out as she read her copy. This email talked about trysts in the basement; was it her? How could anyone have seen her and Dhruv? She was so careful! She looked around her house, everything seemed normal. Amitabh was at work and Aryan in school. For the last week, in fact, they had continued to live a normal life. True, Dhruv had been messaging to meet again but she had ignored him.

She was waiting for Amitabh's birthday to pass before telling him the truth about her and his former best friend. And now someone knew. She was extremely concerned. Could it be one of her friends? They had told her to check her email, was it for this reason, to humiliate her? She read the first line of the email again: Husband's brother? Friend's son? How desperate could they be?

Aarti decided that despite this email and the gossip that may be presently doing the rounds of the Towers, Amitabh's party would push through. None of this pertains to my friends, she thought. They would have a good laugh over it and have a great night. And her secret was still safe.

Sarita saw the mail and was nonchalant. She didn't have a brother-in-law, she had never done—and will never do—anything in the lift or the basement. And it couldn't be any of her friends, no way! She saw them almost every day, they knew every aspect of their lives. As for her and Jai, well yes, they'd been naughty but all of their experimentation with crotch-less panties and whipped cream—which they loved!—had been happening only in their marital bedroom. No, this mail had nothing to do with her. They would gossip about it for sure at Aarti's party tonight. She was sure it was that co-pilot from A wing, the petite slut who kept eyeing her husband.

Gita knew it was the beginning of her doom as the words of the email slowly sunk into her brain. Again she read it. Once more. Yes, she was sure, the writer was referring to her and Sahil. She was guilty. She was shocked. And she was scared, now everyone would know. And she was livid. She knew there could only be one person behind this. Natasha. For so long she had thought Natasha was her friend. She spoke so sweetly. Was so supportive. That back-stabbing bitch. There will be another email, the sender said, and names would be revealed. My God! How could Natasha do this to her? She was going to kill her. Gita didn't really care about who the others were in the mail. It had nothing to do with her life. Her life was going to change forever. Hot tears formed in her eyes. If Shailesh found out, he would kick her out. She would lose face with her daughters.

Oh God, she'll lose custody of her girls? Where would she go? Gita was in panic. How could she face the girls at Aarti's party now? But if she didn't go, they would suspect. They'd think it was because of this email and that Gita was guilty. No, she must put up a brave face even if her life was falling apart. Gita sat and bawled her eyes out. She could almost hear her heart break.

Natasha read the email and thought the sender couldn't be Gita. Gita didn't know that she and Rahul had sex in the lift. She didn't even know that she was seeing Rahul. It had to be Sarita! Maybe Rahul had bragged to his friends that he had sex with an older woman, and through whispers amongst the stupid teenagers, it had come back to Sarita. She did not suspect the other women. Maybe this was what she needed, a push to finally take a hard look at her life. What was she doing having this relationship with Rahul? Yes, he gave her immense pleasure. She felt in control. She was happy and free, something that she had not been for a long time. But sneaking behind Vikram was not the answer. Staying in a marriage and 'coveting a friend's son', as the email said, was not the way to go. She needed to take a hard look at her life, to find her own way. Whoever had written this email would come out soon. Before that happened she needed to speak to Rahul and Vikram. She needed to take control of her life again. For tonight, she would pretend there was nothing wrong and she hadn't even read the mail. What email?

31

How do you make a successful party?
Food. Friends. Music. Alcohol. Laughter. Games. Lighting. If this was all, then Aarti's party had everything.

The evening started out well. With help from an event-manager friend she had dolled up the house and engaged a caterer. Aryan had helped, excited about the impromptu party. Her in-laws had stayed out of the way and Aarti was glad. By the time Amitabh would come back, all her friends would be there and would give him a big surprise.

Gita and Natasha came alone and separately. They didn't sit together the entire evening and, whenever Natasha said anything to Gita, she walked away. Sarita came with her husband Jai who said Hi to everyone and went to sit in front of the TV while the girls sat separately. Aarti served them drinks and some starters. They spoke about the tricky weather, and other mundane things. No one mentioned the email.

'I can't believe they're taking so much money from us,' Sarita said. 'Five hundred rupees per person, plus monthly maintenance charges? Maybe they can hire Shah Rukh Khan to dance for the New Year's Eve party!'

'Maybe I can cater for that party, what do you guys think?' Gita said. Everyone agreed it was a good idea.

'You guys remember the last time?' Sarita said. 'There wasn't enough food for everyone, even when we paid through our noses!' She had a hunch. 'I'm sure they're pocketing most of the money. Where do the lakhs go? Can't we complain to someone about it?'

Aarti said, 'Do you know what I heard happened during the Holi party? Gupte took advantage of a few people. During the rain dance. Everyone was enjoying themselves. We all had a bit to drink. But he was completely drunk! He came over to where the women were dancing and started dancing with the group. We all kind of danced for a bit and went away but he followed some who joined other gangs and started grinding with them.'

They gasped. Jai, who had been sitting quietly in front of the TV, looked at them. It was an unwritten rule that a solitary man amongst a group of women was supposed to keep to himself. And even though Sarita had asked him to join, how could he? He would be labelled a 'lech' if he did. He turned back to the TV wondering if this party was ever going to pick up.

Soon Aarti announced that Amitabh was on his way up. She quickly called his parents from next door, who came and greeted everyone as they sat down.

Aarti switched off the lights and everyone held their breaths. Aryan was most excited and could hardly contain his giggles. They heard the door click. When Amitabh entered, Aarti flicked the lights on and everyone yelled 'Surprise!' Amitabh was truly surprised. Aryan ran into his arms. 'Were you surprised, Papa?' Amitabh gave Aarti a hug. 'Hey guys! Thanks, babe. I have to get my breath back.' He leaned over and gave his parents a kiss. They got up and said they were going back to their house because they wanted to turn in early. Amitabh's father had to get up for his morning walk ritual. Aryan was packed off to bed because there was school the next day.

Aarti set up the karaoke machine. Sarita asked Jai to take the mike but he was coy, 'No, I'm not singing!' They coaxed him and finally, he did take the microphone, chose an old Hindi song from the big songbook and started singing, standing awkwardly at the far corner of the room. He was off-key a few times but was not too bad at all. Sarita looked at Jai as if he was her Michael Jackson. She clapped the loudest when he was done, and the mike was passed to Gita who refused. She quickly handed it to Aarti who looked for a song. Meanwhile, Amitabh came out of the bedroom wearing new clothes and a spicy cologne. Aarti belted out a number and everyone thought she was amazing.

'You should try to sing professionally, Aarti. I never knew you sang so well,' Natasha remarked.

Aarti blushed, 'Years of practice in the bathroom.'

They all laughed as the party slowly picked up.

For a few hours they sang and laughed and danced. Karaoke was a hit, the food was good too, and the birthday boy was happy. He decided to take a break from the partying and sat down to check his phone. 'Hey guys, have you seen this email?'

The elephant in the room had finally woken up. The girls looked at each other and had nothing to say.

'What email?' Aarti asked.

Amitabh began reading out the email and Aarti stopped him midway. 'It's okay, Amit. There's nothing to it.' Amitabh looked at them suspiciously and turned to Jai, 'Do you know anything?' Jai shrugged his shoulders and concentrated on his food. He loved parties. What did he care about gossip from a silly email? He and his wife had roaring sex nowadays. He was sure the email didn't concern his family at all.

Gita had been containing herself so well but she finally burst out. She turned to Natasha. 'How could you? I thought you were my friend!'

'What are you talking about?' Natasha was surprised at Gita's rage. 'Are you saying I wrote that email? No, Gita, I didn't.'

Sarita looked up. 'Gita? Are you telling us that the email is about you?'

Gita took a long time to reply. They waited.

'Do you know what it feels like to have a family that hates you?' she said. 'Your husband compares you to a pet that he was attached to? No! So stop judging me. I have been living with a husband and a set of in-laws who are horrible and have pulled me down for years.'

They kept silent, waiting for Gita to continue. When she didn't, Aarti asked, 'So you slept with someone's son? Who?'

Gita threw her hands in the air. 'No, I didn't sleep with anyone's son, for chrissakes. I wouldn't go so low.'

'Hey!' Natasha burst out, too quickly, and regretted it immediately.

Everyone looked at Natasha as she looked away.

Sarita asked, 'So, whose son?'

Natasha didn't say anything. She looked down as tears welled up in her eyes. Gita guessed and told Sarita, 'Yours.'

Sarita and Jai shrieked in unison, 'WHAT?!'

Natasha shot Gita a dirty look and said, 'Well, I'm not running between floors with men on two floors. And that too, brothers! How disgusting are you, Gita?'

Gita got up from the dining-table and kept her plate in the kitchen. She was done with this party. She wanted to go home and never see these women again. They knew nothing about her life. How can they judge her about Sahil?

Aarti got up and stopped her from walking out, 'Gita, wait. Let's talk about it.'

'Oh my God, I knew it!' Natasha said, as she pointed a finger at Aarti. 'You were the one who wrote that email, weren't you, Aarti? You wanted all of us to get into trouble and you can be the good girl.'

Amitabh remarked, 'There's no need to accuse Aarti. She's only trying to help.'

Jai then said, 'Well, ask her what she was doing in the

basement parking with a man. Maybe she was the woman in the car.'

Amitabh was about to run to Jai and throw him a punch but the women prevailed over them and they stepped back. Aarti said to Amit, 'Let's talk about this later?'

'No, wait, Aarti, was it you?' Amitabh said. 'Say no and I'll whack this asshole.' Aarti kept quiet. Natasha looked shocked. Gita was smug. And Sarita wondered how Jai had got this information and not told her; she would deal with him later.

Amitabh was heartbroken. It was his birthday, and he had been humiliated. 'I'm going. I'm sleeping next to Aryan.' To the others he said, 'And I suggest you take your fight elsewhere.'

Aarti pleaded with him not to go. 'Baby. I'm sorry,' she said, as she reached for Amitabh's hand. He dismissed her and walked to the bedroom. Aarti was frustrated; she wanted to speak to Amit but clearly he was in no mood. She turned to the other women and spit our her venom, blaming them for ruining her husband's birthday. Natasha went outside to the balcony to have a smoke, and Sarita and Jai followed her.

Sarita spoke angrily but in a low breath, 'How could you sleep with Rahul, Natasha? He's just a boy. What the hell were you thinking? You filthy whore!'

Natasha didn't reply. She stubbed out her cigarette and walked inside the flat. Sarita and Jai followed her there, too. Jai was about to speak but Sarita cut him off. 'I think you should go home. I'll take care of this.' Jai left without another word. The four women were left to themselves.

'Natasha, answer me,' Sarita said, as she started to cry. 'How could you have spoiled my little boy? What kind of a monster are you?'

Natasha let Sarita's abusive words come. When Sarita had finished she spoke, 'He's not a little boy, Sarita, and it's time that you recognize that. He approached me. He wanted to be with me. Go ask your little boy why he did what he did instead of calling me a whore.'

'But you already have a loving husband!' Gita shrieked. 'Your pati does so much for you and you're still not happy?' Gita wondered why a woman would covet another man if she had everything she wanted in her home life. At least *she* had an excuse!

Natasha took a deep breath and spoke. The truth must come out. They needed to free themselves of the burden of all the secrets they had carried in their hearts for so long. 'Vikram beats me up. Black and blue,' she began. Everyone sat still. Sarita looked up, wiped her tears. 'He's a horrible husband. I'm miserable in my marriage. But that's not the reason why I did what I did with Rahul.'

Sarita now recollected the times that Natasha would come to their meet-ups wearing full-sleeved tops, or not come at all, making an excuse of some sort.

'Rahul needed attention, Sarita,' Natasha said. 'I gave it to him. I made him stop drinking. Do you know he was a borderline alcoholic?'

'You shut up!' Sarita was livid. 'My boy wasn't alcoholic!'

Natasha kept her calm, 'He was. Every day he drank. And he slowly started loving booze more than life. You hadn't seen that. Jai hadn't seen that. But I did. I saw that he needed to paint, draw, be allowed to talk about his dreams without being told there was no money for such inane things.'

'Don't bring my family's finances into this.'

'I'm just saying maybe you should stop pointing fingers and start looking at where you went wrong as a parent. Rahul is an adult. He's turning nineteen in a few days. He is mature for his age. He doesn't fit in with his peers. He needs help. I just gave him what he needed.'

Sarita almost picked up the coffee planter to throw it at Natasha's face. Natasha was stunned at the violence. But Gita stopped Sarita's hand and spoke gently, 'Let Natasha be. Anyone who has gone through what she's had deserves a break.'

But Sarita was still upset and looked away. Natasha's sharp words stung her more than the fact that she had sex with her only son. Were Jai and she so involved with themselves that they hadn't seen what was happening to Rahul? She refused to believe it!

Aarti said, 'So you go after your brother-in-law?'

'What?' Gita replied. 'It wasn't...I mean...I love him. It wasn't just...' Gita stammered. She didn't want to have to explain herself to her friends.

But Aarti shook her head and told Gita, 'This will devastate your family.'

'Really, now,' Sarita said in mock-pity before saying, 'And what you did in the car with some stranger won't?'

Aarti didn't know if she should justify her actions, or protect her husband. She needed her friends for the next step that she was planning.

'Guys, I'm sorry,' she began. 'What I did was wrong. It's just that...Amitabh and I hadn't had sex for years. It was just a need. I'm stupid to have got caught. But stupider to have kept it from you or him.'

'But so what if you haven't had sex?' Sarita said. 'Marriage isn't only about that, right? It's also about companionship, security, respect, trust. All the things that you people have lost.'

Natasha shook her head. 'No, Sarita. It's also about love. If you don't have that, then those other things you said won't come.'

'It's also about an emotional bond,' Gita said. 'A husband can still want his wife like furniture in the house. But that's not love.

There's no emotional bond. That's not a marriage. He doesn't ask about your day, if you're sick he's not there to look after you, he has to be forced to take you out for dinner, you almost need to beg for some time to talk. And when he's not bothered and continuously puts you down, you feel like shit. There's no companionship left then. Only duty towards your family. At least when people are fighting, you know they still care. Nonchalance is the death of a relationship. And if you're married, where do you go? When there's nothing left. And you're dying inside. What do we do then? Why is it even called a marriage then?'

'That's emotional abuse,' Natasha said. 'And sometimes, it's as bad as domestic abuse.'

'But there's nothing wrong with duty,' Sarita said, unable to understand her friends at all. 'Every marriage goes through its ups and downs. That doesn't mean you go after another man, Gita. Or Natasha, that you find a young boy. Yes, what Vikram does to you is awful. But *you* need to take a stand. Go to a women's cell and complain. Threaten him with dire consequences. Hit him back, for God's sake, so that he will never lift a finger again. Put him in the hospital rather than being a helpless wife. Or even get a divorce. But why go after someone else while you're still married?'

It was Aarti who replied, 'Because divorce sometimes is not an option. We are stuck in our family life. Because of society. For the sake of our children, or our parents who are too old to see this great tragedy befall us. We are scared. We don't make any money to stand on our own two feet. What will neighbours say? Who can we talk to about what really happens inside our bedrooms? It's not easy, Sarita. For years we just let things be. We involve ourselves in family life, making ourselves feel happy that we *at least* have good children, our health, and our friends. But one day we realize our souls have been emptied. And when that germ plants itself deep inside us, you can't run away from it. And then what do you do?'

'You find happiness,' Gita replied. She completely understood what Aarti said.

'Find happiness, sure. But with another man?' Sarita was contemptuous. 'That's disgusting. You have betrayed your husband, Aarti. Did you see the look on his face? You've hurt him beyond repair. Why pursue happiness that causes hurt to someone else, your husband, in fact.'

They all stayed quiet. No one seemed to have figured out who had sent the email. But they had said plenty of hurtful things to each other. Promises were broken and betrayal ran deep.

Gita broke the silence. 'I think we've said enough for one night.' She gathered her things. 'Thanks, Aarti, for the party.'

Natasha and Sarita also thanked Aarti and left. They looked away from each other as they took different ways to get home. They needed space from each other. The next time they would meet would be under dire circumstances, where a life would be hanging in the balance and they would say goodbye to each other forever.

32

A hangover may be a severe headache following the consumption of too much alcohol; it could also be a feeling that persists from your past. The morning after her husband's party Aarti definitely woke up with a hangover of the latter kind. The bitter taste in her mouth was coming from all the secrets revealed the previous night, the harsh words, and the tears shed. She felt miserable.

She dragged herself out of bed and ambled to the kitchen to prepare Aryan's tiffin. She found Amitabh sitting at the dining-table, having tea and reading the newspaper. He pretended not to see her.

Aarti sent Aryan off to school and she took a shower. She sat in front of her mandir for five minutes longer this morning. Aarti thought of herself as a religious woman. She never proclaimed it to the world, but she believed in God. She had made a little temple inside the house, a corner in the kitchen that faced northeast. She lit an agarbatti every morning and said the Gayatri Mantra three times. Most days she simply counted her blessings. Today she asked for some strength.

She walked out to the dining area and sat next to Amitabh. He didn't look up from his paper. She rested her hand on his. He moved it away.

'Who was he?' His voice was rough, anxious. He didn't want to speak to her but also wanted to know the truth.

'Dhruv.'

She was going to tell him after his birthday but her gods gave her the opportunity before she could change her mind.

Amitabh gritted his teeth, 'Dhruv.' He said it almost to himself, as if trying to see if he heard it right.

Aarti kept silent.

'Why? Are there any more?'

She shook her head. There was no explanation except that Dhruv was an opportunity she needed. A catalyst. He wasn't really the answer.

'Do you love him?' Amitabh's eyes were sad with pain.

Aarti again took his hand; this time he let her. 'Not at all, Amit. The only man I've ever loved is you.' And it was true. She loved Amitabh. Only him. That's why she had stayed with him for so many years. She loved how he looked after her and how he was such a wonderful man. He had given her a lovely home and she appreciated every moment of it. But he could not give her sex and sometimes she wanted it. Amit had been the catalyst in the past for her to break away from Dhruv. And Dhruv was the catalyst now for her to break free.

Amitabh understood but grieved.

'I never regret that I married you, jaan,' Aarti said. 'You're the only one I love. That day when you asked me if I loved you and I said yes. Do you remember that? I meant it, Amit. I've meant the love for all these many years. But...' She paused, searching for words to make the blow to Amit softer.

'But I've always needed more, Amit. I'm sorry, you just haven't been able to give that to me. This marriage is a sham. We need to be honest to ourselves.'

'A sham? What's wrong with it? It's been perfectly fine for so many years. Don't I give you everything you need? Aren't we compatible? Don't we love hanging out? Don't I take you out? Am I not a good father? Is this just about sex?' He was angry and his words fired like endless ammunition.

Aarti wasn't proud of it. 'Yes.' She took a deep breath. 'I need sex. It's an integral part of who I am, Amit. I am young and healthy. Yes, darling, we are compatible as friends. I love hanging out with you and you're a terrific father. But I don't need a friend as a husband, Amit. I need a lover. Someone who wants my body. Who desires me.'

She let the words sink in before continuing, 'Our foreplay is half-hearted. Once a month, maybe. Because I initiate it. Do you realize that we haven't even kissed for a few months now?'

He got up and fetched her a glass of juice. She drank and spoke again. 'I've killed the expectation inside me for so long, Amit, but I can't keep doing it anymore. How can I deny myself this forever?'

Amit pondered. 'If I allow you to see Dhruv,' he said, 'and we still remain married? Would that solve the problem?'

'That would be dishonest,' she replied, after quickly considering. 'And what if Aryan found out, what will we tell him? He'd lose his respect for me. Isn't it better to bring him up with both parents being friends rather than bitter enemies? That our son learn that a real relationship is based on truth and honesty rather than lies and deception, just for the sake of society?'

She realized as she spoke that she was the biggest hypocrite and liar of all: Amit still didn't know that Aryan was not his son but Dhruv's. She decided it could wait for another time.

'What are you saying, Aarti?' Amitabh asked. He wasn't dumb, he understood it, but he wanted her to say the words.

'I think we should separate.'

Amitabh refused to reply.

'I'm not saying divorce,' Aarti continued. 'I'm just saying we need to start living separate lives. Have physical space between us. Maybe I could move out to a smaller place within this building itself. Start over. Take Aryan with me. Or maybe he can stay here with you. Whatever you choose. As long as he doesn't think I abandoned him. But explain to him and your parents that we need some space to sort out our issues. To understand ourselves better. To make myself whole again.'

'And what if you find someone else or want to marry Dhruv?'

'Then we'll take it from there. Let's cross that bridge when we come to it, Amit. But for now let's live our lives the way we should. And you know what,' Aarti paused, 'I want you to know that this separation is not just about sex for me. It's about being desired as a woman. About knowing that I'm not just a mother and a daughter-in-law. I'm a woman with a basic need to be treasured and touched! This is about the soft kisses a man gives with a promise of something more. A stolen cuddle, a caress that lingers, a look that burns your heart. I need all that, Amit. I need to feel wanted. You have a problem and you need to get help for it. I've tried talking to you about it for years but you've shut your mind to any possibility after the first few years of marriage. And I didn't push you.'

Aarti hesitated, fighting back her tears. 'So what I really want to say to you, my love, is…I'm sorry.'

He looked up, his dark eyes showing the tortured dullness of disbelief. Aarti started crying. 'I'm sorry I slept with Dhruv. It was stupid. I should have told you I was attracted to someone else. I'm sorry I hurt you, Amit. You've been such a good husband to me. And God knows how I've wanted to stay married to you for the rest of my life. I love you, Amit. But I can't do this anymore. Please forgive me. Please let's be friends. But please let me go.'

Amitabh held his wife as she wept on his shoulder. He smelt her fresh dewy skin and combed his fingers through her hair. He relished the feeling of having her in his arms. He felt a dull ache of foreboding. A nauseating, sinking feeling of despair overtook both of them. They sat for a long time, in each other's embrace, a realization slowly spreading through their veins. This would be the last time they would ever touch each other. From the next day onward they would lead separate lives.

33

Jai and Sarita didn't wait until the next morning to confront their son. They found Rahul asleep when they got home after the incident at Aarti's house. They woke him up and immediately started yelling at him. Despite Rahul's grogginess he realized it was about his affair with Natasha.

'But she's so hot.' Those were the first words that came to him.

It riled up his parents even more. 'Shut up!' Jai screamed.

This time Sarita was completely on her husband's side. The scandal had rocked both of them and they needed to teach Rahul a lesson.

'I thought I had raised you well but I was wrong,' Jai said. 'We tried to inculcate some values in you. But you. You filth! You go off and sleep with an older woman!'

Rahul stayed quiet. He wondered if his father was angry because of the perceived immorality of his deed, or was he jealous that it was not him who had bedded Natasha!

Sarita's in-laws were asleep in their own room and so was Rhea. But all the ruckus awoke them, and now they could hear everything.

'This is not about how you brought me up, Papa,' Rahul said. 'This is not about values. Love *is* the value! And it has no boundaries.'

Sarita went up to him and slapped him hard across the face. 'Love? You call sleeping with her love? It's just your hormones, son. You are just a boy. What do you know about love?'

Rahul remained calm and let his parents be angry with him. Sarita dropped to a sofa, tired from the yelling, and for having slapped her son. She clenched her jaw to kill the sob in her throat. She had never hit her children in her life. She had always used stern words when she was angry. And she had always been on their side! She protected them from their father's wrath, she would even sneak in treats for them when they were young and her in-laws didn't allow it, spend her own money on birthday parties. She did everything for them. Loved them more than herself. And now Rahul had smeared their good name.

She had especially looked after Rahul because she wanted him to do something great in life so that she would be proud of him. Like Hrithik Roshan who had made Pinky Roshan's name so famous. Kambaqt Rahul had shattered her dreams. Eighteen years of hoping he would do something great, and the best thing he could do was to have sex with Natasha! What a waste!

'Mama, please,' Rahul said softly. 'It's not like that. I really love Natasha.' He sat down next to her, as she moved and kept a distance.

'Don't take her name,' Sarita's voice was ice-cold. 'She's Natasha *Aunty* to you!'

Rahul was sure Natasha wasn't his aunty. She was the source of his most intense orgasms. He was about to say, 'It's too late for that!'—but he really didn't want another slap.

Jai stormed off to his mini-bar and took out a bottle of whiskey. He brought out a glass. Sarita immediately went to him and said, 'Jai. Don't do it. Not the RC!'

Jai dismissed her. It had been quite a while since he had been drunk. He needed a stiff one tonight. It was two in the morning and the entire family was awake, listening to the outburst.

Sarita turned again to her son, 'Your Dadaji gave you this name. Do you know that? You come from a good khandaan.

You were the first son born into this family and everyone worships you!' She hoped it would bring some shame to the boy who didn't look apologetic at all.

'What son–shun? Please get over these traditional roles your generation wants to play. I'm not interested. No one from our generation cares who gave us our names. We can change it as we wish. Worships me? That's a joke. You guys can't even buy me new Nike shoes! What kind of a khandaan is that? Natasha loves me. That matters more than being a son or firstborn or whatever rubbish you guys indulge in.' His words were sharp, abandoning all pretence of filial respect.

'So tell me about this love,' Jai asked, as he sat down opposite Rahul, whiskey in hand, a look of mockery visible on his sad face. 'What do you feel? And is she leaving her husband and child to marry you? What do you think, is she going to have your babies?'

He paused and let his son ponder such an idea.

'That old woman won't be able to give you anything, Rahul!' Jai said, again his voice rising. 'You're just fooling yourself. This is not love, it's lust. And with the wrong woman. She's your mother's friend, for God's sake.'

'WAS my friend,' Sarita corrected.

But Rahul still didn't feel ashamed. He was mortified, of course, that his parents had found out in this manner, before he could tell them himself or make plans with Natasha. But he wasn't afraid of his feelings. It wasn't lust, he knew it. He was in love with Natasha. Maybe he hadn't thought about the future, but he had definitely wanted what they had in the present.

'She understands me, Papa, Ma,' he said to them. 'She gets me, for chrissakes! We do fun things together. She makes me feel alive! She makes me want to leave all the bad in the world behind because I want to improve myself for her. She knows how badly I want to hone my skills as an artist. And where I want to take it. And that I've applied for a school in New York.'

Sarita and Jai were hearing this for the first time.

Rahul let them wonder, and spoke again. 'I bet you didn't even know that, did you? Of course not. When did you ask us about our dreams, anyway? Think about Rhea. Do you know how frustrated she is?'

'You keep Rhea out of this, Rahul.' Sarita tried her hardest to keep herself from slapping Rahul a second time. She stood up, clutching the edge of the sofa for support. She was frazzled. She could not believe her son was saying all this, how ungrateful he was.

'Think about it, Ma,' Rahul said. 'Have you ever asked me what I want to do with my life? Everything about this family is money, money, money! How much does this cost? How much have you spent? How much can we afford? I'm tired of it. We have so much money but we live like beggars. Because you never spend it on your children.' Rahul felt bold and insolent. He met his father's eyes.

'So this is about money?' Jai asked. He downed another large peg of whiskey. The drink began to swirl in his brain.

'No, Papa, you don't get it. It's about the fact that I have applied to New York and got through but I can never do it because I'm too scared to ask you for the money. It's about me wanting to talk about my dreams and hopes and no one in this family is ready to do so. It's about me being taken seriously and looked at as an adult rather than a child who needs to be fed parathas. I'm not ten! I'm nineteen on Tuesday. And you haven't even realized that.'

'Yes,' Sarita said, in mock agreement, 'Natasha realized that very well.'

'That woman has completely brainwashed you,' Jai said. He was sure his son was just an innocent victim. He had always thought Sarita's friend was a vamp who cannot be trusted. He turned to his wife, 'You should be more careful, Sari, who you choose as a friend.'

'So now is this my fault?' Sarita said. It was too much for her to bear. What had she done wrong?

Rahul wanted to defend Natasha but he couldn't say anything. They weren't understanding his viewpoint at all. He still lived with his parents and needed their support. He wanted their love. He backed down, softened his voice. 'Please Ma. I love her. Natasha didn't want this. I initiated it.'

Jai thundered, 'And she was quick to let it happen. The bitch.'

'Papa,' Rahul said firmly. 'There's no need to cuss her. I love her. Why isn't anyone still listening to me? She's a wonderful person. She has given me confidence. She has pushed me to do art and because of her I've got into this school. I'm happier. I...' He paused to say that he had given up alcohol but decided it was unnecessary. He just repeated, 'She's wonderful. I don't care about the future. We'll figure it out together.'

'Rahul, beta, you're right,' Sarita said. 'You are no longer a child. You are an adult. You have hurt your parents very badly. This has been very embarrassing for us. At least say sorry before we kick you out of the house.'

Kick him out of the house! Rahul couldn't believe what he heard. He muttered a rather unapologetic, 'Sorry.' But he didn't shut his mouth. Instead, he said, 'It's not as if you two don't do kinky things in your bedroom! You don't think it's embarrassing for the whole family to see a harness stuffed inside a drawer? You don't think we all could hear you every night? You wouldn't even know, would you? Rhea and I use ear plugs to go to sleep!'

Jai got up and went straight for Rahul's face, slapped his son so hard it sent him flying to the sofa. He was drunk and he knew it but he wouldn't take such words from his son. 'Don't you dare talk about us like that again. You are an ungrateful little wretch. What we are doing is legal. I'm married to your mother.'

Sarita felt like her lungs were about to explode. There was nothing left to do. Obviously, Rahul was not understanding why they were angry and why he must end his affair with Natasha.

She stood up and said to Jai, 'Don't hit him anymore. It's not going to help.'

She turned to Rahul, 'There is no place in this house for you anymore. I think you should leave tomorrow.'

She turned and walked into her room. She had made up her mind. She would give Rahul money to live separately but she didn't want to see his face every day, knowing that he was in love with her friend—no, ex-friend—and had done dirty things with her. And after what he had said about hearing her and Jai during their lovemaking, she could not sit pleasantly at the breakfast table with him anymore. If he was old enough to have sex, he was old enough to live on his own.

Little did she know that this decision of hers would haunt her for the rest of her life.

34

Love makes you forgive easily, Natasha thought. And marriage makes you almost blind.

She had forgiven Vikram again and again, for so many faults of his, because she loved him madly. Then one day she realized that perhaps she was madly in love with the idea of him rather than him as a person. She loved the fact that he had taken her away from the model world and given her a home to look after. She pardoned him for all that he did *to* her because of all that he did *for* her. When the lines blurred, she stopped forgiving.

A few hard truths had hit her and she knew she needed to start finding herself now, or it would be too late. How had she let herself get to this point? Her self-respect eroding over the years, small ways in which he dominated over her, without question, almost like a god. Cruel words that corroded her dignity, actions she excused him for. Silently, she accepted it all, because she loved him and because she was married to him. That was what a wife should do, for so long she thought. Keep the marriage intact, even at the risk of losing yourself.

For how many more years would she take Vikram's abuse? He controlled her life. Did she have any strength left to control it herself? Was her life with Rahul? Did she see a future in it? What would she do with Diya? What did she want to do with her own life? Did she have enough money?

Slowly and surely, she found the answers within. Since she didn't have the help of her friends anymore, she felt a little lost. But that email, this disintegration, the fallout with her friends— all of that was allowing her to finally face her problems. To discover her strength and be the woman she could be proud of. She needed to let Vikram go. But how?

Natasha felt alone. She wanted to reach out to her friends but they weren't interested. They would rather let Time make the problems go away.

It was the Friday following the party and there had been no second email yet about the names of the women involved in those scandals. Clearly, the sender was waiting for the right time. All the wives were on tenterhooks. Natasha was unable to concentrate on her housework, and Vikram had been behaving dreadfully.

One night at dinner, Diya said, 'I don't want to play the violin anymore. I'm bored with it.'

Natasha was aghast. 'But you love it! You've been playing it for three years now and are so good at it.'

Diya played with the roti and chicken that Natasha had experimented with that day and disregarded her mother. She said, 'What crap are we eating? Isn't there any salad?'

'I made that dinner,' Natasha glared at her. 'Eat it. We'll talk to your teacher tomorrow about your violin classes. I want to know why you suddenly want to quit.'

Vikram pushed his plate away, too. 'If the child wants to leave it, let her be, Natasha.'

'She has talent. Children would always like having it easy, so as parents we must help them stay on the correct path.'

'Oh, like you stuck to your modelling after you got married?' His sarcasm was obvious. He knew how to needle Natasha about giving up her career after getting married.

'That was different,' Natasha said, wondering how he never took her side on anything. 'And I wasn't a child who needed to be pushed then.'

Vikram ignored his wife and turned to Diya. 'It's okay, sweetheart, whatever makes you happy.'

'But Vikram...' Natasha began.

That was all that Natasha had to say and Vikram erupted. He got up and threw his plate of food across the room. Diya was stunned, seeing her father for the first time like this. But Natasha had become so oblivious to his outbursts, she kept eating.

Vikram sat down. 'Now go get me more food,' he said to his wife.

'No.' Natasha was calm.

Vikram reached across the table and aimed to slap Natasha. Diya screamed, Natasha managed to move away just in time but not before Vikram's daughter saw what he was capable of doing. Natasha turned to her daughter, 'Go to your room right now.' Diya nodded, about to cry, and finally, perhaps for the first time in her life, listened to her mother.

Vikram sat back in his chair, still fuming over his wife's attempt to speak up. Natasha refused to serve him any food. She cleared the table and stood behind the chair. He got up and stood in front of her, waiting for her to apologize. She looked at him and said, 'Now look at what you've done. You've shown your daughter what a monster you really are.'

Vikram lunged across to hold Natasha by the throat but swiftly she caught his hand and twisted it behind his back. He grimaced in pain, stunned at his wife's show of strength. She shouted, 'Don't you ever raise your hand at me again or I will have you thrown in jail forever!' She didn't let go of his arm. 'You do not know that I have evidence of your violence! Your daughter was a witness just now! I have photographs from when you hurt me. So don't try anything funny when I let your hand go.'

She let go and he slowly turned to face her. She saw a different Vikram, not angry, but afraid. Finally. She had stood up for herself. She was repulsed by him. 'I want a divorce, Vikram. And as much alimony as will make me comfortable in my new life. I don't want any arguments about it. Because the lawyer I've hired will not only throw you in jail, but let me keep every single piece of your property. And that's not the worst of your troubles.'

Natasha felt a power within her to stand up for herself. She had always known she had rights, but she never had the courage to demand for them. Now was the time. If she didn't stand up for herself now, she never would. She would fall victim to a cycle of endless abuse and she would only have herself to blame.

'What about Diya?' Vikram asked finally, when he found his voice again, unable to understand how Natasha had thought about all this in such a short time.

'Diya will be sent to boarding-school in Panchgani. Which you will pay for. And once a psychiatrist says you are well enough to see her, she can stay with you during vacations. Till then I will have custody and she'll come stay with me.'

Vikram snorted. While stunned, he knew his wife would not have the guts to carry out these plans. She was too lazy! She depended on him, would be nothing without him. He had made her and he would wreck her! 'You can't make me do all this. You're just threatening me.' He went and sat on the sofa as Natasha followed him with her hands on her hips.

'Trust me, Vikram, if I show those photographs to the Women's Cell and NGOs, not only will your career be over, but your reputation will be ruined forever too. I suggest you do as I say. And till I move out, you can get out of this house as well.'

Natasha continued, 'You have ten minutes to pack your things or all these photos go up on Facebook, so that all your friends can see what you've done to your faithful and loyal wife!'

Vikram decided Natasha was serious in her threat. He walked to the bedroom to prepare to move out, as Diya came out of her own room. He wanted to give his daughter a hug but Diya went to her mother, taking her hand. She whispered, 'Bye, Dad.'

Vikram didn't take long. He came out of the bedroom, looked at his wife and daughter, and wheeled his small bag out the door. Natasha hoped he had learned his lesson, that the most precious possessions are neither money nor fame, but love and family.

Her heart broke as she watched Vikram leave. One tiny part of her wanted to run after him, ask him to come back, forgive him. They had survived so many years, after all! But the more she thought about it, the harder she was convinced that Vikram had lost all respect for her. Why should she still love him? Vikram needed to be alone. Only then would he change to be a better father for Diya. Because the best thing a father can give to a child is respect to the mother.

35

The lawns of Sapphire Towers looked different without the presence of the Lovely Ladies group. Preparations were on for the New Year's party, and if the women were around they would have complained about the same old lights being used, or the waste of money for the extra face-painting artist the committee had brought for the children for that night. They would have made comments on the songs that others were performing to, and even practiced a few numbers for the cultural program for the evening as they laughed and fumbled along with the steps.

Alas, while the poles were being erected, the women looked down from their own houses and refused to join the celebrations. It didn't feel right at all. Natasha was most upset that she had lost her friend Sarita in the aftermath of the email's revelations. She honestly wished Sarita would realize that sex was just a small part of all of us. If you didn't get the larger picture of a person, the sex would never matter. But Sarita had blamed Natasha and she knew Jai would never let Sarita become her friend again. How she wished she could tell her it was because of Sarita that she took the necessary steps to change her life. Natasha wished she could help Sarita with her problems as well.

Gita waited patiently for Sahil to return. She was too afraid to go out of the house except to cook and send pre-ordered parcels to her customers. The orders were pouring in and her business was taking off. She never anticipated it and soon was overwhelmed with the work. Both her children were so excited for her that they wanted to help. And Gita made sure that as soon as they came back from school, they would sit in Sahil's house and help out. The excitement didn't permeate to Shailesh or her in-laws, who all thought she was wasting her time and bringing a bad name to the family. A bahu in their khandaan never worked! It would give a bad reputation to the men, who were supposed to look after the women. But for Gita, it was never just about the money. It was about her independence. If Shailesh didn't understand that, then there was nothing she could do. She had tried to explain to him why she was doing her catering business. He had refused to accept it. 'This was not the agreement we had when we got married. You had promised to look after my family.' She had begged, 'I *am* still looking after your family. But I need to do something with my own life.' He had thundered, 'Why? You're just making a fool of yourself and me.'

Gita did not reply any more after that. She even did not make any excuses when he wanted sex, thinking it would appease him. Even though it killed her to lie still while this vile act was happening. She had surrendered her body to Sahil, and now Shailesh was using it because he had a 'right' to, as a married couple. How she hated that thought. But even after that, he didn't change his mind and continued to belittle her work. She kept quiet, choosing to run away to Sahil's place to work. Her in-laws were also waiting for Sahil to return from his shoot to scold him. How could he go against family tradition and let his sister-in-law take up a profession? How could he allow his brother's wife to enter his kitchen to work while he wasn't there? They were upset and wanted to stop this nonsense altogether.

Chatting with her own set of friends Mrs Patel made sure to insult Gita. 'Bahu has decided to work!' she said to her friends. She dramatically added, 'And no one seems to have time for us anymore. My daughter-in-law is out cooking for other people like a common maid, and our son is out at work. She used to be so nice. Used to sit and talk to us. Now she's not bothered to look after us anymore.'

The other women, as old as she was and themselves mothers-in-law, would agree. So Mrs Patel would ramble on, 'She's not even bringing money back into the house. If she can't spend time with us, at least she should buy us gifts. All my son has done is look after that woman and her children for so long, working so hard.'

This was one reason why Gita couldn't go out to lounge in the lawns, even if she wanted to. There would be too many people looking at her as if she was a monster of a daughter-in-law.

Gita checked her mobile phone for new posts on the Lovely Ladies group; nothing. But no one had exited the group, either. The group was still there, and it appeared they all wanted to stay there. Maybe the good memories were holding them back from leaving.

Gita missed her friends. She could sure use their help. But she was badly hurt by the way they had spoken to her. They did not bother to comprehend her situation and they refused to sympathize. She had expected a little more graciousness from them.

Aarti's life quickly swirled into her worst nightmare. Amitabh, her loving husband, had now become an unsupportive roommate. He had released her from his mind as his wife, and he didn't want to help her. He said it was her choice to leave, so she should be the one to speak to their parents. Not only did she have to explain to her own set of parents, who were extremely upset with her, she also had to bring up the topic of impotency to his parents, who didn't understand the subject at all. 'But he gave you a son. What is the problem?' they had asked.

But that was nothing compared to the agony of sitting with Aryan to explain to him why she needed to move out. Aryan was obviously angry and for several days completely withdrew. Aarti knew that she would have to spend more time with her son to at least help him with the transition when she and Amitabh finally separated.

Dhruv, meanwhile, kept calling her but she ignored him.

She wished she could speak to her friends, have them help her feel better just by talking about the most inane things. But she had been caught in an extramarital affair and she just couldn't face them at the moment. It was not something she had ever done. Or would ever do again. But her friends had judged her for it and she felt betrayed. She had given everything to her friends. So much time and effort had been spent on nurturing these three relationships and now they had fallen apart. Now Aarti needed to rebuild her life and she had no support from anyone.

After Sarita told Rahul to leave, he packed his things and went to stay with a friend. Sarita almost cried again as she watched her firstborn leave. This was not how she wanted things to be. She had hoped that he would grow up in the same house, go to college, get married, and bring his wife home to her. She had even started thinking of how she could renovate the house to make more space for her future grandchildren. Obviously, Rhea would have got married and left for her sasural. And her in-laws would be dead, thank God!

But that was all just a dream. Today Rhea embraced her Bhaiya and sobbed when he was leaving.

Rahul turned to Sarita, 'I'm sorry, Ma.'

Sarita looked at him, unable to understand where she had gone wrong. 'You've not only ruined this family, Rahul, but you've spoiled my relationship with a dear friend.'

As the door shut behind them and Sarita sat down in her room alone, her daughter came inside and stood at the entrance without saying a word. Sarita wiped away her tears. She opened her arms and let her daughter fall into them as she sobbed uncontrollably. She held Rhea closely and wondered if there was still one more chance at bringing up a good kid.

Rhea whispered, 'Mama, I have something to tell you.'

'What?' Sarita wiped away a tear.

'I know who did this. I know who sent that email.'

36

Sahil returned after ten days of being away on a shoot. Gita had given him some details on the phone whenever he had a signal, but she filled him in on all the facts as soon as he landed and before he met his parents. Sahil was shocked that somebody knew about him and Gita. But he didn't say anything and listened patiently while she told him about the loss of her friends and how she was feeling scared to speak to Shailesh about the situation.

'No one knows about it,' Sahil finally said. 'You don't have to tell them.'

'But what if it comes out? The email said that names would be revealed next. What will I do?'

Sahil asked her a question that blew her mind. 'Then how about we just tell them?'

'What?' Gita was incredulous.

Sahil took her hands. 'Gita, I love you. I want to be with you. I will be happy if you leave Shailesh and stay with me.'

Gita stood up and paced the room. 'You're mad! What will people say? What will they think about me? What will my girls say? Renu would be so embarrassed in school. Shailesh would never forgive you. Your parents will die of a heart attack.'

Gita was unable to find logic in Sahil's statement.

Sahil replied, 'If you want this…if you're on my side…we can deal with all that together.'

On his side? Wasn't this issue about her?

'Your problems will be my problems,' he said. 'I want to be the person who solves your problems, Gita. Not give you more. Just say yes.'

Gita couldn't. Although she loved Sahil and wanted to be with him, she couldn't take her children away from their father. She would stay in that bad marriage and deny everything between Sahil and her. She would endure the pain of her in-laws and give up her job, if need be, to prove to them she was a good daughter-in-law. She couldn't betray her children. Her love, her needs weren't worth the devastation it would cause her family.

'I can't, Sahil. I love you too. But I can't do this to the kids. It's best that you move to another place and we never see each other again. If this comes out, I'll deny it. There's no proof. At least, I hope there isn't.'

Sahil held her closely. 'Please think about it, Gita. Come. I've already got two calls from my mother asking where I am. Let's go upstairs. I'll help you with dinner.'

When Sahil and Gita entered the house, they immediately knew something was wrong. Shailesh was sitting with his parents at the dining-table. They were speaking in murmurs. Shailesh got up, pulled his wife towards him and asked her with a loud voice, 'Where do you keep going, Gita?'

Before Gita could compose her lie, Sahil said, 'Leave her alone, Shailesh.' He picked up the TV remote and tuned in to the news. The voice of the news anchor always drowned out the nonsense of his family.

But today Shailesh's anger knew no bounds. He shouted at his younger brother, 'You stay out of this! You're the one who's helping her with this stupid catering business and ruining our family name.'

'What?' Sahil threw his hands in the air. 'Grow up, Shailesh! She just wants to do something with her life.'

'What are you now? Her lover? Why are you doing all this for her?' asked Shailesh.

The split-second pause between Gita and Sahil was enough for Shailesh to understand what was going on. He took one step forward, picked up his younger brother from the collar and punched him in the face. Gita screamed and her in-laws got up from their chairs.

'You son of a bitch!' Shailesh shouted, as he punched Sahil again.

'Shailesh, stop it!' Gita screamed, trying to break up the brothers. 'What will the neighbours think?' Just then, her two children walked into the house with the maid. Shailesh backed down. The maid left and the girls ran to their mother. They were still small but intelligent, and they could tell that something was wrong.

They saw their uncle bleeding from the mouth and left their mother to run to him. 'Sahil chacha what happened? Who did this to you?'

Gita took them aside. 'Please Renu, take your sister inside and lock the door.'

Renu did as she was told. Gita ran to the bathroom to get some cotton and Dettol for Sahil. Shailesh hissed at her, 'I knew it! I knew that email was about the two of you. You thought you could hide this from me?'

Gita trembled in fear. Her in-laws looked at her in disdain. 'You've brought shame to our family,' said her mother-in-law. 'We'll send you back to your parents. What kind of a woman are you? Dirty randi.'

Sahil, pointing a finger at his parents, said, 'Apologize right now to her.'

Shailesh stood between his parents and Sahil and answered for them, 'Don't talk to Mummy and Papa like that. Why should they apologize? Both of you have besmirched our family name. You don't deserve our love. Or our respect.'

Gita and Sahil didn't know what to say. Gita stood between her husband and the man she loved, unsure of what to do. She folded her hands and told Shailesh, 'I'm sorry, Shailesh. Please forgive me.'

Shailesh replied by slapping her across the face. Gita fell to the sofa, holding her cheek and crying in pain. Sahil and Shailesh lunged at each other. Their mother screamed at Gita, 'See what you've done? You've ruined our family. You've broken up brothers. You've made everyone unhappy.'

Renuka came out of the room with Anu, and they both stood at the door surveying the scene and crying loudly. Gita ran to them and held them tightly. Sahil and Shailesh stopped fighting and straightened themselves up. Gita told her kids softly, 'Come. Let me lie down with you. Everything will be okay. Don't worry.' She took them inside her room and closed the door. Her first priority was her children and she didn't want them to be upset.

'Why were Sahil chacha and Papa fighting?' Anu asked innocently.

Gita had no answer but Renuka spoke for her, 'Because Mama loves Sahil chacha more than Papa and it made him mad.' Gita was shocked. How had she heard? Had she seen them together or was it in the last few minutes that she had figured it out. She had no explanation for her daughters. It was the truth. She couldn't deny it. So she kept quiet. Sometimes, silence is the only thing that gives clarity when no amount of conversation helps. Renu gave her mother a tight hug.

Anu said, 'Even I like Sahil chacha more than Papa. He's nice to me. He takes me to different places. And he buys me toys and sweets. Papa never has time for me.'

Renuka nodded and held her mother's hand tightly, 'Even I, Mama.'

Gita was shocked. She pondered and asked them, 'Who would you prefer to be with for the rest of your life? Papa or Sahil chacha?' She knew she needed this answer even more than any gold in the world.

The girls had one answer, the one that Gita wanted to hear, 'Sahil chacha.'

She knew then what she had to do.

'Then let's go. Let's go be with the person who loves us and wants to look after us. And not with someone who is just your biological father.'

Gita walked out into the drawing-room with both her children. Sahil looked at her in deep sorrow. He knew that she would take Shailesh's side. She was a faithful wife and her duty lay with Shailesh. This was probably the last time he would be seeing these three girls who made his life so special.

'Shailesh, I'm leaving you,' Gita said to her husband. 'And I'm taking the children with me.'

Sahil thought he misheard her.

But Shailesh said, 'You can't do that, Gita, you have no place to go. You have no money.'

Sahil stood up. 'Yes she does. She has a thriving business and she has me.'

'Then go,' Shailesh said. 'I never want to see your face again. Either of you. You've been a disgrace to our family.' Sahil's mother came and held her child and beseeched him, 'Beta, don't do this. She's not worth it. I've given birth to you. You're a part of us.'

Sahil looked at his mother. 'You will always be my mother, Mama. So why don't you forgive Gita and give us your blessings?'

His mother looked in contempt at her daughter-in-law and said, 'Never!'

Sahil embraced Gita. 'Then I'll look after her. We don't need your blessings.'

Shailesh turned to the girls and said, 'I will come and meet my children. Renuka and Anu, you will always be important to me.'

His children looked at him in disbelief. 'Really, Papa?' Renuka said, 'How come you never showed it?' Almost eleven years old in a few days, Renuka was far more mature for her age. Gita smiled at her children. They had given her the impetus to move forward with her life. They would give her the support to lead her life freely and with dignity. They were her pillars of strength.

Gita had entered Shailesh's house with a bag full of clothes and a handful of jewellery. And after twelve years of marriage she was leaving with her most precious belongings, her daughters. She knew that their lives had changed forever that night. But from that moment on, she felt a great burden release from her soul. That of being Shailesh's wife.

Sahil wrapped his arms around Gita and walked out with her. He was ashamed of how his family had behaved towards Gita. He knew that his parents had disowned him forever. And he felt great relief that he didn't have to live up to their expectations anymore. He would start a new life with the love of his life and raise her children as his own.

37

As soon as his parents kicked him out of their house, Rahul moved in with a friend, a few years older to him. He had a plan, though. That plan involved asking Natasha to move in with him. They would live with his friend for a while and then get their own place once he had finished college and started working full time. He was determined to do right by Natasha. It didn't matter if his parents didn't understand him. He was in love.

Part of the plan was the art school in New York. He hadn't submitted his letter of acceptance, though, and was still figuring out his finances. He had a month to do that. Maybe he and Natasha could go together? She had told him about the time she lived as a model in New York. He was dying for her to show him all the places that meant something to her. They would begin a life together.

He sent her several messages but they were all unanswered. Figuring she was just busy, he decided to go visit her. He took a bouquet of flowers. She liked flowers.

Natasha opened the door. 'Oh God, Rahul!'

Rahul was puzzled with her reaction to seeing him but walked in when she opened the door wider. He immediately tried to grab and kiss her but she pushed him back. 'Hey, what is wrong with you? Let me go, will you! You've ruined my life. How could you tell people about us? You've ruined my friendship with your mother!'

Rahul didn't understand what she was saying. 'What? I would never tell anyone about us! You're very precious to me. Why would I ruin what we have by tattling?'

Natasha walked in and waved her hands in the air, 'Because you're a fool. You might have bragged to someone and it would have leaked out. Who wrote that email? Only someone who was involved. Otherwise, how would they have known about us in the lift?'

Rahul looked heartbroken. 'Natasha! I would never tell anyone about us. I know I would lose you!'

Natasha was not sure whether to believe him. She moved away from him and sat down. If it wasn't Rahul, then who? Who could have possibly seen them? She tried to recollect when they had got out of the lift, if anyone had been there. She couldn't think of anyone's face. It had been the middle of the night and the halls were empty. Even Diya and Vikram weren't home that evening.

'Believe me,' Rahul pleaded. 'I would never tell anyone. And even I am suffering.' He gulped before continuing, 'My parents have thrown me out of the house.'

'What?'

'Yes. I've moved in with a friend of mine. I've taken up two art classes, to make enough money. I want to do right by you, Natasha.'

Natasha came and sat next to him, gently placing her hand on his. She felt sorry for him.

'I want to take you away from this life,' Rahul said to her. 'I want to look after you, protect you, love you like you should be loved and take care of you. I want to marry you.'

Natasha almost burst out laughing but she understood adolescents by now. She knew he wasn't joking. His feelings were real and he meant every word. To laugh would be to insult him, to dismiss his feelings and see him as nothing more than a boy.

She replied calmly, 'Rahul, I think you are very sweet. But

I can't get married to you. I have Diya to look after. And by the way, I am already married.'

Rahul shook his head. 'I don't care. You get a divorce and we'll get married. Or at least, you separate from him and stay with me. We'll figure out Diya.'

Natasha knew he was speaking from his heart but she needed him to be rational. 'Rahul, we won't have enough money. I'm not going to move in with you.'

Rahul looked at her with exasperation. 'We can't stay here. Everyone already knows about us. People whisper. It's going to get worse. I'll find the money.'

Natasha couldn't believe what she was hearing. 'Rahul, if you and I are together, what will happen to your dream about going to New York?'

'I'll give that up,' he said, in defiance, to prove his love for her. 'Or we could travel together. I'll get a loan from a bank.'

She was getting exasperated. 'Student loans will suck your life away! Okay, so you'll give up your dream, move in with me, and what if you find some new girl to be with? What will happen to us?' She tried to reason with him, trying to show the folly of his ways.

'I don't want a new girl. I won't be in love with anyone as much as I am with you. You understand me. You've changed me. And I've had such mind-blowing...' Rahul said, while Natasha interrupted with 'Yeah, yeah yeah! I get it.'

Natasha had to figure out a way to let him go easily. She didn't want to hurt him. But she couldn't let this continue. She could not handle love and passion anymore. She had just spoken to the boarding-school and they had agreed to interview Diya later that week. Realizing that she had failed as a mother and had chosen a school to look after her only child had sent a wave of mixed emotions in Natasha. She couldn't deal with Rahul and his range of emotions as well. She would be moving to a new building. He husband was in therapy and her life had fallen apart. Couldn't Rahul see that the best way for them was to go their separate ways?

She spoke softly but firmly, 'Rahul, you and I are over. We cannot work. You are too young to be in love with me.' He started interrupting her but she put her hand up and continued, 'It's a good opportunity for you if your parents kicked you out of the house. Look at it as a challenge. I would say, earn enough and start a new life away from your parents. Look, here's what I know. You don't need me. You just think you do. Don't interrupt! I know this. Right now, you might think you love me, but you don't! It's infatuation. Your mother was right. It's been lust from both our sides. And I am sorry I initiated it. I am sorry I gave you the vibes that this was a relationship that was meant to be forever. I ask you to forgive me for leading you on because that was not my intention.'

He said, 'I knew that when we started. You didn't initiate it. I did. I came on to you. I forced you. You don't need to apologize.'

But he still couldn't let her go. 'But I had hoped that maybe our lust would turn into something else. That you would want to spend your life with me.'

Natasha said, 'You'll have a better life without me. You're just starting life. I've already seen it.'

His countenance was immobile, 'But what will I tell my parents? I told them that I love you.'

Natasha shook her head and replied with deep regret, 'I lost Sarita as a friend because of you. So many years of friendship just down the drain. Lost forever. You have to tell them that it wasn't love. They'll believe you. They'll take you back. I promise.'

'Are you more worried about your friendship with her or

your feelings about me?' Rahul felt insignificant in this entire equation.

Natasha smiled and responded to the best of her ability. It had been a tiring two weeks. She had started speaking to Diya slowly about her choices and building a bond. Diya had thrown a fit in the beginning but Natasha had found her groove as a parent and started ignoring her. The last two weeks had been tumultuous for both of them. Vikram had been staying with his aunt and had given her till the end of the week to move out. He had told her he was seeking therapy but needed to stay in his own house. He had found a lawyer as well. Natasha just wanted him out of her life and no more fracas. She had agreed to shift. She needed to start afresh. She wanted to leave the ghosts of her past behind. So she spoke to Rahul, as delicately and lovingly as possible, to explain to him why their relationship could not work.

'Of course, I'm worried about you. But I know you're strong. You'll get over this. You will live your life to the fullest. And your parents love you deeply. They might be angry with you now but they'll ask for you to come back home and everything will turn out just fine. I, however, will never have my friends in my life again. And I have no idea how my life will turn out without them.' She turned away, not wanting to show the fear and insecurity in her face. The nagging feeling at the back of her mind about her future refusing to be still.

His misgivings increased by the minute. Rahul tried one more time, 'Let's run away together. I'll look after you and you won't even need your friends!'

'Rahul!' Now she was getting really frustrated. 'Didn't you hear a word of what I just said?'

'I did!' And Rahul was angry, too. 'I don't believe that you will give up all that we have. I don't know why. You said yourself that the age doesn't matter between us. Did you just use me?'

'Use you?' She stared at him. 'Use you! I'm the one who's left without a husband or child. I'm the one who everyone is gossiping about as the wanton old aunty. I'm the one who has lost all my friends, who were my support system. I'm the one who was just trying to help you find yourself. Make you realize that you can be a man in this world and not a mama's boy. I was the one who listened to you whine about how you hated that house. I gave you wings to fly. No, Rahul, I didn't use you at all. I gave you a piece of myself, my life, my heart. Just because I didn't fall in love with you doesn't mean I didn't care. I supported you. I was there for you. I understood you. And that's what should matter. So don't say hurtful things to me.'

Rahul hung his head in shame. This wasn't going anywhere. He didn't believe her. A muscle quivered in his jaw. He pleaded, 'Let's have sex. Maybe you'll understand you love me then!'

She shook her head sadly. She was wrong; she hadn't taught him anything. It had all been a waste.

'No, love. Let's not. I'm really tired. It's been a long day. I think you need to go, Rahul. Let's catch up some other time.'

She got up and walked to the door. Rahul couldn't believe what was happening. 'But, Natasha, I gave up my family for you. I told them I want to be with you. Please. Even if you don't want to marry me, why can't we continue what we have?'

Natasha felt tired. She had tried to reason with him, show him logic, help him understand but he was adamant about having only his way. 'Rahul, we never had any commitment towards each other. Why are you doing this? I thought we've talked about this. That the spontaneity in our lives gave us wings to do more. But that has gone with everyone knowing. And it has died in me. I'm not a person who wants anything with strings attached. I never have. I told you. Please, just go. Go live your life to the fullest. I wish you all the best.'

'But I don't want to live a life without you,' he insisted. Natasha thought he was going to start to cry like a little boy.

Her head throbbed in pain. She could not sit and talk to Rahul anymore. She requested one last time, 'Please, Rahul, I think you should leave. I just want to be alone now.'

There was nothing Rahul could do. He went back to his friend's house that day and looked at the calamity he had caused. He had broken a true friendship, he had ruined his reputation, he had no money to support himself, and the woman he thought he loved had spurned him. There was no alternative to his decision. He couldn't continue like this. He couldn't show his face in college if it leaked out what he had done, and no parent would send their child to learn art from him again if they knew his dirty little ways. He felt cheap, used, abandoned, and unloved. There was only one way out. He found a piece of paper and wrote his goodbye.

Then with no hope for a future, feeling the darkest he had ever felt, like there was no tomorrow, Rahul Gidwani searched the drawers, overturned them, found a blade, sat on the edge of his bed, and slashed his wrists.

38

Every parent's worst nightmare is a call from a hospital asking if you're the parent of a patient. At that moment your heart starts to race wildly, your brain loses control of logic, and your knees feel like jelly. You don't remember the next few moments, and for the remainder of the time to the hospital, you wonder how you could have changed the scenario a hundred times since the last time you saw your child.

When Sarita got the call from the hospital, she was putting away the freshly ironed clothes into everyone's cupboards. The hospital staff told her that her son was in the ICU. That's all. Why was he there? Who got him there? Who was with him? How did this happen? Questions that she asked but the attendant only said casually—as if it was the most normal thing in the world because it happened every day—that she had no answers for her and if Sarita could just come as quickly as possible.

She rushed to tell her in-laws, who were sitting at the dining-table, and immediately they asked her the same questions. She told them she didn't have any answers. Sarita called Jai and told him, howling and clutching onto her sari to wipe her tears. Jai tried to calm her down in his most controlled voice, 'Sari, you get to the hospital. I'll be there soon, too.'

As he hung up Sarita sent a message on her Lovely Ladies group Whatsapp: 'Rahul critical in hospital. Help.'

The first person to call was Natasha. 'Sarita, come outside to the gate. I'll drive you to the hospital. I'm leaving the house now; see you in five minutes. Everything will be okay.'

Sarita nodded into the phone, 'Okay,' dazed, forgetting that it was Natasha who had snatched the innocence of her boy, the same boy now fighting for his life in a hospital. The doorbell rang as her in-laws were getting ready to go with her to the hospital.

'Sari, what happened?' It was Gita. Sarita held on to Gita and told her what she knew.

Gita turned to Sarita's in-laws, 'Aunty, Uncle, it's best that you stay here. Rhea will be coming back from school. You can give her something to eat. No one is allowed into the ICU for now. We'll call you. Don't worry. I'm sure Rahul will be fine.' They nodded, uttering a little prayer that she was right.

Gita guided Sarita, still shaky, downstairs where Natasha was waiting in her car. They didn't waste any time. Natasha and Gita kept quiet while Sarita went on and on about how she should never have let Rahul leave the house. Between her sobs and her recollecting all the good that her son had done for her, they reached the hospital.

At the ICU the doctor asked in their direction, 'Who is the mother of Rahul Gidwani?'

'I am,' Sarita replied, bracing herself for the worst.

'Your son is in a critical condition,' the doctor said. 'He's lost a lot of blood.'

'Blood?' Sarita didn't understand. 'What happened to him? Was it a car accident? Was he drunk?'

'No, Mrs Gidwani. Your son tried to commit suicide. He slashed his wrists.'

Sarita's head spun. Why would my baby do something like that, take his own life? This doctor must be lying! Then a thought struck her. She turned to Natasha, 'What did he say, Natasha?' The colour drained from Natasha's face.

Sarita said to the doctor, 'There must be some mistake. I'm asking about my son, Rahul Gidwani. Tall, brown hair…'

'Warm smile, hoarse laugh,' Natasha filled in. 'Delicate hands, mole on his right arm, mouli on his left hand, loves wearing sneakers, always carries his sketch pencils.'

Sarita looked at Natasha: this woman knew Rahul better than she did. The thought pinched her heart.

'It's him,' the doctor said, 'We've given him blood transfusion and we're closely monitoring his condition. The next twenty-four hours are critical. We'll keep you posted.' He turned his back to speak to another patient.

Natasha blurted out, 'Can she see him?' Sarita again looked at Natasha, her friend, her enemy? She was grateful. The doctor nodded, 'Only one person can. And only for a little while. You're not allowed into the ICU.'

Sarita followed the doctor to see her son. Gita called out, 'Stay strong, Sari.' Sarita turned to look at her two friends and was glad they were there.

She almost cried again when she saw Rahul, hooked up to machines, his deed obvious with the bandage around his wrists. She composed herself and did not let her tears fall. She took his one hand and whispered softly into his ear, 'I love you, Rahul. I forgive you. Come back to me. We'll do whatever you say.'

She came out to find Aarti waiting with Gita and Natasha. Aarti ran to Sarita and held her tightly. Now Sarita bawled. Aarti let her cry some, then led her to a seat. She went and got a bottle of water for Sarita, and went to find a nurse to ask about Rahul. As she was walking back to Sarita, Natasha stopped her and set her aside, 'Aarti, I have to tell you something.'

'What?'

'Rahul came to me to say he loved me. I told him we weren't going to work out.'

'Shit, Natasha! What is wrong with you?' Aarti said, figuring out the reason why Rahul would have tried to commit suicide. 'I just found out that he slashed his wrists. His roommate brought him in.'

Natasha looked forlorn. 'Aarti, I never meant for anything like this to happen, I promise you. He wanted to have a relationship with me but I never told him I was going to be committed to him. He's just a boy. And Sarita's friendship with me means the world, why would I jeopardize it?'

'Then why did you sleep with him?'

'I didn't come onto him, Aarti. He was all over me. I stopped it for so long. And when it finally happened it was because he needed it. He needed me to help him find his way. He wasn't getting that from his family. Sex hardly mattered. It was just a manifestation of freedom.'

'But why didn't you stop it, Natasha?'

'I tried, believe me. But you should have seen him. He was so happy. To be honest? We made each other happy. There was joy in his face, freedom in his heart. He told me how much his family made him claustrophobic. His parents never understood him.'

'He didn't know better, Natasha. He's just a child!'

Natasha shook her head, 'No, Aarti. That's where you, and Sarita and Jai, you all got it wrong. He wanted to be a man, to be taken seriously. I gave him that.'

Aarti was not convinced.

'I'm not defending what I did,' Natasha continued. 'Maybe it is wrong and I'm sorry. Now I have this terrible guilt that I caused him to do this to himself.'

'And why did you reject him after doing all this?'

'Because he wanted to marry me!'

'What?'

'Obviously, that was absurd. Also, I knew that Sarita would forgive me if I let him go. So I did. But now she never will!'

Aarti began to understand more clearly. She held Natasha's hand, knew that friendships meant the world to her and what happened wasn't entirely her fault. Natasha had tried to help a young man in distress in the only way she knew how. Maybe we were all being too harsh in our judgement of her folly. She lived by her own terms, she had helped Rahul in her own way.

They walked back to the waiting area to find Jai running to his wife.

'What happened?' Jai asked Sarita. 'What did the doctor say?'

Sarita looked at him tearfully, 'Jai, Rahul slashed his wrists. He tried to commit suicide. They'll have to monitor him for the next twenty-four hours to see if he wakes up.'

Jai covered his mouth with a hand to stifle a gasp. 'Suicide,' he mumbled. 'But why? And what does that mean, to see if he wakes up? What will happen in twenty-four hours if he doesn't?'

'He could slip into coma,' Sarita replied, 'What will we do then?' Sarita was beside herself with grief.

Gita said to the two, 'We're not going to think about if he doesn't wake up. We're going to think about when he wakes up!'

Just then, a young man in his twenties walked towards them. He had bloodstains on his shirt. He looked straight at Sarita, 'Mrs Gidwani, I'm Ravi...' Sarita immediately knew who he was. She got up and walked to him. 'How did this happen, Ravi? Were you there?'

'No, Mrs Gidwani,' Ravi replied. 'If I were, this wouldn't have happened. I promise you I did everything as fast as I could.' He started crying softly as Sarita took him in her arms. Although he was a whole foot taller than she was, it seemed like he fit into her arms perfectly.

'It's not your fault, Ravi. And you're the one who brought him here. If not for you, I don't know what would have happened.' She let him go and they both sat down. The others kept silent.

'I don't understand why he did this,' Sarita said. No one had anything to say.

Sarita said to Jai and her friends, 'This is Ravi. He lives with Rahul.'

Aarti asked, 'Could you tell us how you found him?'

'In a pool of blood,' Ravi replied quickly, but in a whisper. 'I immediately tried to revive him but I couldn't. I called the ambulance but they said it would take time. So I picked him up and rushed him here in my car. I gave them your number while they treated him in the emergency room. I'm so sorry, Aunty. I wish I could have done more.'

'You did all you could, beta,' Sarita said. She was calm.

But Jai was not, and he stood up. 'This is all your fault,' he said to Natasha, taking all restraint not to scream in a public place. 'If you hadn't slept with him, we would never have had a fight. And we would never have thrown him out of the house. He wouldn't have felt so depressed as to try to take his own life.'

Natasha looked down, her tears falling silently. 'I am sorry. I just wanted to help him.'

Aarti said to Jai, 'She didn't mean it, Jai. And she's said sorry a hundred times. Maybe Rahul should have stopped running after her, too.'

Sarita was aghast. Her son was lying in a bed in the ICU and he was being spoken about like this? 'Leave my son alone, Aarti!'

Gita stepped in, 'Sarita, please, calm down, we're in a hospital. Let's all calm down.'

Ravi spoke, thinking it was as good a time as any, 'Rahul left a note.' He retrieved a crumpled note from his pocket. 'I haven't read it. I just grabbed it while carrying him. Here, Aunty.' He handed it to Sarita, who at first didn't know if she could bear reading what her son had meant to be his last words.

Finally, she took the note. First she read it to herself, then she read it for Jai and her friends: 'Love is the greatest thing in the world. But without friendship, love is meaningless. I made a mistake. I realized that I broke up a beautiful friendship between two people who cared about each other. I made the best women in the world hate each other. And I lost my parents and their love in the process. I was selfish. I wanted it all. I pushed Natasha and took advantage of her. It was not the other way around. I love you, Mama and Papa. I wanted you to be proud of me. I guess I failed you.'

Sarita looked at Natasha, feeling her resentment dissolve. If her son could forgive her, she needed to as well. She went to Natasha and held her tightly.

'I'm sorry, Natasha,' Jai said. 'We were wrong.'

Natasha shook her head, 'I'm sorry, too.'

By this time night had fallen and Jai got another call from home. Sarita told him to go and check on everyone to let them know about Rahul. She would stay and wait for her son to wake up. Ravi said he needed to go home, too.

'Thank you, Ravi, really,' Sarita said. She embraced him before letting him go, imagining her own son, still fighting for his life.

Sarita looked at her friends, 'I think you should go back as well. Your families are waiting for you.'

They all thought she was mad. 'Our families can manage themselves, Sari,' Gita said. 'We're staying here with you.'

Sarita was touched. She watched them retreat to their own corners, speaking softly into their mobile phones, giving instructions to their kids or maids about what to do. All of them were putting their own lives on hold to give her support.

Jai asked as he was about to leave, 'Do you want me to come back?'

Aarti replied for Sarita, 'We're here through the night, Jai. You just take it easy. I'll call you in case anything happens.' He nodded, grateful for his wife's friends, finally understanding what Sarita meant when she said friends were like gold. They were priceless.

As relatives of other patients left and the waiting-room emptied, only the four of them remained sitting in the lounge, munching on sandwiches that Aarti had arranged for.

Gita asked the question that had haunted them for weeks. 'Guys, this was all set off by an email. If neither of us wrote it, who did? Who's behind all this?'

The girls looked at each other as Sarita cleared her throat, 'I'll tell you.'

39

Teenagers, crop circles, aliens: they all fell into the same category for the housewives of Sapphire Towers. They were a puzzle, something very difficult to comprehend.

'They're just going through a phase,' they would say about their teenagers. It could also be any of these: 'I have no idea what she's thinking!' or 'Why doesn't she know how to spell correctly in a text message, what does "lyk dis" mean?'

With parents unable to understand them and their peers in stiff competiton with them, teenagers were often left alone to fend for themselves.

One evening not too long ago, Diya was showing off her latest Samsung Galaxy phone to her friends. Rhea took it. 'This is really cool, Diya. But didn't you just get a phone three months ago?' Rhea was envious: how come her friend kept getting new things from her parents when she could not get anything, even when she begged?

Diya tossed her hair back. 'Yeah, but my Dad just came back from Greece and brought this back for me.'

All the girls loved Diya's father; they could tell that he gave her everything that she asked for. Diya said to Rhea, 'You should tell your parents to give you a phone. After all, you're fourteen. It's time you stand up for yourself!'

Rhea sighed and gave the phone back to Diya. What was the use of understanding technology so well? She came first in her class in computers. She could decipher any phone and she could even hack into email accounts. She was a genius when it came to gadgets but her parents were so busy with their own lives that they hardly noticed Rhea and her needs. Even Rahul had not given her any attention in the last month. He was always in and out of the house.

Diya said, 'Don't worry, Rhea. I can give you my old phone. After all, God tells us to share things with the less fortunate.'

Diya and the group giggled, making Rhea feel slighted. She hated Diya and her friends for making her feel poor. She hated her parents more for being so stingy. She would get even. She would make all of them suffer, she thought. She had to figure out a way how.

She was crossing the office of the building when she overheard two people sitting in front of the computer. 'It's jammed, I tell you,' one of them said. 'We'll have to call the engineer.'

The other man said, 'It's not jammed. It's on loop. And we need to erase this before it causes a scandal.'

A 'scandal'? Rhea salivated at the thought. She walked inside the office and twirled her hair, 'Hi. I'm Rhea. I am a computer engineer.'

The two men, who had been hired by the society to manage the office, looked at her. 'You're too young to be an engineer.'

Rhea approached the desktop. 'I can fix anything. Just tell me. What has my age got to do with my skills?'

'I don't think you are allowed to see this,' one man said nervously to the other.

Rhea insisted, 'You want your computer fixed for free or not? Or I can give you the number of the engineer who will come tomorrow and charge you money.'

The men thought, 'What the hell does it matter if this girl fixes it.' They gave her free reign over the computer.

What Rhea saw on the computer screen made her eyes pop out. It was video footage taken from the CCTV camera in the lift in C wing: a woman and a man were having sex, the woman facing sideways and the man had his back to the camera. She could see how he lifted her leg, wrapped it around his arm and balanced himself while they had intercourse. The woman had long hair that was loose and she seemed to be giving instructions to him and moaning loudly.

For a minute Rhea couldn't make out who the people were. But as the two lovers moved a bit Rhea took a sharp breath in and realized that the man was her brother Rahul and the woman was Diya's mother, Natasha!

Rhea thought for a minute and gathered her wits about her. 'Yes, I can fix this. I can delete it from the system, if that's what you want, and unlock the code so it looks like there was no one in the lift at the time. Would you like me to do that or set all timers to zero and pretend it was never recorded?'

The men looked at each other and gave it a thought, 'Make it look like there was no one there. Setting to zero might make it suspicious.'

Rhea thought that suspicion would be the least of their worries if this came out. Then she had a thought. What if this video *did* come out? Not only would Diya be humiliated, but also her family would realize that Rahul wasn't the golden boy they thought him to be.

'This will take a little time. In case you want to go have lunch, I'll sit here,' Rhea told the men, who thought it was a good idea. They left, saying they'd be back in fifteen minutes.

But Rhea couldn't copy the video or email it. While Rhea was erasing the video she also saw two more videos that left her stunned. One was from the basement with a car entering and parking in the darkness and then moving. Then a woman getting out about half an hour later and walking up the steps. It was

Aarti Aunty. In a very disheveled state. That could only mean one thing. A slow smile spread through Rhea's lips.

Another video showed an encounter between Natasha Aunty, Gita Aunty, and Sahil Uncle. Rhea had plenty of gossip to blackmail the entire group! She knew exactly what to do. If she couldn't email the videos, at least she could insinuate what was happening and burn a hole in their friendship. And when everyone would be gossiping about it, she would reveal the truth, leaving Diya shamefaced in front of their peers.

She wrote an email from the society group, revealing the dirty little secrets. She knew that she would create a scandal big enough to finally give her some attention.

Triumph flooded through her as she pressed the 'Send' button to everyone in the Sapphire Towers email group. She wished she could see Diya's face when she realized her mother was a reckless slut!

She deleted the video, kept the lift to a blank screen, and finished the work for the managers. By the time they came back, she had already spread the fire. All she needed to do was wait for the consequences to take effect.

40

Rhea didn't tell her mother why she did what she did. She apologized profusely. Her tears overtook her explanation. And Sarita was too shocked to ask questions that evening.

As she told her friends that it was her daughter who had set off the unfortunate chain of events, she wondered if it was indirectly she herself who was responsible for her son lying in the ICU. She wondered where she had gone wrong with Rhea. But as a mother she needed to protect her daughter. So when her friends asked her questions, she only said, 'I don't know. She was mumbling something about her and Diya having a squabble, and that she wanted Diya to learn a lesson, something, I don't know really. I'm sorry on her behalf for what it's done to you. I never meant for this to happen.' Her chest was about to burst.

Natasha was sorry about her own child, too. 'I'm going to slap Diya when I get back home.'

A chill black silence surrounded them. Finally, Gita surprised everyone by saying, 'Maybe I should thank Rhea.'

Everyone looked at her with incredible surprise. The tension between them began to melt. She nodded at them. 'I was living a lie for so long. Unhappy with my life and unable to find a voice. Finally, I could do something for myself and my children. I've moved in with Sahil. Shailesh kicked me out. But I'm finally free. I can be with Sahil openly now. I know it's going to be a long process but I'm finally with a man who loves me, who supports me, who gives me confidence instead of taking it away.' A thoughtful smile formed on her lips as she recollected how he had made space in his house, his heart and his life for the three of them. Gita and her daughters had felt more at home in his small apartment than they ever had in Shailesh's big one. Gita had never felt more optimistic about the future.

Sarita took Gita's hand, 'This must be really tough for you.' Gita had never been a woman who had taken a stand on anything. Seeing her blossom from a scared housewife to a budding entrepreneur was a revelation. Sometimes, the support of someone who loves you does give you wings to fly. And when you find that, there is no need to define the equation. True Love is what it is.

Gita nodded, 'It is. My parents are shocked and have refused to talk to me. My in-laws don't talk to Sahil. Shailesh and he had a big showdown and Sahil has a bruise because of that. But the bruises in our life will be deeper. We've probably lost our families, who will never speak to each other or us again. But if we can't live our life without the fear of being judged, then we haven't lived a full life at all.'

'So true!' Aarti said. 'But what about the girls?'

Gita's eyes lit up at the thought of her children. 'You won't believe it, but it was their idea. They wanted to be with their Sahil chacha more than their father. I wouldn't have been able to take this decision if it hadn't been for them.'

'That's wonderful, Gita,' Natasha said. 'I'm so proud of you.' She thought it was a good time to tell them too, 'Guys, I'm moving out of the building.'

They were shocked. Sarita didn't ask why. Maybe she had forgiven Natasha but it was probably a correct decision on her part to stay away from Rahul. Natasha continued, 'Vikram is getting therapy but this is his house. I don't want to get into property disputes. He's going to give me a divorce and alimony. With that I'll support myself and Diya. I've decided to put her in a boarding-school for now. God knows I've tried my best with her but maybe I need some extra help in raising her, and this distance will do our relationship some good.'

Aarti nodded, 'This is a wise decision, Nats.'

'Thank you. It's so difficult though,' she replied, as she felt a flicker of apprehension.

'New beginnings are as difficult as endings. But they come with hope and great excitement, while endings just come with a bag of memories.' Gita took Natasha's hand and squeezed it tight.

'What about us?' Sarita asked. 'Is this the end? Do we go away with a bag of good memories?'

Natasha hugged Sarita, 'Sari, I'm sorry about Rahul.'

'Stop,' Sarita said. 'I've been blaming you for so long and haven't looked at his point of view at all. I've just thought he was a boy but he's not. I wanted to be his mother so hard that I forgot to see he had become a man. This wouldn't have happened if he didn't want it. He's taken these decisions. I get it now.'

Natasha felt as if a rock had been lifted from her chest. The fact that her friend had forgiven her felt more liberating than taking the bold decision to leave Vikram. It was a release that Natasha needed.

'Thank you, Sarita,' Natasha said. 'That means so much to me, you have no idea.' Soft tears rolled down her cheeks. She cleared her throat, 'I need to ask you one more favour, Sarita.'

Sarita nodded. Natasha continued, 'When he comes home...'

Sarita looked up to say that her child was lying in the ICU and might never come home, but Natasha was sure that he would prevail. 'He will. And when he does, listen to his dreams and help him follow it. Don't let *your* dreams become his. You can't live your life through your children. They're separate human beings whom you can only cherish and nurture to fly.'

Sarita understood. She could not turn away from him anymore, simply feeding him or controlling him. She had given whatever values she needed to, and now she had to start becoming his friend and helping him.

Aarti cleared her throat, 'Amit and I have separated.'

'Why?' Gita asked.

'Because I need some space from him for a while. I've done my duty for so long, being the perfect wife and mother. But it can't remain if he doesn't get help. I can't live with the fact that my husband is impotent any longer. I will help him when he wants to help himself. I'll take him to the doctors. But it needs to come from him. All this while I felt like I was living in a pressure cooker ready to burst. All my emotions suppressed deep inside, building up over the years because I wasn't allowed to say anything. It was my fault. I should have done or said something long time back but I wanted to prove what a good wife I was, or a good daughter-in-law, so everyone would be proud of me. And all I did was deny myself a chance to live completely.'

'So you're still friends?' Gita asked, not seeing the resemblance with her own situation.

'Sort of,' Aarti said. 'Not completely. Things always change when you stop pretending. An expectation dies. While it gives you relief in some ways, it brings new forms of sorrow. I'm still going to be in the same building. My in-laws were surprised and disappointed and I think the backlash will come later, but for now they haven't said anything. Aryan will stay with me at night but spend time in the day there with his father and grandparents. I will spend as much time with him as I did before. I just won't pretend that this is a happy marriage any longer.'

Natasha said, 'I'm proud of you, Aarti. That was a bold decision.' She could have spoken for everyone.

Aarti surprised herself with the sense of fulfilment that came over her. It was an awakening experience that left her reeling. And the conversation with her friends gave her tremendous courage. If she had even a flicker of doubt before, it vanished as she spoke truthfully and confidently to her friends. They strengthened her resolve and confirmed her choices. The love and support from her friends was exactly what she needed.

'I'll help you, Aarti, with whatever you need,' Sarita said.

'We'll all help each other, no matter where we are,' said Natasha. 'Hey! We're the Lovely Ladies.'

It was the lightest they had felt since rushing to the hospital with Sarita. The lightest perhaps in a long time.

'I think we should change our name to Strong Sisters,' Gita said. They all laughed.

'Look, guys.' Sarita said, as she directed their vision to the window looking outside. It was dawn. Slivers of warm, pink light streamed through the curtain.

Sarita looked around and saw that the three women who had been with her throughout her terrible time of tragedy were the most solid friends she could have. And no family member could ever take their place.

As Aarti came back with a second round of coffee and some fresh sandwiches from the deli, the girls sat quietly reflecting in the night all that had passed. They mused on their private memories of the past, and their heads swam with thoughts about their future. They knew that from that day on they would no longer just be simple housewives. They would be women who did right for themselves, first of all.

'Mrs Gidwani,' the nurse came out to speak to Sarita. All the girls got up and held her tightly. The shadows deepened under Sarita's eyes as her whole body was engulfed in tides of weariness and despair.

Sarita nodded, 'That's me.' Her throat was suddenly dry.

The nurse smiled, 'Rahul has woken up. He's going to be fine. Would you like to see him?'

Sarita blinked back her tears of relief. The girls shouted with a loud cheer. They embraced Sarita, their happiness reaching the depths of her heart and flowing with her own joy. Sarita then let go of her best friends and followed the nurse to see her son. She felt a warm glow flow through her. She would take the teachings of this night and become a better mother to Rahul and Rhea.

She knew that the memory of this night would never leave her, and from this moment on their friendship was stronger than ever.

41

One Month Later

Aarti put up the last frame of Aryan and her in her new drawing-room and took a few steps back. Aryan stood by her side with his fingers folded on his chin looking at the frames his mother had put up on the wall. It was a collage of photos from his birth to the present with the important members of his family. A wall that would remind Aryan that this was his new home, with the love from everyone who didn't stay there.

'Does it work there?' Aarti asked.

'Yup!' Aryan said happily, without giving it any more thought, as he went to take out more toys from his box and unpack them in his cupboard. 'But tell me again why you are staying here, while Papa is moving in with Dadu and Dadi?'

Aarti went inside her new bedroom and opened Aryan's cupboard to check if there was some space there. 'Well Mister, since your toys have just increased over time, we needed more space to keep them in a new place.' Aryan made a face at her as she continued speaking a little more gently to help him understand, 'And Papa needs to stay with his parents. They're getting old and he needs to look after them now.'

'But why can't you stay with them too?' Aryan asked logically, handing some books he had packed for himself. Aarti and Amitabh had decided that Aryan would stay with her and visit her in-laws and Amitabh on a daily basis. Whenever she travelled, he would sleep at Amitabh's house, and Aarti had promised to keep her travelling to a minimum. Aryan had been

upset in the beginning but when Aarti included him in the
house-hunting and packing, he was most excited to have his
own space and make a new home for himself.

'Well, Mama needs some space too, baby. And sometimes
mamas and papas don't stay together. But that doesn't mean they
don't love you and want the best for their little brats!' Aarti said,
hoping Aryan would understand for now.

'I'm not a brat!' Aryan replied with a smile. And Aarti started
chasing him around the house, as Amitabh used to when he was
young. Aarti would explain to him about the separation and hope
that he understood in time, but for now she needed to give him
assurance that he was safe and loved by everyone. The maid rang
the doorbell and Aarti told her to get some vegetables. She told
Aryan to go downstairs with her, buy vegetables and go to the
lawns to play. The nanny would supervise his playing before
Aarti reached downstairs for her kick-boxing class.

Just as they left and Aarti went about unpacking, the doorbell
rang. 'Oho Aryan, I'm sure you've left your ball!' she said loudly,
as she picked it up from his toy drawer and opened the door.
She threw it just as Dhruv caught the ball and said, 'Are we
playing catch?'

'Dhruv!' Aarti was shocked. He smiled as he leaned against
the door. Aarti felt confused and pleased at the same time. 'How
did you find me?'

'Can I come in and explain?' he asked, as he ran his fingers
through his hair, looking deliciously appealing.

She opened the door wider. He walked in. 'By the way, I
just met Aryan. He reminds me of someone.'

She walked to the sofa and sat down. 'Come, sit. We need
to talk.'

✳

Sarita and Jai packed their bags, preparing to leave for America that night, as Rahul bounced around the house singing a love-song from an old Shah Rukh Khan movie. He hugged his mother as he crooned. Sarita giggled, happy to see him in such a jovial mood. Rhea sat sulking in a corner, watching TV. Rahul was already fully packed for a week. He had never been so excited in his life.

'Rhea,' Sarita called out, 'Don't forget to give Dadi her medicines every morning. You're in charge of your grandparents, remember.'

Rahul sang as he twirled his morose sister around, 'Tu haan kar, ya na kar, tu hai meri Rheaaaaaa.'

Rhea pushed him aside. She didn't think it was fair that she was being punished for her deeds. She had thought her parents had forgiven her but clearly they hadn't. A part of her was happy that she would have the room all to herself since Rahul wouldn't be coming back from the States. He was enrolling in the Arts program at Tisch School in New York. But she was also sad that she wouldn't have her big brother around.

Jai packed his underwear as Sarita took out the harness from under the bed. He looked at her slyly, 'Do you want to do that again?'

Sarita nodded with glee, 'Of course. We need to pack this. I'm guessing they have stronger hooks in America!'

Jai smiled as Sarita came to him, put her arms around his head, and kissed him passionately, 'And I'm sure we can buy a few more toys while we're there. That's why I've left room in my suitcase.' Jai kissed her back with equal ardour and unpacked his underwear before saying, 'I'll leave some room too.' Sarita looked at him with a twinkle in her eyes and they both glanced towards the open door. Both her children were staring at her with widened eyes and a disgusted look. Sarita remarked, 'You have a problem? Go get your own house!' And as she threw her head back and laughed, a wave of joy and peace washed over her.

Rahul had recovered well and realized that he didn't need Natasha in his life. Sarita, Jai and Rahul had a serious conversation about his needs and where he saw his future. Jai and Sarita decided that there was no point in saving so much if they couldn't spend it on making their children's dreams come true. Sarita's in-laws had protested at first but Jai had stood up for her and Rahul, remarking then that maybe they needed to move to their own house when they returned from the US. In the meantime they would stay in the current apartment with Rhea, who was being punished for sending that nasty email and wouldn't accompany them. They were going to be in New York for three weeks. Sarita knew that when she returned she would spend more time with Rhea and try to get to know her better as well. She didn't want a repeat episode of the hospital scene in her life.

It was going to be the first trip she took abroad and she couldn't wait to sit in first class. She wanted to show Jai what she had learned about the Mile High club. She wore her black lace bra just for the journey. It was going to be a ride they would never forget.

'OMG Mom! Can't believe he said that to you. Will totally discuss this with you when I'm there this weekend. P.S. I don't need an Ipad. I have a phone that is very cool. Thanks for offering to buy me one. I love you.'

Natasha read the message from Diya and felt a lightness in her heart that had not been there for a long time. Boarding had worked wonders for their relationship. Diya had cried when

Natasha had driven her to Panchgani. Natasha was thankful that before that they had spent many days talking to each other about their feelings, what had brought on Diya's resentment of her mother, and how Natasha had tried but failed to understand her daughter. They bonded, and by the time Diya was to leave for boarding-school, the bitterness that surrounded their relationship had gone away.

It was in one of those conversations that Natasha told Diya that it was Rhea who had sent the gossip email. Diya was furious. Natasha told her the truth, not hiding her reasons for doing what she did. Diya appreciated her honesty and realized that it was probably because of her that Rhea had acted that way. She learned the folly of her ways.

Natasha and Diya were facing a new beginning! When she had gone to meet her the previous weekend, she took a promise from Diya that she would call Vikram every day to talk to him. Diya had promised. Natasha didn't want her only child to break away from her father and Diya needed to help Vikram as well. By giving answers to his only child she hoped that Vikram would learn to start respecting women again and, in the process, understand himself better as well.

Vikram had started his anger management therapy and moved back into the house. Natasha had moved to another building in the meantime. She had enough from the alimony but she was still searching for what she should do with her life. She discussed her plans with Diya on a regular basis and her daughter helped her think her ideas through. She had been thinking of becoming a counsellor for adolescents and their parents, teenagers who needed guidance and parents who didn't understand them.

She knew she could do counselling from home, as she had enough space in her roomy two-bedroom apartment in Malad.

It was walking distance from the malls and close enough to visit her friends in Sapphire Towers.

She grabbed her purse to head out of the house for an evening walk by herself. Even though she had friends who cared for her, Natasha finally felt alive because she was alone. She wasn't ever meant to be a housewife, she knew that now. She had fallen into it accidentally. She was happy to be single and a mother. Being alone completed her more than being with someone.

She entered the lift and pressed G. Just as the doors were closing, a young man stopped it and entered. His shoulders, a yard wide, were moulded in warm, golden bronze. His dark eyes framed a handsomely square face, while his light hair was a sharp contrast to his deep tan. He turned and looked at her as a smile turned the corners of his mouth. His attire was simple but sophisticated, and Natasha immediately grasped that only a man who was working could afford such an expensive outfit.

'Hello Aunty,' the warmth of his smile echoed in his voice.

Her tone was as smooth as single malt, 'Call me Natasha.'

Gita and Sahil moved out of the building into another colony. Her in-laws had disowned both of them, and Shailesh had agreed to give her a divorce immediately. Gita had promised Shailesh that he would have access to his children but they seemed to be quite happy with their new surroundings and with their Sahil chacha. They travelled by bus to their school while Gita continued her catering business. Sahil rented a large flat with a massive kitchen for Gita to employ three servants and a nanny to manage her business and their children. With his support her business grew, and word of mouth made Gita's Kitchen the best catering service in the area. She started two new bank accounts in her childrens' names and deposited money into them every month. She finally had a purpose that was more than being a wife. She loved her career as much as she loved looking after her family. And she had never felt as much bliss in her life as she did when she was wrapped in Sahil's arms every night as he whispered in her ear before he slept, 'I love you.'

'Sangeeta,' Gita called out to the house-help as she wiped her hands on a kitchen towel, 'Will you go pick up the girls from downstairs? They've gone for tennis.' Gita was delighted with the ample space of her new complex. There were five towers of apartments, two pools that were uncovered because no one cared if the women were in their bathing suits, a billiards room, a large dance hall, and two tennis courts. 'I have to go for my zumba class. I'm running late. Give them milk and let them start their homework. Sahil should come any minute.'

The maid said 'Yes' to her mistress's instructions. She left the house as Gita peeped into the kitchen on her way out, fully dressed in track pants and a bright green Nike shirt that she had bought. With her own money! Oh, how that made her feel good. She had asked Sahil if she could join the zumba class and he had looked at her, confused, 'Why are you asking me for permission, darling? If you have the time, go right ahead!' He had taken his wallet out immediately and said, 'How much do you need for the class? Will you dance around in your kurtas or shall I give you some money for sports clothes?' Gita had looked at him and wondered how she had got so lucky. Maybe God had heard her prayers after all. Or maybe she had finally got the courage to listen to her own prayers and do something about them. She held his hand and said, 'I think I can afford it myself!'

Financial independence liberated her. She knew she could always count on Sahil, but knowing that she could support herself gave her immense self-respect. Her children saw that she was earning and spending her own money, and involuntarily, she was instilling in them the power of choosing to do anything they wanted in their own lives.

She knew at heart she was still a housewife. But she understood how powerful that was as well. A woman who chose to sacrifice her life for the sake of her family was the greatest woman on earth. A housewife is the backbone of any society. It is because of her that men can go out to have a career, and children grow up to be good human beings. Without her support there would be complete chaos in the house. But a housewife needs to be nurtured and appreciated. Only then can she give from her endless reservoir the love and encouragement to make this society healthy. Gita was extremely proud to be a housewife.